WHO BY
FIRE

A DAME POLARA MYSTERY

WHO BY
FIRE

GREG RHYNO

Cormorant Books

We acknowledge financial support for our publishing activities: the Government of Canada, through the Canada Book Fund and The Canada Council for the Arts; the Government of Ontario, through the Ontario Arts Council, Ontario Creates, and the Ontario Book Publishing Tax Credit.

LIBRARY AND ARCHIVES CANADA CATALOGUING IN PUBLICATION

Title: Who by fire : a Dame Polara mystery / Greg Rhyno.
Names: Rhyno, Greg, 1976- author.
Identifiers: Canadiana (print) 202305628 5X | Canadiana (ebook) 20230562892 |
ISBN 9781770867420 (softcover) | ISBN 9781770867437 (EPUB)
Subjects: LCGFT: Detective and mystery fiction. | LCGFT: Novels.
Classification: LCC PS8635.H97 W56 2024 | DDC C813/.6—dc23

United States Library of Congress Control Number: 2023949972

Cover and interior text design: Marijke Friesen
Manufactured by Friesens in Altona, Manitoba in February 2024.

Printed using paper from a responsible and sustainable resource, including a mix of virgin fibres and recycled materials.

Printed and bound in Canada.

CORMORANT BOOKS INC.
260 ISHPADINAA (SPADINA) AVENUE, SUITE 502,
TKARONTO (TORONTO), ON M5T 2E4

SUITE 110, 7068 PORTAL WAY, FERNDALE, WA 98248, USA

www.cormorantbooks.com

For Min & Ged

What is forgotten is not extinguished.
— Sigmund Freud

CHAPTER ONE

IT STRUCK DAME as particularly cruel that West End Fertility offered, among other magazines, *Today's Parent* as reading material in its waiting room. As she flipped through the pages, the glossy images of young families smiling and celebrating their good fortune left her feeling vaguely nauseous. Dame dropped the periodical back on the table in front of her and selected the safety of *National Geographic* instead. When she opened the magazine to a picture of a gorilla piggybacking its infant, she whapped the cover shut again.

After a small forever, she heard her name called. She spent another ten minutes sitting in the examination room, breathing in the faint menace of rubbing alcohol, and facing the narrow bed with its cruel metal stirrups. The last few months came back to her in flashes of banal horror: blood tests, hormone injections, follicular growth evaluations, the cold jizz of ultrasound gel.

Next to the bed was a cabinet, newly plastered with a constellation of cartoon stickers. The messy evidence of children. Dame hoped it was a good sign.

Eventually, the door swung open and the doctor came in carrying a clipboard. He was in his early sixties, with sad, penetrating eyes and wavy hair combed away from his forehead.

"Good morning, Dame," he said. "Hope we didn't keep you waiting too long."

"Not at all." Maybe if she kept the conversation buoyant, he'd have no other choice but to deliver good news. "Gave me a chance to admire the new artwork."

The doctor turned and looked at the mess stuck to the cabinet. "My wife's a pediatrician," he said. "She uses the office sometimes."

"You two really have the market cornered" — Dame kept treading water — "manufacture, maintenance, repair …"

He gave a small, unconvincing smile and cleared his throat. In the instant he looked down at his notes, Dame could see the truth in his eyes.

"So," he said, "I'm afraid it looks like this most recent transfer didn't work —"

She felt herself slip beneath the surface and sink into the familiar abyss.

"— and as this was your last viable egg, I think it might be a good time to reassess your current situation."

"My current situation?"

"Well, you're" — the doctor lifted a page on his clipboard — "thirty-six years old. You've had three miscarriages. Five failed transfers. You've listed your marital status as separated —"

"Divorced," she corrected him. "And?"

"And, maybe it's time to start considering alternative options."

"I thought this was the alternative option."

"I mean options besides in vitro fertilization." He paused for a moment. "There are a number of very credible adoption agencies in the city, and I think —"

Dame shook her head.

"Look, this is an expensive process. You've already spent thousands of dollars, and there are no guarantees."

She adjusted her glasses. "Are there ever?"

"I know it seems unfair." The doctor crossed his arms. "After everything you've been through, it must seem like the universe owes you a child."

But as Dame stared at the half-peeled Spider-Man sticker clinging to the cabinet, she knew her doctor had got it wrong. The universe didn't owe her a child; if anything, it was the other way around.

CHAPTER TWO

MEERA BANERJEE POINTED a finger at the clock. "You forget to set an alarm?"

Dame walked through the office and put her backpack down beside her desk. "I had a doctor's appointment."

"Well, it meant I had to spend the entire morning alone with Lewis."

The man eating a breakfast bagel paused mid-chew. "You always used to be so nice to me, Meera," he said through a mouthful of egg and cheese. "What happened?"

"We got married."

Lewis swallowed his food in a gulp. "Right."

"So, anyway" — she turned back to Dame — "I started listening to a new true crime podcast. It's about this guy who may or may not have murdered his whole family. But I've got a theory that —"

"Maybe later, okay?" Dame said. "It's been kind of a rough morning."

She sat down in front of her desk. Pinned to the back wall of her cubicle were photocopied memos striped with bright highlighter. Beyond that, there wasn't a lot of colour in the Heritage

Planning office. The room was a barren slot of municipal tedium, complete with a slouching fern whose best photosynthesis days had come and gone.

"Did I miss the meeting?"

Meera shook her head. "Peggy's running late. She went down the street to get us some decent coffee."

Dame turned to look at them. "Uh-oh."

"What do you mean, '*Uh-oh*'?"

"She's got bad news. Remember how last year she got us free tickets to see *Stomp*?"

"Yeah," Meera said. "I had to spend the next two weeks convincing Lewis not to join a drum circle."

"Well, the Monday after, Peggy announced that City Hall was starting mandatory performance appraisals. And, do you remember last month when she brought in that huge batch of homemade scones?"

Lewis nodded. "Orange-cranberry."

"That was the day she told us we'd have to share our photocopier with the Accounting Department."

"Oh yeah," Meera said. "Weird."

"She was the same way when I was a kid. She'd show up at my folks' place with a strawberry pie and warn us the city was tearing up our street for a new water main."

"God, she's like chocolate-covered raisins," Lewis said. "All sweet on the outside and then *bam* — the nightmare begins."

"Be nice," Dame said. "Sometimes, I think this job is all Peggy has left."

The office door swung open and the team leader of Heritage Planning came bustling through it. "Sorry I'm late!"

With one hand, she balanced a tray of steaming paper cups; with the other, she carried a plain brown file folder. Her silver curls bounced with every step.

"Meera, here's your Americano. Lewis: hazelnut Frappuccino. And Dame, you're still off coffee, right hon?"

"Sadly."

"I got you a London Fog. Hope that's okay."

"It'll do." She took it in her hands. "Thanks."

"All right, so" — Peggy flopped into the nearest empty chair — "I'm afraid this is going to be a bit of a tough one."

Dame snuck Meera a look over her glasses.

"We've got a hearing next week with the Municipal Review Board, and Sharon Fischer is presiding."

Meera groaned. "The Fish? What does she want to turn into condos this week? Casa Loma?"

Peggy opened the folder and applied a pair of bifocals to her face. "The Atkinson Theatre. Over on College Street."

"The Atkinson?" Dame said. "I thought they designated that place years ago."

"Only the facade is protected." Peggy handed the file over to Dame. "They've got grounds to bulldoze the rest."

"Shit. I love that old theatre." Dame flipped through the report. "Dodge used to take me there when I was a kid."

"I went to go see *Jesus Christ Superstar* there when I was sixteen." Peggy smiled. "Carl Anderson was so handsome."

"Well, it's not gone yet," Lewis said.

"I wouldn't hold my breath." Dame passed the file to Meera. "The Fish never met a developer she didn't like."

AS DAME WAS packing up to leave that afternoon, Peggy stopped by her desk.

"Hey," she said. "Are you feeling okay? You seemed — I don't know — a little off this morning."

Dame could hear the real question loud and clear. Even when her friends tried to tread lightly, she couldn't help but feel trampled by their concern. "Just more bad news from the doctor."

"Oh, hon." Peggy leaned against her desk. "I'm sorry."

"It's all right."

"Try to put it behind you, okay? All we can do is keep moving forward."

"You realize we work for Heritage Planning, right? Our whole job is to prevent things from moving forward."

"*We celebrate the past to awaken the future.*"

Dame raised an eyebrow. "Who said that? Oprah Winfrey?"

"John F. Kennedy."

"Well, the future didn't exactly work out for him, did it?"

DAME TOOK THE elevator up to the sixth floor of Sunset Apartments and made her way down a long hallway that smelled of cigarettes. When she got to her father's unit, she let herself in.

"Dodge?" she called out. "I didn't feel like going all the way to Shangrila." She kicked off her boots. "I know you like their chili fries, but Rice & Noodle have been pretty good, lately. They do that killer sesame chicken."

The paper bag in her hand had already started to darken with grease. She put it on the kitchen counter and listened. The television babbled in the living room.

Dame shrugged off her backpack and, from it, dug out a book she'd brought for her father: *Encyclopedia Brown Gets His Man*. She'd come across it Saturday, on the time-stained blanket Mrs. Carnegie usually draped outside the Dollarama. ("*Oh, that's a good one,*" Mrs. C. had said in the low gear of her smoker's throat. "*My boy liked that one a lot.*")

Dame found Dodge sitting in the La-Z-Boy, eyes glued to *Murder, She Wrote*. Around him, bookshelves lined the walls, shoved full with Raymond Chandler, Elmore Leonard, Walter Mosley, and the rest of the sneaky canon. On the wall were a number of framed newspaper clippings. Two were from her father's high school glory days: "*Polara Leads Panthers to Championship*" and "*David 'Dodge' Polara Named* MVP." Beside them was a bigger article in a bigger frame. It wasn't as yellow as the others, but it was spiderwebbed with lines, as if someone had once crumpled it up: "*Local Investigator Saves Three from Fatal Hotel Fire.*"

"Good show?" Dame asked.

Dodge kept his eyes on the screen.

"I don't know if you heard me, but I brought some food from —"

He put an index finger to his lips.

"Fine, then," she said. "More sesame chicken for me."

Dame was into her second helping of garlic ribs when Dodge finally joined her at the table.

"So?" she said. "Did J.B. Fletcher solve whodunit?"

Dodge nodded and cleared his throat. He took a couple runs at saying something, and soon, out of the murky, muttering static, there was a word. "*Prick.*"

"Prick? Makes sense. I imagine most murderers are probably pricks."

Dodge shook his head and tried again. "*Pre-dick.*"

"Pre-dick? Pre —" She thumbed through her mental dictionary: *Predicament. Prediction.* "Predictable?"

The old man's face broke into a smile. He nodded.

"Well, you kind of have an unfair advantage," she said. "Most people who watch *Murder, She Wrote* aren't private investigators."

Dodge shrugged. Dame put some sesame chicken and chop suey on his plate.

"You look thin," she said. "I hope you're not spending all day cooped up in here. Is Homecare bringing you enough food?"

He waved the question away and flexed his biceps. The pink and purple tissue that tattooed his arms writhed and contorted. Even after all these years, Dame didn't like seeing her father's scars.

"Yeah, yeah. You're strong like bull. But you need to put some meat on those bones. I don't want you eating canned crap every day. It's too much sodium."

The old man held up a saucy forkful like an accusation.

"Touché."

Dodge smiled and put the food into his mouth.

"I brought you something to read." She produced *Encyclopedia Brown* and put it on the table next to the cartons of food.

Dodge raised a skeptical eyebrow.

"Look, you can't sit around watching reruns all day. It'll rot your brain."

He held up the book and rolled his eyes.

"Well, I'm sorry" — she took the offending literature from her father's hand — "but it's not like you can get through five hundred pages of John le Carré anymore."

She sighed and put the book back down on the table. For a little while, they ate in silence.

"I guess," Dame said, "I should also tell you that the last IVF transfer didn't work. Doctor says it might be time to call it quits."

Dodge took another mouthful of food, chewed, and swallowed it.

"*Egg*," he said at last.

Dame waited. Her father's eyes swept the floor like he'd dropped the words on the ground somewhere.

"*Egg. Eg — gain. Again.*"

She sighed. "Yep. It didn't work again."

Dodge shook his head. "*Try again.*"

"I don't know if I can, Dodge. It's hard. And it's a lot of money. I'm not sure I —"

The old man stood up and walked over to his daughter. He put his hand on her shoulder. "*Try again.*"

CHAPTER THREE

AS DAME TURNED onto Queen, a flock of pigeons cascaded across the streetlit sky from one rooftop to another. She walked past the hardware store and the vegan place and watched a small garbage cyclone twist itself up against the bricks of the library. She waved at Mrs. Carnegie, who toured a parking lot on her motorized wheelchair, smoking and yelling something into a flip phone. Outside the rec centre, Dollar Sixty-Five was running his usual game: *Hey man, any chance I could borrow a dollar sixty-five for the bus downtown?*

Dame made her way east, against the slick wind that blew gelato cafés, yoga studios, designer weed, and eight-dollar coffees into the heart of her neighbourhood. She hung a left when she reached O'Hara Avenue.

But when Dame stopped at her house, she was surprised to find the door to her apartment hanging wide open. She took a step back, adjusted her glasses, and looked up and down the street. The grey October light was already fading, and with the exception of an elderly neighbour trundling his compost bin to the curb, the little avenue was quiet and empty.

Dame waited a moment, listening. Eventually, she climbed the front steps of the house. "Hello?"

A tall, dishevelled man stood in her living room, testing a loose floorboard with his toe. He had his phone pressed against one ear.

"Jesus, Ray. You're supposed to ask before you come in here." Dame closed the door behind her. "At least keep this shut. I'll get mice."

The man held the phone away from his head. "I'm airing out paint fumes," he hissed. "You didn't clear any renovation projects with me."

"It's paint, Ray. I don't have to clear paint with you." Dame took off her boots. "Maybe it's time you and I review the Landlord-Tenant Act."

The man put the phone back to his ear and held up a silencing finger. "Yeah," he said into the receiver. "Yeah, go ahead."

Dame sighed and walked sock-footed down the battered pine that stretched to her little kitchen. On the table sat a stack of unopened bills, stuffed with the usual suspects: hydro, internet, Dodge's Homecare, West End Fertility, and of course, Visa. Her credit card debt was starting to feel like some kind of monster movie blob. No matter how much money she fed the thing, it only seemed to get bigger and bigger.

As she dropped her keys into a tiger-shaped cookie jar, she could hear her landlord's voice getting louder in the next room.

"Did you let that guy in?" she asked the ceramic tiger.

Maybe — Dame allowed herself the faintest hope — Ray was here to fix the dripping tap, or the broken floorboard, or finish one of the countless repair jobs he'd promised to do when she first started renting this place.

She'd finally just painted over all the burgundy in the spare bedroom, but God, the things she would do to this old bay-and-gable if it was hers. Refinish the floors. Replace the cabinets. Definitely change the locks. But she couldn't afford to buy a house like this, and she couldn't bear to invest in some white cube of a condo. The apartment was supposed to be temporary, a nice place to hide while she figured things out. That had been over a year ago, and still, the back porch was jammed with boxes she hadn't unpacked and things she couldn't throw away.

Dame found the bottle of mezcal in the cupboard and poured herself a glass. The sound of Ray in her living room was becoming increasingly unbearable.

"I'm very aware of our agreement," he was saying. "Four hundred dollars a day plus expenses."

A pause.

"But you can't just —"

Another pause.

"Well, I'm sorry Mr. Felski, I'm not entirely sure I believe that."

Felski? It had been a while since she'd heard that particular handle. She leaned against the counter and took a sip of her drink.

"... and I was very clear when we entered into this arrangement that — I'm sorry? What?"

Dame could tell by the way Ray's voice was shrilling up that the conversation was almost over. She was just about to open the freezer and dig around for a frozen pizza when she saw a letter stuck to the fridge door with a magnet. It was addressed to her. Dame tore open the envelope and read it. Moments later, she confronted Ray. "What the hell is this?"

Her landlord was sitting on her couch.

"I'm sorry, I have to go," he said into the phone. "No, I don't think there's anything left to discuss. Goodbye, Mr. Felski."

"*I regret to inform you ...*" Dame started reading from the letter "*... sixty days to vacate the premises* — you're evicting me?"

"Look" — Ray pushed himself to his feet — "you knew this would happen eventually."

"Yeah, but I didn't think I'd be out on the street three days before Christmas. That's fucking criminal."

"No, I'm afraid it's all perfectly legal. Check the Landlord-Tenant Act, if you like."

Dame balled up the letter and threw it at Ray. "You're an asshole."

She stomped back into the kitchen. As Ray caught up to her, she was pouring herself another glass. "Jesus," she said to herself. "I can't afford first and last on a new place."

"You've been a good tenant, Dame, but something's come up. I might need a new place to live soon, and I don't have a lot of options."

She fixed him with a look. "You think your wife's cheating on you."

"What? How did —?"

"You were just on the phone with Anton Felski" — she took another pull — "so obviously, you think your wife's cheating on you."

"I'd appreciate it if you didn't listen in on my private conversations."

"And I'd appreciate it if you didn't have your private conversations in my *fucking living room*."

Ray was quiet for a moment. "How do you know Anton Felski?"

"Not a lot of Felskis in the phone book. Especially ones who charge four hundred dollars a day. You're probably better off without him, though. My dad used to say the guy couldn't find his ass with both hands and a flashlight."

"Your dad? Who's your dad?"

Dame took another sip of mezcal. "David Polara."

"David Polara," he repeated. "Why do I know that name?"

Dame shrugged.

"He was a cop or something, wasn't he?"

"Private investigator."

"And he saved a bunch of people when the Sainte-Marie Hotel caught fire, right? It was on the news and stuff."

"Yeah. Years and years ago."

"I remember because that poor little kid died. They ever catch the guy who did it?"

"No," she said into her glass.

"Is your father still a private eye?"

Dame thought of Dodge, sitting in his La-Z-Boy, watching *Murder, She Wrote*. "He's got a few cases on the go."

"Would he —" Ray cleared his throat. "Would he consider taking on a new client?"

She snorted. "You think my father would work for a man who's evicting his daughter?"

"Well, what if I didn't evict you?"

Dame hesitated. The truth about Dodge hung around the back of her throat, but she swallowed it down with another mouthful of mezcal.

"Look" — Ray pulled out a chair and sat down at the table — "my wife's family has a lot of money. If we ever went to court, she'd take me to the cleaners. But, if your father could find out what Aki's been up to and bring me something — something tangible, something I could use — you could stay here. In this apartment."

"Why my father?" Dame drained her glass and put it down on the table. "I mean, I know Felski was a bust, but you could hire anybody."

"I need someone I can trust." Ray rubbed his temples. "And soon."

Dame knew what he wanted. He wanted closure. An end to all the uncertainty. But she also knew that when he found it, it wasn't necessarily going to bring him any peace.

"Or you could just let this whole thing play out. Who knows? Maybe it'll all go away."

"Play out? I can't —" He let loose with a lung-rattling sigh. "I need to know the truth."

Dame thumbed the bare skin of her third finger. "Okay. I get that." She grabbed a second glass out of the cupboard and poured them both a shot.

Ray sniffed at the booze. "Do you have any mix?"

She brought his glass over to the sink and ran some cold water into it. She put the drink back in front of him and sat down at the table. Ray sipped at his drink and grimaced.

"So, look. My father doesn't really do domestics. He says they tend to be a little messy. But I could talk to him."

"Okay." There was a flicker of a smile.

"Just don't get too cheerful," Dame said. "I'm not making any promises."

CHAPTER FOUR

"WELL, THE MONEY'S got to be half-decent, right?" Meera dipped one of Dame's fries into a puddle of ketchup. "I mean, those IVF bills aren't exactly covered by insurance. Plus, you wouldn't get evicted, so that's a bonus."

Dame already regretted telling Meera about Ray's offer. "Dodge barely leaves the apartment anymore. And even if he did, there's no way he'd get involved with something like this. The guy is *very* retired."

"Your landlord doesn't have to know that."

Dame had to admit the thought had crossed her mind. "I'm not a detective, Meera. I'm a thirty-six-year-old municipal employee with significant credit card debt."

"But you learned all that stuff from Dodge, didn't you?" Meera adjusted the straw in her root beer. "He took you along on cases and stuff, right?"

"He didn't have much of a choice. We couldn't exactly afford a babysitter."

"So, what's the point of having all that know-how if you never use it?"

Dame looked around the diner. It was one of those new places that was trying to look old. "The point is not ending up like Dodge."

"Hey, I'm not saying you make a career of it. Just follow the wife around. It might be kind of exciting — peeking in windows, taking pictures, snooping through people's stuff — like being in your own true crime podcast."

Dame sighed. "Staking out a cheating wife isn't exactly a triple homicide, Meera. And even licensed investigators can't peek through people's windows or take pictures of them in private places. They still have to operate within the confines of the law. It's mostly a lot of sitting around and waiting for people to walk out of buildings."

"Still though. Maybe" — she cleared her throat — "maybe it would be good for you."

"Good for me?" Dame stared across the table.

"You know what I mean. It's been what — over a year? — since everything happened with Adam? And you never do anything anymore. You look after your dad, you hang around your apartment, and you work. That's kind of it."

Dame shrugged. "I like what I do."

"I know. I'm just saying" — Meera proceeded with caution — "maybe it's time you had something else in your life."

Dame scrounged up the last of her fries and put them in her mouth. She thought it might keep her from saying things she couldn't take back.

"Speaking of time —" Meera looked at her watch. "*Shit.* I was supposed to meet Lewis at a site inspection ten minutes ago." She gathered up her things and raced toward the exit. "See you this afternoon!"

Dame watched as her friend flew out the door. "Guess lunch is on me."

EVENTUALLY, DAME MADE her way back through Nathan Phillips Square and toward what her fellow City Hall employees had long-ago dubbed the Clamshell. She was barely inside the lobby when she heard the *clawk-clawk-clawk* of heels and saw an expensively dressed figure menacing toward her. Dame had to admit, there was something almost admirable about the woman's tidy blandness and the sheer efficiency with which she carried her compact body through space. It was only when the Fish came closer that Dame was reminded of how her too-big eyes, too-big mouth, and overall cold-bloodedness bore an unfortunate resemblance to her nickname.

"Good afternoon, Ms. Polara," Sharon Fischer said. "I understand your team will be presenting at the Atkinson hearing next week."

"That's right."

"Well" — she distracted herself with the strap of her purse — "we both know that Toronto has its share of dilapidated movie theatres. I can't imagine there's a great deal of merit in preserving that particular one, can you?"

"We have to consider its character in the context of the neighbourhood," Dame said. "It's a part of the community's culture and history."

"Really? And how has that community honoured its 'culture' and 'history' since the theatre closed?" Fischer was still fussing with her bag. "By throwing rocks through the marquee? Spray-painting phalluses on the windows?"

"According to our records, the Okusha Corporation has owned that building for almost a year. Maybe they should take better care of it."

"Yes," she said, not looking at Dame. "I imagine they intend to. God*dammit.*" She paused and forced a smile across her face. "I just bought this purse last month and all the stitching is coming apart."

"Guess they don't make things like they used to."

"No, I guess not." She looked at Dame. "Of course, that coat you're wearing has certainly stood the test of time, hasn't it? And those glasses. Are they ... vintage?"

"They were my mother's."

The Fish smiled her wide-mouth smile. "Well, you certainly have an appreciation for ancient artifacts, Ms. Polara." She walked past Dame and toward the exit. "I'll see you at the hearing."

DAME STORMED INTO the Heritage office and kicked the leg of her chair. She looked around to see if anyone had noticed her performance, but the room was empty.

It was maddening that, year after year, Sharon Fischer continued to authorize the destruction of some of Toronto's oldest and most beautiful monuments. Why would you live in a city if you were only going to destroy it from the inside out?

Money, Dame reminded herself. That's why. It was practically an open secret that Fischer was on the payroll of the city's biggest developers. How she still had her job at the Municipal Review Board was anybody's guess.

The file on the Atkinson Theatre lay open on Meera's desk. Dame picked it up and once again scanned through the first few pages. Apparently, the place had been built in 1942, by a guy named Len Atkinson. It featured a roller-skating rink at the back of the theatre, and a two-lane bowling alley in the basement. In 1973, Atkinson tore out the rink, added another screen, and renovated the interior. When he died in the late nineties, some young cinema enthusiast named Todd Sergeant bought it and turned it into a repertory theatre. He wasn't able to shake enough change out of people's pockets to make it commercially viable, so it barely lasted a decade.

Dame went online and found a CBC archive video about the theatre's reopening. There was the usual walk-and-talk through the foyer with Sergeant, but then the video cut to a talking head: a man in his eighties with significant tufts of white hair sneaking out of his ears.

"*I used to go to the Atkinson during the war.*" His voice was an elderly creak. "*We'd go see* Abbott and Costello, *or* Captain Marvel, *and then I'd drop my sister off at the roller-skating rink and I'd go bowling with the fellas. I remember, I'd never seen an automated pinsetter before. I thought it was the damnedest —*"

Dame paused the video. She grabbed the file again and found photocopies of the most recent blueprints. Main floor. Second floor. And, there. Right there in the basement. The reason why the Okusha Corporation couldn't bulldoze the Atkinson Theatre, and the reason why Sharon Fischer couldn't let them.

BY THE TIME Meera and Lewis walked into the office that afternoon, every previously bare surface was blanketed with historical documents. A bankers box stood empty on the floor. Blueprints lay draped over desks. Dame was talking to someone on the phone.

"Well, I really appreciate it." Pause. "Yeah, I hope so, too. Take care."

She hung up.

"Jesus," Meera said. "What happened in here?"

"Did you start drinking coffee again?" Lewis asked.

"No. Take a look at this."

They all crowded around Dame's desk.

"So, I ran over and picked up the original blueprints for the Atkinson —"

"Wait," Meera interrupted, "you went all the way to Archives?"

"I hate Archives," Lewis said.

"Everybody hates Archives," Meera said. "It smells weird and you can never find parking."

"Like I was saying," Dame persevered, "these are the original blueprints for the Atkinson Theatre. And *this*" — she slammed another sheet on top of the first — "is a blueprint of the renovations they did in 1973. Everything's different, right?"

Lewis took a moment and eyed the plans. "Right."

"Wrong. They never remodelled the basement."

"Dame," Meera said, "I know you went out of your way to dig this up and all, but no one's going to save the Atkinson because it has the original scuzzy basement."

"They might" — Dame folded her arms — "if that original scuzzy basement still housed Toronto's very first automated ten-pin bowling alley."

"Wait," Lewis said, looking at the blueprints. "I thought Kingston Bowl had the first automated pinsetter."

Meera shook her head. "You would know that."

"Kingston Bowl opened in 1943," Dame said. "Len Atkinson built his in 1942. Everyone just thought he tore it out when he renovated, but apparently, it's been down there all this time."

"Are you sure?" Lewis asked.

"I just got off the phone with the previous owner. He said the pinsetter was still there when he sold it. Said he and his buddies used to go down there after hours and bowl a few frames. Still worked and everything."

"There's no way they can bulldoze that place now," Lewis said.

Meera smiled up at Dame. "What were you saying about not being a detective?"

CHAPTER FIVE

ON HER WAY out of Heritage that afternoon, Dame ran into Peggy. She was coming from the break room cradling a mug of tea.

"Hey," she said. "Working late on a Friday?"

"Just on my way home."

"Got a minute before you go?"

Dame followed her back into her office. The fluorescent overheads were off, but the last light of day glowed through the west window. From a stereo partially obscured by a small jungle of houseplants, Dame could hear a bleak baritone filling the room.

"Leonard Cohen, right?" Dame said.

Peggy nodded.

"Rosie used to play this song all the time."

"Did I ever tell you your mom and I went to go see him together?"

"Really?"

"He played Massey Hall in the eighties. Great show — maybe a little too much of that new wave synthesizer stuff." Peggy smiled. "Rosie had just started working at the *Toronto Star*, and she convinced security to let us backstage."

"Did you get to meet Leonard?"

"No, but his saxophone player kept flirting with Rosie. Your mother was a real heartbreaker back then. A real troublemaker, too."

"So I've heard."

"Well, grab a seat" — she navigated through a little labyrinth of cardboard boxes and paper — "if you can find one."

Dame moved a stack of binders off a chair and sat down.

"See what the Deputy Speaker brought me yesterday?" Peggy gestured toward a potted plant on her desk that looked like a tiny tree. "Think he might be a little sweet on me."

"Is that a bonsai?" Dame asked.

"Dwarf jade." Peggy turned the plant a few degrees. "But I'm going to try and coax it into becoming a bonsai." She looked around her office and sighed. "It's already so crowded in here, though. And my poor ficus isn't getting enough light."

"I'm sure you'll make a great bonsai mom. You've got more maternal instinct in your green thumb than most people do in their entire bodies."

Peggy laughed a little and sat back in her chair. "So" — she blew steam off her tea — "a little bird told me that you may have single-handedly saved the Atkinson Theatre."

"Was that little bird Meera? Because she tends to exaggerate."

"A historic bowling alley? In the *basement*? I guess all those years of working for your father were good for something."

"Yeah. I guess so."

Peggy sipped at her tea. "Dame, can I ask you a question?"

"Shoot."

"Are you happy here? At Heritage?"

Dame sat up in her seat, surprised. "Of course. I love working here."

"I knew when I hired you, you'd be fantastic, but I just assumed it would be a temporary position. You were always so brilliant, and I know your mom had such high hopes for you. These days you seem — I don't know — a little stuck."

"Yeah." Dame sighed. "You're not wrong."

"I know it's been a tough couple years, what with Dodge's stroke, and the divorce, but —"

"You're going to tell me to keep moving forward again, aren't you?"

Peggy smiled. "*You can't let your past hold your future hostage.*"

"More JFK?"

Peggy shook her silver curls. "LL Cool J."

"Huh. Smart guy."

DAME TOOK THE long way home that evening, Ray's offer clanging around in her brain. In a way, the proposition felt familiar, comfortable. Something she could handle. But at the same time, she'd spent years trying to leave that world — her father's world — behind. She knew the stink of other people's business all too well.

Peggy was right. You couldn't move forward when you were standing still, and in a way, taking her landlord's case seemed even worse. Like walking backward.

If she did get evicted, maybe she could move in with Meera and Lewis for a year or two and help them out with their mortgage. Maybe she could put all the IVF business behind her and save up enough money to afford a decent apartment, or even a down payment on a house. What's more, she wouldn't have to deal with Ray anymore — his unannounced visits, his broken promises, his musty, dead-end bay-and-gable. And sure, she felt kind of bad that he was suffering the slow-motion nightmare of infidelity, but she survived it; he would, too.

Dame walked for a little while down Dundas and eventually cut through Alexandra Park. All around her, dead leaves were falling; everything was frozen and grey. And yet, despite the grim landscape, the place was busy with people. As she made her way south, Dame was surprised to see a disproportionate number of round bellies bumping out of ill-fitting coats and hands pushing into aching backs. Was it always like this here, or had some pre-natal yoga class just let out?

Not far ahead, she noticed a cluster of park moms mid-selfie, their sleek black strollers idling nearby. They posed in slim-fit coats and wide-knit scarves, their leather gloves wrapped around half-fat caramel macchiatos, their faces grimaced in smiles. Dame felt the familiar swirl of nausea. She shoved her hands deeper into her pockets and kept her stare middle-distant as she passed by the women.

"Dame?"

The voice was familiar. And when she looked back and saw who it belonged to, cold bolts of electricity radiated down her spine. Her stomach turned itself sick.

Rachel. Which meant that the little bundle in the stroller was —

"Dame!" the woman called again.

Her heart was racing and she was having trouble breathing. She kept walking, quickly, and then she was running. Out of the park. Away from that woman and her child. She stumbled on the uneven ground, regained her footing, and kept going until her lungs burned. When she collapsed sobbing into a bus shelter, hot tears fogged her glasses. A little man wearing a Blue Jays toque got up and moved a couple seats down.

It took a few minutes, but when she finally caught her breath, when her body stopped hitching and sighing, Dame took out her phone and made a call.

"Ray?" she said when he answered. "Dodge says he'll take your case."

CHAPTER SIX

FOR THE FIRST time in their shared history, Ray Hobart actually knocked on Dame's door.

"Just a minute!"

Dame, of course, was on the can. And by the time she flushed the toilet and washed her hands, her landlord was in the front hall, wiping his shoes on the mat.

Baby steps, she reminded herself. "Why don't we have a seat at the kitchen table?"

They both sat down, and Dame lifted the screen of her laptop.

"All right. I've got a few questions I want to ask, just so we can put together a strategy to meet your particular —"

"Where's your father?"

Dame cleared her throat. "Well, like I said on the phone, I'll be doing most of the administrative stuff. The preliminary interview kind of falls under that category."

"Oh," Ray said.

"So, when exactly did you first —"

"It's just —" Ray looked back at the door as if Dodge was about to walk through it. "I think maybe I'd be more comfortable talking to — you know — a real investigator."

Dame sat back in her chair and looked Ray up and down. "You were born in the States, weren't you?"

"I'm sorry?"

"Michigan, probably — and you lived there until your teens."

"Look, I appreciate —"

"You went to U of T to be an engineer, but you didn't quite jive with the profession and decided to be a high school teacher, instead. I'm guessing math? Physics, maybe? You recently started playing the guitar again, you have a six- or seven-year-old kid at home, and this morning you had breakfast at Sausalito."

"How — how did you know all that?" Ray fumbled. "Did you look it up online, or …"

Dame shook her head. "You never take your shoes off when you come into my apartment. Canadians don't really do that — we're too polite. Plus, I can hear a little of that Michigan accent in your vowels — that flat, nasal *a* sound — but it's subtle, and I've noticed that in anything you've written to me — like, say, an eviction notice — you still put the *u* in all the funny British places, so I'm guessing most of your American habits were bred out of you by a more local secondary education."

"Okay, but what about U of T?"

"You've got one of those Iron Rings on your baby finger that engineers are always so proud of. And I know you got it in Toronto because every other engineering school in the world uses stainless steel. Real iron leaves a little black mark on your finger" — she pointed — "like the one you've got there."

Ray looked down at his hand.

"I know you're not currently an engineer because no firm is going to hire you with that haircut. Plus, every time I see you, you've got that white line on your butt from leaning against chalkboards. I figured high school math because it's up your alley."

Dame reached across the table and turned her landlord's hand over at the wrist. "My ex played guitar. You've got blisters on your fingertips, which means you've just started, but most forty-something beginners are a little more tentative in their playing. Your fingers already know what they're doing — they're just not as tough as they used to be. And you've wrapped one of those blisters in a Pokémon Band-Aid which tells me there's probably a little kid in your life, but if not — no judgement. I'm down with Pikachu."

For a brief moment, Dame thought of another little kid. A kid with curly hair who liked Spider-Man, not Pokémon. She pushed the memory out of her head and cleared her throat.

"As for breakfast this morning, Sausalito's the only place around here that does a decent savoury French toast. They've got that really good onion-pepper compote and I could smell the garlic, arugula, and coffee on you when you took off your jacket."

All of a sudden Ray looked very tired.

"Okay," he said. "Where do we start?"

Dame smiled. "Do you have a picture of your wife?"

He took out his phone and tapped the screen a couple times. He slid the device across the table. "That's Aki."

Dame picked up the phone and looked at the screen. The woman in the photo looked young and happy. She didn't seem to be wearing any makeup or jewellery and her dark hair was cut short. She was dressed casually, in a striped T-shirt and jean jacket. There was something about her that seemed oddly familiar.

"Could you send that picture to me?"

Ray nodded.

She slid the device back. "So, why do you think she's having an affair?"

He leaned forward. "She went back to work last fall — just over a year ago — and for a while, everything seemed okay. But then —"

"Why was she off work?"

"She wanted to stay at home with Hank."

"Your son?"

"Henry Yukao Hobart." Ray smiled a little to himself. "When Aki and I got married, we always said it would just be the two of us. But after she turned thirty, I guess she heard that clock ticking."

Dame knew exactly what that clock sounded like.

"It took a few years, and more trouble than we were expecting, but eventually we got lucky."

"And things were still okay?"

"For sure. I mean, the kid's a maniac, but we love him. We were happy. At least, I thought we were."

"So, what changed?"

"I don't know. A few months ago, she started coming home late from work —"

"Where does she work?"

"The Brickery. It's this bakery and coffee shop in Kensington. She works there a few days a week. Her friend Val owns it."

Dame took this in for a moment. "Okay. So, she started coming home late from work."

"Yeah. Usually, Aki goes in early and does the first bake around four a.m."

Dame let out a low whistle.

"She'd usually be home before lunch, but lately ..." He let it hang in the air for a second. "She said she needed to stay late and help Val up front with sales, but whenever I stopped by to see her, she wasn't there."

"Did you confront her?"

He sighed. "She said she was running errands for Val."

"Well ..."

"It's not just that. There've been so many things that don't add up."

"Like what?"

"Well like, she changed her phone password. For the last six years it was always our son's name, but when I tried to get into her phone a couple weeks ago, I couldn't do it."

"Maybe she just doesn't like you messing with her stuff."

Ray sighed. "You said Dodge doesn't do a lot of cases like this anymore."

"Domestics? No. Not really."

"Do you have any experience with this kind of thing?"

Dame took a deep breath. "Yeah. You could say that."

"So, what happens now?"

She shrugged. "Is Aki working tomorrow? At the Brickery?"

"Yeah. Sunday's the long morning shift."

"Maybe stay out of Kensington, then. At least until we get some things figured out."

"Makes sense."

Dame conjured her father's usual caveats. "Just so you know, we expect you to provide accurate information regarding the investigation, and we're not responsible for unproductive investigation time due to inaccurate information."

"Okay."

"We'll give you weekly updates every Thursday, unless circumstances dictate otherwise. So basically: don't call us, we'll call you."

"I can live with that."

"Daily billing rate is four hundred and fifty dollars plus expenses."

"Four fifty? That's more than Felski was charging."

"Plus, there's a nine-hundred-dollar retainer."

"Nine hundred dollars?" Ray ran his fingers through his long hair. "Can I just subtract it from the rent you still owe me?"

Dame shook her head. "Unfortunately, no" — she couldn't resist — "we'll need your first and last payment upfront."

Ray sighed and took out his wallet. "Is cheque okay?"

CHAPTER SEVEN

DAME'S ALARM WOKE her up early the next morning. It was still dark as she hauled herself out of bed and shuffled her way into the shower. When she was dressed and ready, she walked into the kitchen and admired the neat row of items she'd laid out on the table the night before.

On stakeouts and tail jobs, Dodge always adhered to a very specific list of supplies. Coffee and snacks were usually crucial, but Dame wasn't drinking coffee these days, and she was fairly confident she could find something to eat in Kensington Market. Otherwise, it was all there: the flashlight, the point-and-shoot camera, the map of Toronto, the book of crossword puzzles, the notepad and pen.

Dame was out of practice, but there was something soothing about the old rituals. The ceremony of preparation didn't actually make her anymore prepared for what she was about to do, but she hoped that if she kept going through the motions, the muscle memory would return.

She stuffed it all into her backpack and hoisted it over her shoulder. She was halfway out the door when she realized she'd forgotten her phone. When she picked it up off the front table, she held it in her hand for a moment. Flashlight, camera, map, puzzles, notepad. Suddenly, the bag on her back felt unnecessarily heavy. She let it slide off her shoulder and left it on the hardwood floor.

FOR MOST OF the morning, Dame bivouacked in a window seat at a juice bar called Main Squeeze, nursing a pot of Earl Grey and keeping an eye on the bake shop where Ray's wife worked. The Brickery was a ramshackle mess on Augusta Avenue that, even by the most bribable inspector's standards, couldn't be up to code. The once-yellow brick was now a peeling mustard, and its airbrushed sign the work of some talented amateur: a swooping, pseudo-neon exclamation of purple, pink, and silver.

From the comfort of her table by the window, the whole neighbourhood seemed to have a kind of neutered hipness. Enlightened souls moved along the streets, past unsolicited murals, grocer awnings, and curio shops. On outdoor racks, used clothing stores flew bright flags of vintage tees and army surplus.

Dame watched a woolly-bearded dad browse a fruit stand with his young daughter. He let go of the girl's hand to thump a cantaloupe and smell it at one end. He handed the melon down and directed her to do the same. Despite the fact that it was late October and that cantaloupe would probably taste like nail polish remover, Dame felt a familiar longing burrow into the sinewy meat of her heart.

Suddenly, she was aware of a burly, tattooed arm reaching across her line of vision. It took hold of the steel teapot in front of her.

"More hot water?" the server asked.

Dame said sure.

IT WAS AFTER one o'clock when she finally put eyes on Aki. Despite her best efforts, she'd almost missed her. She didn't understand how people did this kind of thing. Dodge always had an impressive mastery of his bladder, pissing in Pepsi bottles or irrigating alleyways when circumstance permitted. Dame on the other hand, had been making anxiety-fuelled sprints to the tiny bathroom in the basement every hour or so. Next time, she'd have to remember: less tea.

She was returning from one of these runs when she finally saw Aki, her red toque pulled down over her black hair. She was smoking, stretching her legs, and she was halfway up Augusta.

"Shit."

Dame pulled out her wallet and threw down a twenty. Already, she was hemorrhaging retainer money. She shadowed Aki for three or four blocks. The entire time, Dodge's Rules of Following were running through her head on repeat. *Number One: Don't get too close. It's like fishing. Let out a little slack, then reel it back in. Number Two: Don't stare. Find something besides your mark to look at. Number Three: Don't get caught. If your mark takes three right turns, you hang a left.*

Dame kept back nearly half a block, watching the red toque like a bobber in a sea of pedestrians. Aki took her to College, where she waited for the streetcar outside a gourmet hot dog joint. Wherever she was going, it wasn't home.

Dame risked a little proximity and pretended to be on her phone. She watched the woman cross and uncross her arms as she checked her watch.

When the streetcar finally came, Dame hung back until Aki got on, and then hurried to climb aboard. For nearly fifteen minutes, she considered the back of Aki's head and wondered what was happening inside it. They travelled past Sneaky Dee's and the Atkinson Theatre, through Little Italy, stopping every couple of minutes or so to let people on and off. And then, as they got closer to Dufferin, Aki pulled the cord.

By the time Dame got her boots on the asphalt, Ray's wife was heading north and covering ground. The street was wide and relatively empty, so Dame let her swim a length upstream. As they neared Dufferin Mall, the sidewalks got a little more crowded and Dame picked up the pace. Just outside the mall entrance, Aki stopped. She was talking to someone, some young hairdo in a tailored jacket. He was clean-shaven and handsome, with a broad smile and swimmer's build.

As Dame watched, he patted his pocket and produced a phone. He lined up beside Aki, shoulder to shoulder, and held the phone at an arm's length. He took a picture of the two of them standing together, and then checked the screen. Smiling and seemingly satisfied with the result, they shook hands and parted company.

What was all that about?

Aki continued on, cutting across a parking lot and taking another turn down a dead-ender that ran up against the back of a red-brick building. Dame recognized the place immediately as Loyalist Collegiate, an old high school built in the 1920s. It had been decommissioned for ages, but Meera had managed to save it a few years back when developers tried to have it demolished. As far as Dame knew, it had stood empty since then.

Ray's wife climbed the chain-link fence that circled the property. It rattled and rang with her weight, and she landed catlike on the other side. Dame crouched behind a parked car and watched the woman cross the schoolyard and disappear around a corner of the building.

Silently, Dame counted to ten. Then, she hurried toward the fence and tried to duplicate Aki's feline dexterity. As she swung her leg over the top, she heard the disheartening sound of tearing denim. She landed hard on the ground below, recovered, and made for the same corner. When she peeked around it, there was no sign of Aki.

For the next half hour, Dame walked around the perimeter of the building. All of the twenty-two windows on the first floor were locked and secure, as were all of the six doors. Nothing was broken and there were no signs of forced entry.

So where had Ray's wife gone?

CHAPTER EIGHT

ON THE STREETCAR back to Kensington, Dame mourned a toonie-sized hole in the crotch of her favourite jeans. She could probably fix them, or maybe even buy herself a new pair with Ray's retainer money. The truth was, she couldn't remember the last time she had actually bought new clothes. In any case, she was going to have to choose her sleuthing pants a little more carefully in the future.

Dame checked her watch. It was already past three o'clock and she was starting to feel like she'd wasted the whole day. There had to be something else she could do to justify Dodge's daily fee.

Soon enough, Dame found herself back at the Brickery. She knew she ran a risk showing her face and making herself recognizable to Aki's known associates, but the day had stalled out on her, and she was hungry for something she could use. And also, just hungry.

When she walked in, there was a glass display case stuffed with enough sugar and carbs to keep her going a good while, but it was something more olfactory that commanded her attention. The air was saturated with the smell of good coffee. The Brickery had enough java options for the most discerning of addicts, and it took a significant percentage of Dame's willpower not to order something strong and drown her sorrows. She did notice a fresh pot of decaf brewing, but even in her weakened condition, Dame wasn't going to lower herself to that sad brand of methadone.

A bandanaed woman behind the counter — possibly Aki's friend Val — leaned on pink, meaty arms dusted with flour. "What'll you have?"

Dame smiled and looked at the display case, and then the chalkboard menu. "What's good?"

The woman took a moment, either to consider the question, or to let Dame know it wasn't one worth considering. "It's all good."

"I'll try a couple of those Boston Creams, then."

As the woman tonged the donuts into a crackling paper sack, Dame glanced at a bulletin board covered in ads for rock shows and spin classes. One caught her eye.

PUMP & DUMP
Kid friendly bitch sessions.
Wednesdays 4:30 to 5:30
Alexandra Park Community Centre
New moms welcome.

The bottom of the poster was fringed with tear-away phone numbers. Next to each number was a name: *Aki*. Dame took one of the paper tabs between her finger and thumb and gave it a thoughtful tug.

"One of our bakers helps run that," Maybe-Val said, handing her the bag of donuts. "Sometimes we donate our day-olds."

"Interesting."

"Are you a new mom?"

Dame's smile froze on her face. She felt her head nod up and down.

"Well, maybe you should check it out."

"Thanks." Dame tore the tab free of the poster. "I just might."

THAT EVENING, WHEN she had finished sewing up the hole in her jeans, Dame did something she hadn't done in months — she went on Facebook. Sure enough, when she signed in, her home page was flying a lot of angry-looking red flags. Notifications and messages ran into the high double digits. Meera Banerjee. Adam Hoffman. Rachel Suarez. Some of the names seemed like characters from a story she'd finished reading a long time ago. She ignored the messages and plugged Aki's name into the search field. She found three Akiko Miyamotos, but only one located in Toronto. When she clicked on the local Aki, her privacy settings were high, and the only posted images were stock photography — flowers and sunsets — none of it too recent. She ran the same name through Twitter and Instagram and Snapchat without any luck.

Dame cast a wider net to see what Google had to say about Ray's wife but came up with almost five hundred thousand search results. A mess of names and faces. Digging through all of it would take hours. Days maybe. But then, even before she could click on the first link, her phone buzzed. It was Meera.

"Hey!" She sounded out of breath. "Any chance you're following the news?"

"No. Why?"

"You remember that old high school I worked on years ago? In Bloordale?"

"Loyalist Collegiate?" Dame was unsettled by the coincidence.

"Yeah. It's currently on fire."

"WHAT DO YOU see?" the detective asked his daughter.

The kid looked around the Skyview Restaurant. "I don't know. What am I supposed to see?"

The detective waved down the waitress, and a moment later, she appeared at their table, hair pulled back into a bun, notepad peeking out of an immaculate apron. "Can I start you two off with something to drink?"

"Two coffees, please," he said.

The waitress looked at the thirteen-year-old girl and kept smiling. "Two?"

"Yeah," the kid said. "I'm trying to stunt my growth."

The waitress laughed. "Okay, then. Two coffees. Did you need some more time to order?"

The detective looked at the woman's name tag. "Uh, Edith? Could you tell me what kind of pie I saw in that display case when we walked in?"

"That would be lemon meringue," Edith said. "Baked this morning."

The detective looked at his daughter. Her eyes were wide and she nodded her head.

"We're going to think on it a bit."

The kid sighed as Edith headed back behind the counter. "What's there to think about? It's lemon meringue."

The detective took a pack of Dominions out of his coat pocket. "Hold on, partner." He leaned back and lit one. A wreath of blue-green maple leaves circled the cigarette above his knuckle. "First, let's play a game."

The kid rolled her eyes.

"I want you to look around this restaurant and tell me one interesting thing about every person in it. If you can do that, you can have a piece of pie. Deal?"

She scanned the room. It was early still, and quiet. She counted six customers. Before she could agree to the terms, the waitress returned with their coffee.

The kid tilted her head. "Does that include her?"

The detective nodded.

"Okay," the kid said. "I can tell you that her name isn't really 'Edith.'"

The waitress froze. A white ceramic cup steamed in each hand. "It's not?"

"Uh, no. It's not," the woman confirmed. She smiled a baffled smile and set the cups down on the table. "My real name's Linda. I forgot my name tag today, and the owner gets mad if we don't wear one."

"How did you know?" the detective asked his daughter.

"I came here once before. With Rosie."

"Oh," he said.

"Edith — the real Edith — was our waitress."

"Well, now that my secret's out," the waitress said, "have you folks made a decision about that pie?"

The kid poured sugar into her cup. "Still thinking on it, Linda."

CHAPTER NINE

CAROL JANUARY STOOD smoking a cigarette on the sidewalk outside Loyalist Collegiate. She looked tall and rangy in her old firefighter's coat, her arms a bit too long for the sleeves. On her head, the middle-aged woman was sporting a black ball cap. Above the brim were the letters "OFM," below was the kind of weary disdain worn by understaffed emergency room doctors.

"I think they used to make the students smoke out here, too," Dame said as she walked up to her. "You know, after they couldn't smoke on school property anymore."

"Nice to see you, Dame," Carol said.

They shook hands.

"Sure is a lot of smoke on school property now," Dame said, looking around.

"Uh-huh." Carol dropped her cigarette butt on the sidewalk and crushed it under her boot. "Visibility's been terrible. Traffic was rerouted for hours. They were putting out spot fires until about four in the morning."

Dame blew heat into her hands and rubbed them together. She looked over at the school. The pump trucks were gone, and the front yard was a swamp of muck and detritus. Black skeletons of once-venerable trees clawed up at the ash still floating above the wreck. Two of the school's exterior walls had collapsed into minor avalanches of scorched brick and timber. On the second storey, the fire had chewed the classrooms back to steel beams and cinder blocks.

As she surveyed the ruins, Dame couldn't help but think of the Sainte-Marie Hotel. A cruel memory was creeping its way back to the surface. "Was anybody hurt?"

"No." Carol's eyes were briefly sympathetic. "Not this time." The muffled sound of a radio crackling came from her coat pocket, but she ignored it.

"Well, I'm kind of surprised to see you here so soon," Dame said. "Usually takes a couple days for the Fire Marshal to send out an investigator."

"Uh-huh."

"You must be pretty sure it was arson."

"Fire department seems to think it was accidental, but I'm not convinced either way. We're collecting samples to test for accelerants."

Down the sidewalk, a crowd of teenage destruction enthusiasts gawked and gestured toward the building.

"Isn't the Fire Marshal usually supposed to wait for hard evidence before they assign personnel?"

Carol pinched the bridge of her nose. "What's with all the questions, Dame? You working for Dodge again?"

"God no. City Hall. This was a designated heritage site."

Carol shook her head and laughed a little. "Figures." She reached into her coat pocket and produced her cigarettes. She lit another one. "Look, I'm just trying to do my job here. Give me a little room to work. And maybe tell your pal at City Hall to ease off a bit."

"My pal?"

"Uh-huh."

"Who's been on your case?"

"That woman from the Municipal Review Board. Sharon Fischer."

Dame squinted up at the fire investigator. "You've been talking to the Fish?"

"She's been sniffing around. Asking a lot of questions." Carol took another drag of her cigarette. "Probably why the Fire Marshal's office got involved in the first place. They pulled me off a case where some guy tried to light up the Guelph Civic Museum with a blowtorch. That was interesting, at least. But this? A decommissioned high school?" Her radio crackled again and she took it out of her pocket. "This is just a giant headache."

"Sharon Fischer has a reputation for causing headaches. But anyway, good luck with" — Dame gestured toward the building — "whatever happened here."

"Thanks." She softened a little. "And listen, tell Dodge I said hey. I know he's been having a tough time lately."

Dame nodded. "I will."

As the fire investigator put the radio to her ear and started walking toward the destroyed building, Dame noticed a car idling a little way up the street. It was a Chevrolet Caprice — a dented old cop cruiser, painted white. Dame couldn't say what, but there was something off about it, something that left her feeling cold. A bad tint job, bubbling away from the glass, kept her from seeing who was behind the wheel. If she could just get a little closer, she might be able to make out the driver. But when she took a few steps toward it, the car peeled out into traffic and was scolded by the horn of an oncoming pickup.

"Jesus." Meera materialized beside her. "Someone's in a hurry."

Dame kept staring down the street in the direction of the white car.

"Everything okay?" Meera asked.

"Yeah." Dame shook off the strange sensation. "Yeah, fine."

Meera turned around and assessed the damage behind her. "God. What a mess."

"Any idea who actually owns this mess?"

"I checked the register last night," Meera said. "It's changed hands a few times since we designated it as a heritage building. Right now, it's owned by some company called 'Titun Developments.'"

"A developer? Any idea what they were planning to do with it?"

"No, but" — a little grin snuck across her face — "I did a little digging, and found out something that supports an online theory."

"What's that?"

"They're making a *School Colours* reunion!" Meera let out a little squeal.

"What are you talking about?"

"Okay, so I found out that Titun was leasing Loyalist Collegiate to a guy named Hugo Howlett. And I thought that name sounded kind of familiar, so I looked him up. Turns out, Howlett was one of the original producers for *School Colours*."

Dame shrugged.

"You know, the classic Canadian teen drama?"

Dame looked up at the building again and it clicked. "That *Degrassi Junior High* rip-off?"

"It wasn't a 'rip-off.'" Meera glared at her. "*School Colours* was far superior to *Degrassi*."

"If you say so."

"Maestro Fresh Wes performed on one of the episodes."

"'Drop the Needle?'" Dame asked.

"'Let Your Backbone Slide.'"

"And they filmed all that here?"

"Yeah, but it got cancelled after, like, one season. Come on" — Meera grabbed her friend's hand and started tugging — "I'll give you the official *School Colours* tour."

Dame let herself be dragged down the sidewalk. Meera was pretty strong when she wanted to be.

"Okay, see? Over there by the flagpole? That's where Crystal and Monique shared their lunch with an old homeless man named 'The Captain.'"

"Heartwarming."

"And then he propositioned them for sexual favours."

"Oh."

"And over there? By that pile of bricks? That's where Justin got Bryan to try Quaaludes for the first time. Then Bryan passed out in Mrs. Garcia's class and she had to call an ambulance. That one was a two-parter."

"Guess it would have to be."

Meera yanked Dame over to the yellow caution tape that cordoned off the damage. "And right there? On the front steps? That's where Sonnet and Sylvie started to become" — Meera pulled Dame's hand to her chest and batted her eyelashes — "more than friends."

Dame reclaimed her hand. "Who are Sonnet and Sylvie?"

"They were best buddies on the show — kind of peripheral characters in a bunch of other storylines — but then in one episode, they were sitting on the steps talking when Sonnet's hand grazed Sylvie's. They looked into each other's eyes, leaned in closer, and then ..."

"What?"

"Mrs. Garcia burst through the front door and interrupted them."

"That Mrs. Garcia. Always such a buzzkill."

"The show was cancelled a couple episodes later. I guess a bunch of morons wrote into the CBC to complain. It was the eighties. People were extra terrible. There's a whole thing about it on the *School Colours* fan wiki."

"There's a website for a Canadian TV show that was cancelled after one season?"

"Obviously. That's where I read about all the reunion rumours. Oh, hey." She pulled Dame right up to the yellow tape. "See over there, where that stack of chairs is all melted together? That looks like the exact spot where Darren Masterson gave Jamal James the hugest atomic —"

"*Ma'am?*" a voice came across the schoolyard.

One of the remaining firefighters jogged toward them. His haircut was recent and regulation, and his face marbled with soot.

"Ma'am, you can't be this close to the barricade."

"Sorry!" Meera put her hands up in mock surrender and took an exaggerated step backward. "Sorry about that."

"This is a very hazardous area. We put that tape up for a reason."

"I know. I'm an idiot," Meera said. "Won't happen again."

The firefighter nodded and started to walk away.

"Hey," Dame called to him, "did you work this job last night?"

He stopped and turned around. "No, I'm on *A* shift. Missed most of the action."

"Do you know what time the fire started?"

His green eyes cut through the mess of his face. "Are you with the media? Because if you are —"

"Nope," Dame said. "Just a concerned citizen."

He squinted at them both. "My understanding is it started around four o'clock yesterday."

Dame thought for a moment. She'd lost Aki just after three.

"I noticed the Fire Marshal got here pretty quick." Dame gestured in the direction of Carol January. "Isn't that kind of unusual?"

"You sure you aren't with the media?"

"Why?" Dame raised an eyebrow. "You got a hot tip?"

He smiled, seemingly in spite of himself, then straightened out his face. "We treat all fires as suspicious until we can establish cause. I'm sure Ms. January's here for a good reason."

"If you say so."

As he made his way across the schoolyard, Dame noticed his name stenciled in orange across the bottom of his coat: *G. Morrow*.

"I like his suspenders," Meera said, watching him. "A girl could get tangled up in a pair of those." She sighed. "God, some days I miss being single."

"Believe me," Dame said. "You're not missing much."

CHAPTER TEN

"YOU DIDN'T HAVE any other plans, did you?" Peggy slid into the little booth.

"Well," Dame said, sitting down across from her, "if by 'plans' you mean eating the second half of a soggy falafel I couldn't finish last night, then yeah. Big plans."

"Thanks for keeping me company." Peggy smiled. "Sometimes I just need to get out of that place."

Gimme Sushi was busy with the lunch rush and cold air clung to people's coats as they walked by. A middle-aged man brought over chopsticks and glasses of water.

"I think I'm just going to get the Number Eight," Peggy said.

"Me too," Dame said. "But could I get yam tempura on the side?"

The man nodded. He collected their menus and made his way into the back of the restaurant. A few moments later, he returned with two little bowls of miso soup.

Dame breathed in the salty broth. "God, I'm starting to think I'd starve to death if I actually had to cook for myself."

"You sound like your mom. Poor Rosie could hardly boil an egg."

"We can't all be homesteaders like you, Peg." She swallowed a spoonful of soup and felt the warmth of it flood her body.

"Did I tell you I'm growing pumpkins this year?"

"No, but I hope there's some pie in it for me."

"Could be."

"How'd your tomatoes do? Last time I saw them they were all green and tiny."

"Squirrels got them."

"Aw, no. That's so disappointing."

"Isn't it?" Peggy sighed. "You plant the seeds and water them every day. You watch them grow, you start to imagine all the things you can do with them. And then one day, they're just —" She shrugged.

Dame was quiet for a moment. Her eyes welled with sudden tears.

"Oh, hon." Peggy dug a couple Kleenexes out of her purse and passed them across the table.

"I'm sorry." Dame blotted her eyes with the tissues. "Jesus, what's wrong with me? We're talking about *tomatoes*."

"You know, when John and I found out we couldn't have kids, I'd have a nervous breakdown every time I saw a Pampers commercial."

Dame blew her nose. "The doctor said I should start thinking about adopting."

"And you don't want to."

Dame sighed. "I get that it's a good thing to do. Maybe the right thing. And there are some days when I feel like a bad person for wanting what I want. But Dodge is getting older, and once he's gone" — she took a deep, shuddering breath — "he's the only real family I have left."

Peggy cleared her throat. "You know, I didn't really have a family growing up. My folks died when I was pretty young, and I got bounced around in foster care. I always just figured that, eventually, I'd start a family of my own." She shook her head.

"When John passed, I felt like I'd missed my chance. But your mom and dad" — she smiled — "they looked out for me. They made me feel like family." Peggy reached across the table and squeezed Dame's hand. "That means you're family, too."

Dame smiled. "So, I know you and Rosie were Leonard Cohen groupies, but tell me something else about the two of you."

"Like what?"

"I don't know. How did you meet?"

"Well," Peggy smiled and folded her hands together. "I actually met your father first."

"Really?"

She nodded. "I had just started at City Hall — working for the Auditor General's Office of all things — and Dodge had been hired to investigate some kind of insurance fraud. He interviewed me — you know, for the case — and I thought he was just so smart and dashing, like one of those private eyes from a movie. So, I asked him out for coffee."

"You asked Dodge on a *date*?" Dame was gleefully scandalized.

"Your father was quite a catch in his day." There was a far-away look in Peggy's eyes Dame had never seen before. "But then, he met Rosie, and eventually they got married. We all stayed friends, of course."

"You and Dodge." Dame smiled to herself and shook her head. "I never would have guessed."

"It's funny how things work out. Who knows? Maybe in some alternate universe I might've been your ..."

Before she could finish her thought, a feast of dragon and dynamite rolls materialized in front of them. They snapped their chopsticks apart and got into it.

"You know," Peggy said between mouthfuls, "I was thinking about our conversation earlier."

"The one about how I should really get on with my life?"

Peggy smiled. "There's a new position opening up with the Municipal Review Board. It's a little more responsibility, but your salary would be, well, *significantly* better. If you were interested, I think I could pull a few strings."

Dame was surprised into silence.

"This city's changing," Peggy continued, "and the two of us could work together to make sure it changes for the better."

Dame took a deep breath. "I don't know, Peg. I mean, I really appreciate the offer — and God knows I could definitely use a raise — but this job's been one of the few stable things in my life, lately."

"Just think about it. You don't have to decide right away." Peggy cleared her throat and smiled. "In the meantime, are you going to be okay for money? I know things have been tight."

"I'm okay. I kind of —" Dame pinched a piece of ginger between her chopsticks. "I kind of took a case."

"What do you mean, 'a case'?"

"A Dodge kind of case."

"Oh, hon," Peggy put her chopsticks down. "You worked so hard to get away from that whole business."

"I know. It's just a one-time thing. Typical cheating wife stuff. But listen" — Dame leaned a little over the table — "I followed this woman yesterday from Kensington to Bloordale, and guess where she wound up?"

Peggy shrugged.

"Loyalist Collegiate."

A light seemed to go on in Peggy's eyes. "The high school that just burned down?"

Dame nodded. "And then this morning, when I went back to check out the damage, Carol January was there. If the Fire Marshal's already on the scene, there's a pretty good chance it was arson, right?"

Peggy frowned. "Just try to be careful, okay? You know how you can get." She gave her a pitying look. "You're so much like your mother, sometimes."

"How do you mean?"

"That woman could be so stubborn. She never let anything go."

"Yeah, but, isn't being stubborn what made her a good journalist?"

"Maybe." Peggy sighed. "Maybe it's also what got her killed."

ALL THE WAY home from work, Dame couldn't shake the feeling she was being followed. Something — some phantom outside of her peripheral vision — seemed to appear and reappear, but whenever she looked back to confront it, there was nothing. She thought about tailing Aki to Loyalist Collegiate. Had someone seen her? She thought of Dodge's Fourth Rule of Following: *The follower should not become the followee.*

Then, as she walked west on Queen, a familiar station wagon slowed down beside her.

"Hey!" the driver's voice boomed. "Want a ride?"

It was just starting to rain, a cold, October rain, and Dame weighed being wet and miserable against being dry and miserable. She chose the latter. When she climbed into the passenger seat, she could smell the interior's familiar funk and see that the floor mats were still thatched with damp leaves and muddy gas receipts.

"Sorry," her ex-husband said. "Things are kind of a mess."

"They always were."

Adam signalled and turned back into traffic. He looked different, somehow. A little heavier, his beard a little thicker. He was wearing the same Expos hat he always wore, but a newish-looking coat she didn't recognize. She thought of his old hunting jacket — the one they used to keep hanging on a hook by the back door.

Dame would grab it when she had to take out the garbage bins or make a run to the store. It was a little big on her and a little small on him, but they made it work. Now he'd gone and found a better fit.

"Pretty ugly out there, huh?" Adam said.

Dame nodded.

"It's been a cold October," he added.

"Yep."

"Are those new glasses?"

"Kind of. They were Rosie's."

They drove for a little while in silence as fat drops of rain detonated against the windshield. Dame grasped at conversational straws but came up empty. Did she really want to know about his life now that she wasn't in it? She decided instead to cut to the chase.

"So, why were you following me?"

"Following you?" Adam frowned. "I was just heading home from work and —"

"You weren't at work." She turned and looked him up and down. "You're wearing your work boots, but your nails are clean. And you don't have that little red mark on the bridge of your nose you get from wearing safety goggles."

Adam smiled the guilty-as-charged smile she once found charming. "Never could put one over on you, could I?"

"That's not exactly true."

They were quiet again for another block.

"I'm just up here," Dame said.

Adam turned down O'Hara and double-parked outside her apartment.

"You could've called, you know," she said. "You didn't have to ambush me."

He looked out at the empty street ahead. "Rachel said she saw you in the park the other day. She said you just kind of ... took off."

"Yeah. That sounds about right."

Adam played with the clasp of his wristwatch. "She was pretty upset about it."

"*She* was upset?" Dame stopped herself from saying all the things she wanted to say.

"She's worried about you. I am too."

A bark of laughter escaped Dame's throat. "Well, I appreciate your concern and all, but —" She reached for the door handle.

"Wait."

Dame sighed. "It's been a long day, Adam. Can you just tell me what you want?"

"Okay. It's just —" He pulled long on the inhale, like the speech he'd been planning was finally finding its way out of his mouth. "I really hate that you're not in our life anymore. It seems like a waste of — I don't know — history? I mean, you wouldn't bulldoze an old building, would you? Even if it needed a little work?"

"I think your analogy needs a little work."

"I just mean — how many people do you meet in this life that really get you? That really understand who you are?"

"Just one," she said. "Or, at least, that's how I thought it worked."

Adam sighed. "I know things won't ever be the way they used to be."

"You made pretty sure of that."

A light shifted in Adam's eyes. Dame could see all the sweet contrition fading away.

"Well, it's not like you did anything to stop me."

There he was. There was the old Adam.

"You know," he continued, "so many nights I'd come home and — I mean, yeah, you were there — but you were always so far away."

"I didn't realize you needed so much attention."

"It wasn't that." Adam's face tightened up like a fist. "After that last miscarriage, I thought maybe we could figure it out together, but there were these parts of you I just couldn't access anymore. You were broken in ways I couldn't fix."

"So you traded me in for a newer model."

Adam shook his head. For a moment, he stared quietly at the steering wheel in front of him. "Do you ever think about them?" he said, finally.

"Who?"

"The ones we lost. Do you ever wonder who they might be by now? Who we might be?"

"Of course I do." Dame brushed tears out of her eyes.

"I never meant for any of this to happen, Dame."

A horn blared and a massive suv squeezed past them.

"I think you're blocking the street." She turned to look out the back window, and that's when she saw it — the infant car seat, empty, and facing away from her. Its grey canopy collapsed into itself, a plush monkey dangling from the apex of its carry handle. When she looked back at Adam, the distance between them felt infinite.

"I'm not asking you for anything," he was saying. "I just thought maybe we could grab a coffee sometime."

"I'm sorry" — she pushed her way out of the car and into the rain — "I don't drink coffee anymore."

CHAPTER ELEVEN

WHEN DAME LET herself into Dodge's apartment, her father was in the little galley kitchen, dish in one hand, blue sponge in the other. A cluster of iridescent bubbles twinkled on his wrist. His wedding band waited in the soap dish.

The old man looked up at his daughter and smiled. "*Squeak.*"

Dame raised an eyebrow.

"*Squeak,*" he said again.

Dame waited with a bag of food in one hand while her father riffed through some incomprehensible syllables. Aborted words floated out and haunted the air between them. Finally, she heard, "*Clean.*"

Released from language limbo, Dame smiled back. "Yep. Squeaky clean. Place looks great, Dodge. It's almost like you're a real grown-up or something."

Dodge chuckled a little to himself.

"I brought fish and chips," Dame said, holding the bag aloft as she managed out of her boots. "From Goldie's. And some tallboys from Chez Beer Store."

Dodge's eyebrows went up in snowy tufts. "*Fants.*"

"Very fancy. You finish up and I'll set the table. I think Goldie gave us some plastic utensils so you can give that sponge a rest for the night."

Dame put the Styrofoam cartons and plastic forks into place, while Dodge rinsed the remaining dishes and put them on the rack. When they got down to the business of eating, they were both quiet for a while.

In the silence, Dame debated whether she should tell Dodge about the new case. About the fact that she was using his name and reputation to earn a little extra money. She wasn't quite sure how he'd feel about it all and decided to keep it to herself for the time being.

After dinner, Dame cleared the mess into the kitchen garbage. On top of the microwave, she spotted a pack of Bicycles.

"Two-handed euchre?"

He nodded.

She sat down and began separating out the cards. "I saw your old pal Carol January today. She's investigating the school that burned down in Bloordale. How long did she work for you? Two years?"

Dodge held up three fingers above the scarred mess of his forearm.

"She was always a little nuts, wasn't she?"

Dodge smiled, and then tapped the top of his head with one finger.

"Yeah, she's smart. You can be crazy and still be smart. It's not like the two are mutually exclusive."

Dame dealt the cards. Dodge sipped at his beer, and then picked up his hand.

"Did that new Homecare worker stop by this week?" Dame asked. "What's her name? Fatima?"

Dodge nodded.

"She's getting you to do some speech therapy now, huh?" Dame won the first trick with an ace of diamonds. "What's she like?"

Dodge blushed a little. "*Bam ... bam-bi ...*" Finally, "*Bambina.*"

The word reassured Dame. It reminded her that, despite being stuck with a bad Scrabble rack these days, the real Dodge was in there somewhere. A Dodge who used to embarrass and infuriate her with words like *broad, tamale,* and of course, *bambina.*

"You better be on your best behaviour," she said. "Those support workers probably buy their pepper spray in bulk."

The old man grinned. He snapped down a ten of spades.

Dame looked at her hand and then threw a jack of spades on top. She moved to sweep the cards from the table. Dodge raised an eyebrow.

"I'm following suit, aren't I?" Dame looked at the cards and realized her mistake. "Shit. Left bower." She sighed. "I'm getting rusty."

She replaced the jack with a nine of spades and Dodge took the trick. He gave his daughter a knowing look and pointed at his own head.

"Yeah, yeah. Like I said — smart and crazy aren't mutually exclusive."

Dodge smiled and put down his next card. As he waited for Dame, he played his wedding ring end to end over the knuckles of his right hand.

"You're going to lose that if you're not careful."

Like a magic trick, the ring appeared between his thumb and forefinger. He pushed it back onto the appropriate digit and put his hand over his heart.

"Yeah, I've been thinking about Rosie a lot too, lately. I had lunch with Peggy and she started telling me stories about the old days."

The old man frowned and clacked his cards against the surface of the table.

"She told me she asked you out on a date, once."

Dodge shrugged and tapped the table impatiently. He'd been like this the last few times she mentioned Peggy — cool, noncommittal. If she thought about it, Dame couldn't remember the last time she'd seen Dodge and Peggy in the same room. Was it pride? Was he ashamed of what he'd become? Maybe Peggy just reminded him too much of his time with Rosie. Of the way things used to be. Or, of the way things were now.

"Maybe the three of us could get together sometime. She seems — I don't know — kind of lonely."

Dodge sighed and put his cards down. He folded his arms.

"What?" Dame asked. "What is it?"

The old man shook his head. It seemed pretty clear he was done talking for the night.

AFTER ALL THE autumn air she sucked back on the way home, Dame should have conked out the moment her head hit the pillow. Instead, she lay there in bed, her brain sifting through every detail about Aki Miyamoto and the high school that burned down. There had to be some reason why Aki broke into the place, and she wanted to know what it was. When the bulldozers showed up later that week, it would be too late.

By midnight, Dame found herself standing outside Loyalist Collegiate. Barely twenty-four hours had passed since the fire was contained, but already, there weren't any cops or firefighters guarding it. In fact, no one was paying it much attention at all. It was as if the charred wreck had become some familiar — albeit terrible — part of the landscape. Still, Dame didn't know what kind of surveillance they had on the place, so she turned her collar up and pulled her toque down snug. She circled around to the back of the old school and stopped at the yellow tape that stretched across its perimeter.

This is a very hazardous area. We put that tape up for a reason.

Staring up at the bleak destruction, a sudden sense of dread overwhelmed her — some fractured memory was fighting its way out of the darkness. Dame couldn't shake the feeling that no good would come of all this.

Of course, that never stopped her before.

CHAPTER TWELVE

"YOU HAVE TO *imagine the fire in reverse,*" *the detective said.* "*Work your way toward the point of origin. Start with the perimeter. Check the doors and windows for evidence of forced entry —* *that is, if there are any doors or windows left. Then, take a look at where there's the least damage before you start rooting around in all the black stuff.*"

"*In case they left a clue or something?*" *the kid asked.*

The detective walked ahead and toed at the charred wheel of an ancient Exercycle. "*Well, it's not like some firebug is going to leave a jerry can lying around with his name and number written on the bottom. But yeah, something like that.*"

The roof was gone, and while the walls were still standing, the kitchen was like some kind of Twilight Zone of domesticity. A white fridge was grey with smoke, the plastic of a microwave bubbled like it was being consumed by a dark fungus. A mug on the kitchen table read "World's Best Grandpa."

"*Was anybody hurt?*"

"*No.*" *The detective looked at the floor and shook his head.* "*Fire department got here pretty quick, but even still, the old folks* who lived here were never in any real danger. They were probably the ones who started the fire."

The kid's eyes went wide. "Why?"

"Money, most likely. Insurance money. That's why the insurance company pays me to investigate."

"How do you know that they did it?"

The detective scratched his head. "Well, there's arson that looks like arson, and then there's arson that looks like an accident. Someone tried to make this look like an accident, but they did a lousy job of it, which probably means we're dealing with amateurs."

She looked around the destroyed kitchen. "Seems like they did an okay job to me."

The detective laughed. "Okay, but look over here." He gestured toward the wall behind the stove. "See how the blackness spreads up and out, kind of like the letter V?"

"Yeah."

"Well, think of that V as a kind of arrow. Any guesses what the arrow points to?"

The kid squinted at the stove top. "Where the fire started?"

"You got it, partner."

She smiled. "So, maybe they just burned their dinner."

"Well, that's what they want us to think, but if you'd be so kind as to follow me into the family room ..."

The kid did as the detective asked, and he directed her to look behind the scorched box of what used to be a television set.

"See that?"

"Another arrow?"

"Yep. This one's by an outlet, so it looks like it could be an electrical fire, but the odds of two separate fires starting at the same time are a little on the low side. So, general rule of thumb: If

you've got more than one arrow, you've probably got a case of …?"
The detective looked at his daughter.

"Arson."

He nodded. "A more experienced firebug would probably have a blueprint of the place in his head. Start one fire in the right place and let it burn."

"But I still don't get why you think the old folks did it."

"Someone who was just out for kicks wouldn't be so careful, and a pro wouldn't make such rookie mistakes. But, there is something else — or a lack of something else. Notice anything a little funny around here?"

The kid scanned what was left of the room but didn't say anything.

"What do you see?"

The kid shrugged.

"What kind of pictures do we have in our family room?" he asked.

"Pictures of you and me."

"And your mom," he added.

"Yeah."

"Isn't it kind of strange there aren't any family photos in the family room? Like maybe someone took them all out before the fire even started?"

"That's so sad." The kid looked around the room again. "Things would have to be pretty messed up to burn down your own house."

IN THE BLUE halo of her little flashlight, Dame saw a sprawling horror in brief sketches. Exposed wires like the guts of an animal. The pitted chrome legs of a murdered office chair. Decades of history, now a black grit under her boots, an acrid reek in her nose.

Here and there, Dame spotted the numbered tags left behind by the Fire Marshal's team. A language of clues she didn't speak. From the news she'd gleaned online, she knew that the fire had likely started in one of the old science labs. Methodically, she worked her way around the building. Classroom by classroom. Trying to give some kind of shape to the profanity. At one point, Dame's flashlight found a mathematics problem on a chalkboard, unsolved and half-bubbled by the heat. There was no order or intention, only evidence of a desperate, hungry fire.

By the time she got to the science wing, Dame was starting to think she wasn't alone. A couple of times she had heard a quiet scrabbling as though some dog or raccoon was also searching through the rubble. But now, she was hearing something else — a sharp scraping sound — and then, the sudden groan of yielding metal. Dame's heart started beating faster, and her head started working on a way out, but she ignored them both and followed the sound through the darkness.

The noise stopped when Dame turned down a long hallway lined with lockers. As she illuminated the metal doors and built-in combination locks, she could see that time and rust had done more to damage them than the fire itself. With the exception of their stencilled numbers and the occasional slash of graffiti, the lockers looked nearly identical, oppressively uniform — a never-ending series of soldiers standing at attention.

All save for one.

Fresh scratches and a door slightly bent away from its frame told Dame that someone had recently tried to pry the locker open with a crowbar. But why would someone want to steal something from a locker that — as far as she could tell — hadn't been used in years? Dame crouched down in the filth and put the flashlight between her teeth. She turned the combination dial with her fingertips and found the mechanism still intact. She gave the door a tug to see what she was working with, and then began twisting the dial clockwise, gently, feeling for points of resistance. When she found what she wanted, she started turning the dial in the opposite direction. She was out of practice, and it took the better part of ten minutes — knees aching, glasses slipping down her nose — but then, the metal door sprang free of its frame and swung forward on its hinges.

Dame shone her light up and down the hallway once more to see if anyone was watching. The coast sufficiently clear, she pointed the beam into the narrow space that looked like the inside of a steel coffin. It was empty. Or at least, it appeared to be empty. She ran her fingers around the inside corners and the dented bottom. She stood up on her tiptoes and pushed at the locker's ceiling, pounded on its thin walls.

Finally, she found something. Wedged under the metal lip of the shelf was a small book — a relatively undamaged hardcover edition of Emily Brontë's *Wuthering Heights*. As she stood looking at the slim volume, she could hear the scrabbling noise again. It was close.

Dame painted a bright arc of light across the darkness, until finally she found her: standing still in the middle of the hall, dressed in jeans and a leather jacket. For a moment, the strange woman didn't move, and some small part of Dame whispered, *Ghost*. But then, she noticed the dull metal crowbar in the phantom's hand.

"Okay," Dame said. "Take it easy."

But instead of attacking, the woman shielded her eyes from the flashlight beam and turned away into the shadows. As she did, Dame noticed her short blonde hair and — tattooed onto the back of her neck — the outline of a small deer.

"Wait!" Dame shouted.

She gave chase, the glow of her flashlight a constant tunnel ahead of her. Dame stumbled over a tangle of ruined furniture, and her flashlight spun into the cold sludge of ash and hose water.

"*Shit*," she cursed herself. "Hey! I just — *fuck*. Come back!"

Dame picked up the dripping flashlight and scanned the room. Nothing. Nothing. *There*. Flat against the hulk of an ancient Coke machine. The blonde took off running again and Dame chased her through the dim labyrinth. She weaved in and out of the path of Dame's light, and as they got closer to the inevitable exit, the woman took a hard left into the darkness and vanished. Dame followed, clambering over the remains of a brick wall. Her foot caught some loose masonry and she found herself sprawling on the grit of a particularly unforgiving sidewalk.

"God*dammit*!"

She lay there for a moment, waiting for the pain to arrive and the embarrassment to subside. When she opened her eyes, she could make out five stubby fingers hovering in front of her face.

"Hey there, sunshine," a man's voice said. "Looks like you could use a hand."

It was Anton Felski.

CHAPTER THIRTEEN

DAME SIGHED AND allowed herself to be pulled onto her feet. She wiped her hands on her pants and looked past Felski down the sidewalk. She turned and squinted in the opposite direction. There was no sign of the woman.

"Fuck." Dame pulled the toque off her head. "*Fuck!*"

"What's with the potty mouth, Dame? Everything okay?"

"I'm fine, Felski," she said through gritted teeth.

"You sure? Looks like you dropped something there."

Dame's flashlight rolled down the sidewalk in a slow-motion attempt to escape. The damaged copy of *Wuthering Heights* lay face down on the concrete. She swung her backpack off her shoulder and stuffed them both inside.

Dame paced a little, gave herself a moment to catch her breath and give Felski the once-over. He hadn't changed all that much in the last fifteen years. What was left of his hair was unnaturally black and brilliantined to his scalp. His belly pushed against the turquoise satin of his Miami Dolphins jacket. Clamped to his head were a pair of furry ear muffs.

According to Dodge, some people became private investigators because they had a knack for it. For others, the job was a consolation prize. A few months after Dodge hired Felski, he found out the guy failed the police psychological screening exam on at least three separate occasions. He was never really sure if Felski was crazy or stupid or a little bit of both.

"You know," Felski was saying, "My math was never all that great, but I think you might be a bit old for high school. Especially one that just burned down." He cupped a cigarette against the wind and lit it.

"Did you see a woman run by?" Dame asked. "Blonde. Leather jacket. Tattoo on her neck."

"Can't say I did." The cigarette bounced in the corner of his mouth. "But she sounds like a swell gal. Friend of yours?"

"Something like that."

"I've got to say, Dame, all this poking around behind the yellow tape is a little more up Dodge's alley." Felski took another drag and gestured toward the high school. "You working for the old man again?"

"I work for City Hall now, Felski. You know that."

"Sure, but that doesn't exactly explain why you're playing midnight hide-and-go-seek with Blondie the Tattooed Lady, does it?"

"This building's on my caseload. I caught her trespassing."

"Caseload. Right. Interesting hours you City Hall types keep."

"Why are you here?"

"Professional curiosity." Felski sucked on his teeth and looked up at the destruction beside them. "Been tailing some broad for a few weeks. Couple times she wound up here. Then I hear on the news that the whole place went up in flames."

"What do you think she was doing here?"

"Oh, the usual, I imagine. You know how it is. Some people like satin sheets. Some people like abandoned high schools, am I right?"

"She was meeting someone."

"Never saw anybody, but yeah, probably. I finally caught her with some good-looking guy last week, but it wasn't here. It was at this fancy French restaurant in Yorkville."

"Huh. You think she had something to do with the fire?"

"Couldn't say. But you know, it's funny." Felski smoothed the edge of his moustache with a little finger. "Even before I could show him the photos, her husband — this guy named Hobart — gave me the heave-ho. And now you're here, snooping around, asking all these questions."

She narrowed her eyes. "So?"

"Look, we both know Dodge isn't quite the detective he used to be. Maybe we should all pool our resources, you know? Help each other out. Like we did in the good ol' days."

"The good ol' days? Back when it was Dodge giving you the 'heave-ho'?"

"Ah, hell. You know what they say: *This river I step in is not the river I stand in.*"

Dame squinted. "Heraclitus?"

"Beats me. Saw it written above the Queen Street Viaduct."

"Pretty sure that's Heraclitus."

"Well, either way, it's all water under the bridge." He winked and handed Dame his card. It was bright turquoise, the same colour as his jacket.

"*Anton Felski,*" Dame read, "*Discrete Detection.*"

"Classy, right?" he said. "You be sure and tell Dodge that if he needs some help, he can always give me a call." He stuffed his hands into his pockets and started heading down the sidewalk. "See you around, sunshine."

DAME WAITED UNTIL she got home to take a proper look at what she'd found. Sitting on her couch, she pulled the old novel out of her backpack. If there had been a dust jacket, it was long gone, and the once-navy cover had faded to a brownish purple. The spine cracked in protest when she opened the book, and the paper inside stank of smoke and mildew. There were no messages written on the pages, and nothing pressed between them. It was a perfectly plain 1972 edition of *Wuthering Heights*, and there was nothing special about it except for the fact that it had recently survived both fire and theft.

At least, that's what Dame thought until she reached the back cover. It was there that she found the little paper pocket, with the library card still inside. The borrowers listed on the card were unfamiliar to Dame, with the exception of one. The last one. And according to the date stamped next to Aki Miyamoto's name, the book was almost twenty-six years overdue.

CHAPTER FOURTEEN

THE DISTANCE BETWEEN Dame's wrist and her elbow was the only thing keeping her head off her desk. She had almost forgotten that the worst thing about moonlighting was the daylight that inevitably followed. When Peggy materialized in the Heritage office, Dame did her best to look bright-eyed and bushy-tailed, but she wasn't fooling anyone.

"Oh hon," Peggy said, "you're exhausted. You've been burning the candle at both ends, haven't you?"

"Is it that obvious?"

"If you were flying out of Pearson, your eyes would have to check their own baggage."

"That's funny."

"Thanks. I'm trying to work on my jokes. The Deputy Speaker said he likes a gal with a sense of humour."

"He won't be able to resist you."

"So, what's been keeping you up? Is it the *big case* you're working on?"

Dame looked around to make sure no one was listening. Meera and Lewis both seemed sufficiently mesmerized by their computer screens.

"Yeah," she said. "I actually ran into one of Dodge's old cronies last night. I can't quite figure out his angle. Do you remember a guy named Anton Felski?"

"Felski ..." Peggy thought it over. "Was he the draft dodger from Northern Ontario?"

"No, that was Bluegrass Joe. He went to jail for manufacturing LSD."

"Oh. Was he that awful man with the pet rat?"

"That was Robbie Rabies."

"Whatever happened to him?"

"He became a real estate agent. I heard he's doing really well, now."

"Huh." Peggy shrugged. "Sorry I can't be more help. Could you ask your father?"

Dame sighed. "It's kind of hard to talk to Dodge these days."

"I can imagine." Peggy gave her a sympathetic smile. "Just don't get in over your head, okay? And try to get more sleep. You're going to need it if you decide to interview for that job at the MRB."

Dame frowned. "Yeah, about that —"

Peggy held up a hand. "I don't need an answer right now. Just think about it. Think about how we could make this city a better place, okay?"

It was hard not to admire Peggy's optimism.

"Okay."

BY NOON, THE weather had become unseasonably warm, so Dame and Meera brought their lunches out to Nathan Phillips Square and found a concrete bench not far from where Lewis was trying to hand out flyers. A steady stream of people steered around him — students on break, the business lunch crowd — most of them, Dame noticed, were giving him a wide berth.

"I wish he'd quit with all that," Meera said, watching her husband and digging her fork around in some reheated lasagna. "It's embarrassing enough he started doing it in the first place. Now he's got to advertise?"

"I think it's nice," Dame said. "It's good to try new things."

She hadn't told Meera about taking Ray's case. Not yet. It was one thing to tell Peggy, who knew just how little glamour there was to the job. Meera's inevitable enthusiasm would make it all seem too ridiculous. Or, too real.

"It *is* kind of amazing to have the house to myself once a week." Meera held out one of Lewis' flyers. "Of course, it comes at a price."

Dame looked down at the fluorescent yellow paper. The colour alone was enough to curdle her soul, never mind the words Comic Sansed across the page: "*Tuesday Night Improv Jam.*"

"Do I really have to go?" Dame asked.

"You already told Lewis you would, so don't try and weasel out now. We're picking you up tonight. Nine o'clock sharp."

"Come on, Meera. I hate improv."

"Of course you hate improv. Everybody hates improv. But we love Lewis, right?"

Dame knew when she was beat.

"Don't be so gloomy. It'll be fun." She put a forkful of lasagna in her mouth.

"If you say so."

"*Mmmph!*" Meera hit Dame on the shoulder and then jabbed her fork in the direction of something in the crowded square.

"What?" Dame said.

Meera swallowed her food. "Isn't that Suspenders over there?"

"Who?"

"You know, the firefighter we talked to the other day." She searched her teeth with her tongue. "What's he doing here?"

Dame looked at where Meera's fork had pointed. Bundled in

a red-and-grey curling sweater, the guy didn't look much like a firefighter at all, but as he came closer, Dame recognized his bright green eyes.

"Come on." Meera grabbed her by the wrist.

"Wait. What are we —?"

"Just follow my lead."

They threaded their way through the crowd until they intercepted the man.

"Hey," Meera caught his attention. "How's it going?"

"Sorry" — he tried to move around them — "not interested."

"We met at Loyalist Collegiate the other day," Meera said. "You advised us against unsafe behaviours."

"Oh." He paused and looked at her, then at Dame. There was a flicker of recognition. "Right. Hi."

"Look, I can see you're in a hurry," Meera continued. "We just wanted to invite you to a comedy show tonight." She grabbed the yellow flyer out of Dame's hand and gave it to the firefighter.

"Thanks," he said, "but it's not really my —"

"Free drinks," Meera added. "All night."

He raised an eyebrow.

"Well, for you, anyway." Meera gestured toward her friend. "She's buying."

Dame blushed. The firefighter smiled, suddenly a little red-faced himself.

"Uh, I'll have to think about it," he said, folding up the flyer and shoving it into his jeans pocket. "Thanks for the invite."

He moved past them toward City Hall.

Dame whapped her friend's shoulder. "You're the worst."

"What? Maybe he'll stop by."

"Right," Dame said, "because handing out flyers is such a successful form of advertising."

"I don't think he'd be coming for the amateur comedy."

IT WAS STILL warm as Dame walked home down Queen Street. She knew this weather was temporary. She knew there wouldn't be many more days without ice between her boots and the sidewalk. Already the sky was starting to get that pre-sunset glow, and the early darkness of winter was on its way.

A chill passed through her body and she was once again overcome with the feeling that she was being followed. She looked over her shoulder and half expected to see Adam's station wagon creeping up behind her, but this time, there was no sign of her ex.

When she reached her neighbourhood, she found Mrs. Carnegie sitting sentinel on her motorized wheelchair. There were a few new books on the blanket that day: *T*A*C*K into Danger*, *Basil of Baker Street*, and *Nate the Great*. Dame crouched beside the display and looked at the collection. She thought of Aki Miyamoto's mouldering copy of *Wuthering Heights* lying on her coffee table at home. Seemed like people couldn't give old books away. So, what made that one so special?

"I'll take *Nate the Great*, Mrs. C." She stood up and fished around in her pocket for a toonie.

"*O-oh, I'm sorry,*" came the phlegmy purr of the old woman's larynx. "*My boy's not done with that one, yet.*" The wheelchair whined a few inches forward. The knotted joints of her hand reached out and took the book off the blanket.

"No problem." She scooped up another book: *Nancy Drew and the Secret of the Old Clock*. "This one okay?"

Mrs. Carnegie nodded. "*Jamie never liked them girl books. That one's on the house.*"

The sound of her toonie hitting the bottom of the can made a substantial thud. She walked on.

As the light of day faded, Dame turned down her street. She was almost a block from her house when she saw it, parked on the curb, blue exhaust twisting out of its tailpipe.

It was the white Chevrolet Caprice. The same banged-up cop cruiser she had noticed idling outside of Loyalist Collegiate. Dame's heart started to beat faster. She looked for a licence plate, but there wasn't one to be found. As she got closer, the car turned on its headlights and pulled away from the curb. It drove toward her slowly, and as it passed, Dame tried to make out who was behind the wheel. The peeling tint revealed only the shadowy shape of someone looking back at her.

CHAPTER FIFTEEN

A FEW HOURS later, there was a different car waiting outside Dame's apartment.

"*Improv Jam!*" Meera shouted from the passenger window. She banged on the side panel of her Jeep as Dame made her way down the steps.

"Are you drunk?" she asked as she climbed into the back seat.

"Just buzzed." Meera smiled in the rear-view. "Needed to get a head start. This guy" — she threw a thumb in Lewis's direction — "has been driving me bananas."

Dame looked over at Lewis who was gripping the steering wheel like he was trying to mow a lawn. Even in the dim light of the dashboard, Dame could see his face was pale and his hair was damp with sweat. He chanted quietly to himself: "*Always agree. Don't block. There are no mistakes, only opportunities ...*"

"He's reviewing the rules," Meera explained.

"Rules? I thought the whole point of improv was that there were no rules."

"With Lewis, there's always rules."

THERE WASN'T ALL that much to the Quick Draw Club. Near Bloor and Dufferin, the place was a black box of a minimalist theatre. There was a foot-high stage (no curtains), a lot of folding chairs (you unfolded yourself), and a small bar at the back (thank God). After Meera bought Dame a tequila and soda and got herself a pint of draft, the two of them managed to score one of the few tables planted at the back of the room. Lewis wandered off and found the other members of his improv class who welcomed him with hugs and back pats, like he was a fellow survivor of some obscure catastrophe.

"They seem nice," Dame said.

"Yep." Meera took a pull on her beer. "A very positive people, the improv community."

It took a little while for all the seats to be unfolded, but by ten o'clock it was pretty much a full house.

"Who knew improv was so popular in this town?" Dame said, looking around.

"No sign of your fireman friend, though."

In spite of herself, Dame scanned the room. "Can't say I'm surprised."

Eventually, the stage lights came up and a man appeared front and centre. He was a little older than they were, and some of the aesthetic choices he'd made for himself included a greying goatee and a gold earring circa 1988. He looked like a guy who wanted to run a record store, but possessed none of the required cynicism.

"That's Lewis's instructor," Meera whispered.

"Okay!" the man said, rubbing his hands together. There was no microphone, but his thespian's voice cut through the din. "Welcome everyone, to the Quick Draw's fourth annual Beginner's Showcase!"

The crowd erupted into enthusiastic cheers.

"Our first group of performers describe themselves as a cross between Danger Bay and Romper Room with all the danger and twice the romp. Please welcome to the stage: *The Polka-Dot Four!*"

Cue obligatory thunderous applause. From the back of the room, four people came jogging up the aisle. With the exception of Lewis, all the improvisers were in their fresh-faced twenties, but it was clear that Lewis had found a place among them. As the four positioned themselves in a line across the stage, each seemed to have a signature nervous tic: clapping, or running on the spot. One woman shook the jitters out of her hands like there was no paper towel in the restroom. Lewis, apparently, was a bouncer. They watched as he pogoed with anticipatory excitement. Dame couldn't remember if she'd ever seen him demonstrate this particular behaviour before.

One of the young women — the clothing adjuster — stepped to the edge of the stage and began addressing the audience. "Hi everyone!" she shouted. "To start us off tonight, I'm going to need someone from the audience to suggest a profession. Any kind of profession."

The once raucous crowd found itself suddenly shy.

"Come on! There are no bad suggestions!"

It was at that particular moment of sudden quiet that Dame's phone decided to ring. Its electronic song desecrated the new silence of the little theatre.

"Mother*fucker.*" The word shot out of Dame's mouth like a dart from a blowgun.

One hundred heads simultaneously turned in Dame's direction. From the stage, Lewis's eyes went wide.

Overcome with the hot shame of large-scale faux pas, Dame leapt to her feet and smuggled the device through the crowd like an accused pedophile in a media scrum. Before she left the building, she heard the clothing adjuster concede that profession-wise, "Motherfucker" might not be the best suggestion to start the evening. The slamming door killed any of the ensuing laughter.

Dame found herself in the alley behind the Quick Draw Club, the phone still making its asinine melody. The caller's name lit up the screen.

"Ray," she said, "I thought we talked about keeping business hours. Remember? Don't call us, we'll call you."

"It's just" — there was an edge of panic in her landlord's voice — "she came home late again today, and we had a fight. I stormed off. I need to know what's happening."

"You stormed off?" Dame said.

"Yeah."

"Exactly where did you go when you stormed off?"

"I ..."

"Are you in my apartment right now?"

He didn't answer.

"Jesus, Ray."

"I didn't know where else to go. And I thought Dodge might, you know ... have something for me."

Dame sighed. "Look, I'll give you my weekly report on Thursday. Like we agreed. In the meantime, you need to keep your shit together."

"Okay."

"And I want you to stay out of my apartment. Seriously."

There was a pause. "Okay."

"Good night, Ray." Dame ended the call and took a deep breath. She looked up. Between the two buildings, the city's never-dark sky cut a glowing swath.

"Something the matter?"

Dame froze. Twenty feet into the dimness, she could make out the imposing figure of a large man smoking a cigarette.

"Uh, no," Dame said. "Everything's fine."

The man flicked his butt across the alleyway and started moving toward her. Dame was calculating how quickly she could get back inside the club when she realized just who the man was.

"Sorry," the firefighter said. "Didn't mean to eavesdrop."

"Hey, no, I'm the one who should be sorry. Here I am interrupting —" Dame paused. "What exactly were you doing back there? Lurking? Brooding?"

"Lurking," he said. "I do my brooding behind Yuk Yuk's. The lighting's better." He held out his hand. "I'm Gus, by the way."

She shook it. "Dame. You about to go inside?"

"That was the plan." Gus looked at the door to the Quick Draw. "How's it going so far?"

"I might be the wrong person to ask. I'm really just here for moral support."

"Haven't been converted yet, huh?" He reached inside his sweater and brought out his cigarettes.

Dame noticed the familiar package. "You smoke Dominions?"

"I do."

She reached over and coaxed a little white cylinder out of his pack. It was identical to what Dodge used to smoke, right down to the blue-green maple leaves above the filter. She held it to her nose and breathed in. It smelled like home.

Gus held out his lighter, but Dame shook her head and gave the cigarette back to him.

"Not a lot of people smoke Dominions anymore. Used to be my dad's brand."

"Mine, too. After he died, I found a half-finished pack in one of his old coats. That's kind of how I got started." Gus put the cigarette in his mouth and thumbed the butane.

"Oh," Dame said. "Sorry."

"It was a long time ago." He took a drag and blew smoke into the sky. "What was Dominion's motto again?" He took on the corny voice of a broadcaster: "*Dominion: For Smokers with Daddy Issues.*"

"I thought it was, '*More Doctors Smoke Dominion.*'"

"Well that's not very catchy."

"Might explain their decline in popularity."

"That and, you know, all the cancer and heart disease."

The door to the theatre opened and laughter spilled into the alleyway. Two women stumbled out and the door swung shut behind them. They looked at Dame and Gus, simultaneously decided they were irrelevant, and then headed toward the street. One paused to throw up between her shoes.

"Guess they're not improv fans," the firefighter said.

"Speaking of which, I should probably get back."

"Any chance you'd want to go someplace quieter instead?" Gus asked. "I seem to remember some talk of you buying me a drink ..."

"My friends are waiting inside. Rain check?"

Gus smiled. "Only if you give me your number."

There was a flickering in Dame's sternum. "Okay. Sure."

She told him and he tapped the digits into his phone. As she watched him leave the alley and turn the corner, she immediately reconsidered his offer. She was about to catch up with him when a cloudburst of sudden applause sounded through the back exit. Meera stood holding the door open.

"What are you doing out here?" she asked.

"I didn't want to interrupt the show."

"*Again.* You didn't want to interrupt the show *again.*"

"Is Lewis pissed off?"

"No, Lewis loves you."

Dame took a breath. "I met that firefighter guy."

"What? Where is he?"

"You just missed him."

"Who is this guy? The Polkaroo? Come on inside and tell me all about it before I catch my death out here."

Dame smiled. She followed her friend back into the club and closed the door behind her.

CHAPTER SIXTEEN

THE PAPERWORK REQUIRED to remove Loyalist Collegiate from the official register of heritage designated sites was as much hassle as it was heartbreak. So instead, Dame spent her Wednesday morning reading through all the less-than-urgent-looking email she had avoided in the past few weeks. If you let it, procrastination could come full circle.

Meera also seemed to be avoiding any real work, but the sunglasses she hadn't bothered to take off her face when she collapsed into her chair that morning suggested it was for a different set of reasons.

"Ugh," she said, her voice muffled by the crook of her elbow, "whose idea was it to drink on a work night?"

"That would be yours."

"Can I blame Lewis, anyway?"

"You can, but he's out getting us Starbucks right now."

"Good point," Meera said, sitting up. "I'll wait 'til he gets back."

Dame clicked on another email in the shared folder. "Did you hear that they're painting the break room on the fourteenth floor?"

"I didn't even know there was a break room on the fourteenth floor. What colour are they painting it?"

Dame squinted into her computer screen. "Casual Khaki."

"What colour was it before?"

Dame squinted again. "Wilmington Taupe."

"And they say change is the only constant."

"This river I step in is not the river I stand in."

"Who said that?" Meera asked.

"Some dead Greek guy."

"Guess he's not in any kind of river these days."

"Guess not."

Meera turned back to her computer, and for a few moments there was only the sound of quiet machinery. A photocopier warmed up in the room next to them.

"We should really read this stuff more often," Meera said. "I mean, look at this lost opportunity. We could've signed up for a team-building conference at Lake Couchiching. Campfires, canoe lessons, free Wi-Fi."

"That actually sounds kind of nice."

"Ooh, there's a strategic-planning seminar and keynote address by Sharon Fischer."

"Maybe not so much." But then, a little light went on in Dame's head. "Where are you reading that?"

"Uh, it's from a while back. I think we may have missed the boat. Or canoe, as it were."

"Can I see?"

Dame stood up and read the email over Meera's shoulder. "That's this weekend."

"I know. Who gives up their Saturday like that?"

Dame sat back down in her chair. "So, the Fish will be out of town for a couple days."

Meera looked at her. "And?"

"Just interesting, is all."

"Since when were the Fish's weekend plans 'interesting'?"

Dame shrugged.

"What's going on with you?"

Dame leaned back in her chair. "I took the case my landlord offered me — well, offered Dodge. So I guess, technically, Dodge took the case. He just doesn't know it, yet."

"Seriously?" Meera put her sunglasses up on her head. "Why didn't you tell me?"

"I didn't want you to make a big deal about it."

"A big deal?" Meera's eyes were wide. "This is better than a true crime podcast. You're like, a real detective. Solving mysteries and shit. We need to get you one of those hats. And a trench coat!"

"Meera, this isn't a career change. I'm just trying to earn a few extra bucks."

"Whatever you say, Miss Marple." Meera picked up a pencil and tapped it on her desk. "But, I don't get it. What's the connection between your landlord's wife and Sharon Fischer?"

"Loyalist Collegiate," Dame said. "Apparently, Fischer was asking all these questions about the arson investigation. And I caught my landlord's wife sneaking around the school on Sunday just before the fire started."

"Jesus, how do people have the energy to lead these double lives? I can barely make it through an entire episode of *Grey's Anatomy* most evenings."

Dame smiled.

"Is there anything I could do to help?"

Dame thought for a moment. "Actually, there is one thing."

Meera flicked her sunglasses back down over her eyes. "Name it."

"Is there any chance I could borrow your wedding ring?"

CHAPTER SEVENTEEN

BEFORE SHE WENT inside the Alexandra Park Community Centre, Dame pushed Meera's ring onto her finger. As she fought the thing past her knuckle, she hated how familiar the cold metal felt against her skin.

Adam never bought her an engagement ring — they were both too poor — but she remembered liking the simple gold band she wore on her finger for three years. Liked it well enough to resist throwing it into a High Park duck pond after she found out about Adam's affair. She'd lost track of it when she moved out, and she hadn't seen it since.

All the way down the community centre's hall, Dame reviewed her backstory and tried to embrace the weird theatre of the task before her. At the door to Meeting Room B, Dame could hear the participants of the Brickery-sponsored Pump & Dump, a Dump already in progress.

"— and I swear, it was just like someone stomped on a mustard bottle."

The group sounded with disgust.

"It went flying across the room and landed in a brand new pair of shoes."

Disgust turned to horror.

"Luckily, they were Pete's Reeboks, so I didn't have to deal with it."

Horror evaporated into laughter. When it faded, Dame pushed open the door. "Sorry" — stupid grin clamped to her face — "just running a little late."

Heads swivelled. Seven adults. Two kids. And shit. None of them were Aki Miyamoto.

"No, no!" A woman in her early thirties stood up. She was round-faced and had the cheerful demeanour of a cooking show host. "Welcome! Please, grab a seat. I'm Paula."

"Uh, Nancy." She gave a little wave to the rest of the group. "Nancy Marple." They were organized in a loose circle of folding chairs, and with the exception of a tattooed teenager hunkered over a cooing infant, none of them seemed to be responsible for any children. Next to the chairs, one mystery child played by himself. The dark-haired boy rummaged around in a plastic bucket that, by the unmistakable clatter of it, contained a load of Lego.

Dame sat down beside a woman wearing a homemade knitted sweater.

"I'm Jill," the sweatered woman said.

"Do you live in the neighbourhood, Nancy?" Paula asked.

Dame smiled. "We just moved here. I got hired on as a —"

"*Dun duh-duh! Dun duh-duh!*" The unaccompanied minor improvised an urgent score as he sailed a blocky spaceship in swooping figure eights.

"— a receptionist at an insurance company downtown. I've got two kids —"

"*Prepare for stealth mode!*" the boy commanded.

"— a girl named Meera and —"

"*Activate mega laser!*"

"— a boy named Lewis."

"Oh no! Engines failing! Self-destru-u-uct!"

The woman beside Dame stood up and walked over to the boy, who was now smashing the spaceship back into the bucket from whence it came.

"Hank?" Jill said, crouching beside him. "Try to be a little quieter while we're talking, okay buddy?"

"Okay," the boy said, "but can you find one of those blocks with the wheels on it?"

"Your mom will be back soon. She knows how to find that stuff better than I do. Plus," she said in a stage whisper, "she's bringing treats."

The boy gasped. *"Pan old choco-lot?"*

"Maybe."

Dame took a closer look at the boy. *Hank*. Or, Henry Yukao Hobart. Maybe this wasn't going to be such a waste of time, after all.

With the boy temporarily pacified, Jill came back to her seat. She gave the others a knowing smile.

Paula cleared her throat. "Well, Nancy, I'm so happy you were able to make it." She turned and surveyed the group. "While we're waiting for coffee and snacks to arrive — Nancy, I'm so sorry we took orders before you got here — I was thinking maybe we could talk about times when we've had to pick our battles."

"Pick?" A large woman across the circle sat up in her chair. "I don't get to pick, Paula. My girls are all-battle-all-the-time."

"I guess what I mean, Reggie, is when do we let our kids get away with things that we probably shouldn't?"

"Food," a red-haired woman offered. "I'm sorry, but I am *done* fighting with my kids about what they can and can't have for dinner. If they don't like what I make, they don't have to eat it. It's not like they're going to starve to death."

"Last night, I was so tired after work, I let my kids share a bowl of popcorn for dinner," Jill said. "In front of the TV."

"Oh, do not get me started on television," Reggie got started. "It is *embarrassing* how much television I let those girls watch. And the stuff they pick? Like that *Paw Patrol*? Bunch of talking dogs operating heavy machinery — who lets a puppy fly a plane?"

The women laughed and Dame dug her nails into the palm of her hand. It was hard not to resent them. She wanted so badly all the things they took for granted. Their exhaustion. Their boredom. The new strangeness of their own bodies. She wanted to worry about latching and sleep cycles. Tummy time and screen time. She wanted to possess an intimate knowledge of another person's bowel movements. She wanted to wake up in the middle of the night and listen for the sound of her own child breathing.

"Nancy?"

Dame reacted too slowly to the bullshit name.

"What about you? What do your kids watch?"

"Um, *Sesame Street*?"

"Classic," Paula said. "Anything else?"

What did kids even watch these days? "*Mr. Dressup*?"

"That's some old school shit," Reggie said. "Good for you."

"*Lazer blaster!*" Hank was levelling a Lego-made semi-automatic at the women. "*Pew! Pew!* Now you're all dead like Grandma and our budgie, Samsonite."

"Nice work, Hank," Jill said. "Why don't you try building something else, now, okay? Something that doesn't kill people?"

It was then that a familiar woman backed into the room, balancing a paper bag on top of a tray of coffee cups. "He-ey," she said. "Sorry I'm late!"

Hank chucked his most recent invention back into the bucket and burst through the circle of chairs to hug his mother's legs.

"Hey, Chief," the woman said.

"Did you bring treats?"

"I did. I brought some custard brioche, some *pain au chocolat*, a couple cherry Danishes, and an extra apple tart for Jill because she was nice enough to pick you up after school."

"Yum," said Jill.

"And I brought coffee. Come on people, don't leave me standing here all day."

Everyone got to their feet and worked around Hank. When her hands were free, the woman scooped her son up into her arms. She turned to Dame.

"Hey, sorry," she said. "I didn't think anyone else was coming."

"It's okay."

"That's Nancy," Hank said.

"Hi, Nancy," the woman said, squinting at her. "I'm Aki. Have we met before?"

Dame felt a flush of sudden exposure. "I — I don't think so."

Aki snapped her fingers. "Kensington Market. On Sunday, right?"

Shit. "Uh, yeah" — she took a chance on the truth — "I was there."

"I thought so." Aki smiled. "I never forget a face."

Dame realized she was going to have to be more careful.

AFTER THE PUMP & Dump, Dame made sure to head home the same way Aki did. Following her was different now. On Sunday, it almost seemed like a game — one she hadn't played as well as she thought — but now, as Dame watched the woman walk hand in hand with her little boy, there was a thorny tangle of guilt and resentment blooming in her guts. On one hand, Dame felt dishonest and predatory, but on the other, she wanted to reveal Aki's selfishness to the world.

It was unfair. How could this woman — a woman who had everything Dame wanted — risk losing it all? Of all the mothers she had met that day, Dame disliked Ray's wife the most. The way she came in late and made other people responsible for her child, the way her parenting was so casual, so laissez-faire — as though Hank was a minor inconvenience, a bag of groceries she couldn't put down.

The sudden howl of a passing siren caught Dame's attention, and when she turned back to her strange quarry, she saw a different child walking with Aki. A curly-haired boy wearing Spider-Man pyjamas. Dame shook the past out of her head until the curly-haired boy was gone.

Aki and Hank moved east toward Spadina. They would probably hop the streetcar downtown, and Dame knew she needed to catch up with them before it happened. She switched on her phone's voice memo recorder, put it back into her pocket, and then jogged ahead. This time, she wanted to make sure Ray's wife noticed her.

"Aki?" she said as she caught up.

For a moment the woman seemed startled, gripping the hand of her child a little tighter. Then she recognized Dame. Or at least, who Dame said she was.

"Nancy, right?"

"Right," Dame said. "Hi, Hank."

The boy looked up at her with mute skepticism, then returned to driving a Lego car down some invisible, mid-air road.

"Are you on your way home?" Aki asked.

"No, not yet. I'm just running some errands. My husband" — she felt the ring biting into her third finger — "he's looking after the kids tonight."

"Ah. You've got one of those too, huh?"

"A husband?"

Aki nodded.

"Well, kind of. We're not exactly, uh — we're not together, right now."

"Vrrmmm — *hrrrmmmm*," Hank hummed the music of shifting gears.

"Oh," Aki said. "Sorry. That must be tough. Especially with little kids."

"Yeah," Dame-as-Nancy took a deep breath. "I didn't want to get into it at the meeting. You know, first impressions and all."

Aki looked at her. "Nancy, half of those women are single moms."

"I know. It's just — I haven't really figured out how to talk to people about it."

"Well, you know, that's what the group is all about. Nobody's going to judge you."

"They might, when they hear the whole story. It was all kind of" — Dame borrowed one of Dodge's favourite words — "messy."

The three of them crossed at Dundas and turned onto Spadina. Dame followed as they made their way over to one of the metal and glass shelters that lined the streetcar route.

"Well, this is us," Aki said.

"*Eeerk!*" Hank screeched the tires of his toy car.

"You don't live in the neighbourhood?" Dame played dumb.

"No, I just work close by."

Hank tugged at his mother's hand and she let him go.

"Stay close, Chief," she said. "It's busy here."

"Where do you work?"

"At this place called the Brickery."

"Oh, I *love* the Brickery," Dame said. "That's where I found out about the Pump & Dump. Are you a baker?"

"Yeah," Aki said. "It's not exactly glamorous, and the hours are a little bit tricky, but I love being able to —"

And then, from the corner of her eye, Dame saw it happening. A whole scene that didn't make sense. As Aki stood in front of her with her back to the road, the 510 was coming toward them, a little faster than it should. It was one of the new ones, Dame noticed. All round and sleek like a mechanical snake. And Hank — why was Hank there? He wasn't supposed to be there.

The little boy was standing right in the path of the oncoming streetcar.

CHAPTER EIGHTEEN

AS THE STREETCAR barrelled toward Hank, Dame lunged past Aki and grabbed the boy's arm. She yanked him up onto the curb as one hundred thousand pounds of glass and steel came to a screeching halt. Lego broke apart against the asphalt.

"My *car*!" Hank said. He glowered at Dame. "She wrecked my car!"

Dame let go of the boy's arm.

Aki's eyes were wide. For a moment, she didn't move. The commuters who had watched it all play out slowed down and stared, but eventually, they made their way to their seats. By the time the crowd cleared, Aki was wrapped around her son.

The driver stepped out, his safety vest reflecting the last of the sunshine. "He all right?"

Dame was crouched and picking up the scattered pieces of Lego. "Yeah. I think so."

The driver shook his head and muttered to himself. A moment later, the streetcar clanged and trundled away on its route. Dame looked down at the plastic blocks in her hand. She was flooded with endorphins. Swimming in them.

Aki knelt on the ground, her arms around her child. Another silent minute passed before Hank recovered from his confusion and squirmed out of his mother's embrace. Aki grabbed him by both shoulders and looked him in the eyes. "Never, *ever* do that again. It's not safe. You always stay *right beside me*. Okay?"

"Okay," Hank said quietly. He didn't seem to understand what had happened, only that it carried some pretty serious weight. "Are you mad at me?"

"No. I love you." Aki wiped tears from her eyes with the heel of her hand. "Just — hold on to me, okay? Tight as you can. Don't let go."

Aki looked up at Dame. "Thank you. I can't — I can't believe I wasn't *watching* him. If you hadn't —" Her face collapsed in realization, and she buried her face into her son's shoulder.

Dame wanted to hate her. She wanted to believe that this woman was negligent and irresponsible, and that she didn't deserve to be a mother. But watching her hold the little boy, watching her suffer the possibility of his loss, Dame couldn't believe for an instant that Aki didn't love her child enough. And in that moment, Dame understood that she had never loved anyone as much as Aki loved Hank.

"It was just a fluke thing," she said, offering what little comfort she could. "I was distracting you, and that driver was coming in way too fast."

"Jesus." Aki stood up. She was shaking.

"Maybe we should go sit down somewhere."

"Yeah. Good idea." She heaved a sigh. "I know just the place."

AKI POURED SOME bourbon into a cup that read "*Old Bakers Never Retire, They Just Stop Making Dough*" and put it down where Dame sat at the stainless steel table. "I always keep a couple bottles of this stuff back here. It's really good for gingerbread. And Friday afternoons." She poured herself some and bellied up beside Dame.

In the back of the Brickery, they clinked each other a cheers and took a pull. At the other end of the table, Hank sat engrossed in what must've been his third *pan old choco-lot* of the day.

"Did you want anything to eat?" Aki asked. "We've got lots of stuff in the freezer."

"This is good for now," Dame said, taking another sip.

She looked around the little bakery. The space was crowded with a massive fridge, empty cooling racks, the sinister corkscrew of the industrial mixer, and of course, two brick ovens that gave the place its name. Compared to the grungy storefront she'd visited on Sunday, the back was surprisingly tidy. "So, this is where it all happens, huh?"

"Pretty much," Aki said. "Hank, show Nancy how we get the ovens ready."

The little boy shoved the rest of his snack into his mouth, chewed noisily, and then swallowed. He slid off the stool and crossed the room.

"First, she starts a fire in here." He gestured to the inside of the oven. "And then it gets really hot and the bricks turn white."

Aki nodded. "And then what do I do?"

"She takes this big thing here." Hank tried to lift a long rake that leaned beside the oven, but it was too heavy. His mom jumped up to help him steady it. "And she scrapes all the ashes out and puts the dough and stuff in there."

From her seat, Dame eyed the inside of the oven. "They're really not that big, are they?"

"No, we have to do five or six bakes a day."

Dame adjusted her glasses. "You must have to start a lot of fires."

"*Mo-om?*" Hank said. "Can I watch *Odd Squad* on your phone?"

"Yeah, but use my headphones so we don't have to listen to it, okay Hankerchief?"

The little boy was already digging around in his mother's purse. "Okay."

Aki watched him until he was sedated by the shifting light of her device. She sat back down beside Dame. "I need a cigarette," she said quietly, "but I can't with you-know-who around."

"I quit when I got pregnant," Dame lied.

"So did I. That boy's the reason I quit, and the reason I started up again."

Dame laughed.

"Your kids are how old?" Aki asked.

Shit. In her head, she reconstructed her fictional family. "Three and five."

"Right in the thick of it, huh?"

Dame reached into her pocket and put the Lego pieces she had collected on the steel surface. "Yeah."

"Seems like your husband picked a great time to leave."

"He didn't — it wasn't really his fault." Dame drained the rest of her cup. The dishonesty was getting harder and harder. "I had an affair."

"Oh," Aki said. Without asking, she poured Dame a refill and topped herself up as well.

Dame sighed. "This guy — an old friend of ours — started paying more attention to me. Told me he loved me. I thought I was in love, too, whatever that means."

"How long did it go on for?"

"A while," Dame said. "Months, I guess."

"How'd your husband find out?"

"Same way everybody finds out these days," Dame said. "He looked at my phone."

Dame remembered the text that Rachel had sent Adam. The one she saw when he was in the shower. It was only two words long. Two little words that fucked up her entire universe: *I'm late.* All the old hurt welled up, and she had to fight it back down.

"I catch my husband looking at my phone sometimes," Aki said. "I think men are more suspicious than women because they assume we have the same capacity for bullshit they do."

Dame smiled. In spite of everything, she was enjoying Aki's company.

"It's funny," she said. "Adam's a smart guy. Good problem solver. Always great at reading people. I tried to throw him a surprise party once, but he knew the whole time." Dame took another sip. "And still, the only reason he found out about the affair was because of a text message."

"Sometimes people just don't want to know the truth." Aki drummed her fingers on the steel surface of the table. "What happened with the other guy?"

"Didn't work out." Dame cleared her throat. "Sorry. I really shouldn't lay all this on you. I mean, you barely know me. You must think —"

"No," Aki said. "I get it. Marriage is a locked room. Everybody outside it wants in. Everybody inside wants back out. Someone hands you a key, of course you're going to think about using it. Especially if there's a couple of screaming kids locked in there with you."

Dame laughed.

Aki picked up the pieces of Lego from the table and rolled them around in her hand like dice. She looked over at Hank, who was still fixated on the screen. "Ray — my husband — we've been having some problems this past year."

Dame tried to look interested, but not too interested. She hoped her phone was still recording.

"I'm pretty sure he thinks I'm seeing someone else."

Dame took another sip of the bourbon and eased into the question. "Are you?"

Aki kept her eyes on her cup and rotated it slowly on the table. For the first time, Dame noticed the word printed across its porcelain: "*Alcatraz.*"

"The thing you have to understand," Aki said, "is that when Ray and I first got together —"

"*Battery's dead!*" Hank shouted. He took out the ear buds and waggled the phone at his mom. "Screen's blank. Can't see anything."

Aki reached over and took the phone. "Shoot. Do you know what time it is?"

Dame looked at her watch. "About seven thirty."

"Dammit." Aki stood up. "We should probably get going. It's almost Hank's bedtime, and Ray gets kind of twitchy when I don't stick to the plan."

Dame drained her drink. "I can imagine that."

Aki shelved the bourbon and put the dirty cups in the sink. She let Dame and Hank out the back door of the bakery before she locked it. They walked a little way in the cool weather, and Dame felt the booze boiling in her veins.

"So," Aki said, "are you taking your kids trick-or-treating on Saturday?"

"Probably."

"Well, if you're up for doing something after, my friend is having a Halloween party. You should come."

"Same crowd as today?"

Aki laughed a little and shook her head. "Kind of a different scene. It's a costume party at my friend Hugo's condo."

"Hugo?" The name pinged in Dame's brain.

"You'd love him. He's a TV producer. Has this great place in the Distillery District. His parties are always super fun."

Hugo Howlett. It had to be. The producer of Meera's favourite TV show, and the guy who happened to be leasing Loyalist Collegiate when it burned down.

"Are you going with your husband?"

"Ray?" Aki said her husband's name like it tasted funny in her mouth. "I didn't exactly tell him about the party. He just thinks I'm dressing up and watching *The Rocky Horror Picture Show* at Val's like I do every year."

"Okay." Dame shrugged. "Let me give you my number, and I'll see if I can find a sitter."

ON THE STREETCAR back to her neighbourhood, Dame pulled a tangle of headphones out of her coat and reviewed the conversation with Aki.

The thing you have to understand is that when Ray and I first got together —

Battery's dead!

She kept listening.

… a costume party at my friend Hugo's condo … He's a TV producer …

Dame hit pause. A couple things came to mind. The first was what Anton Felski had said outside of Loyalist Collegiate: *I finally caught her with some good-looking guy last week … at this fancy French restaurant in Yorkville.* The second was the photograph Aki posed for outside of Dufferin Mall. Who would ask a stranger for a selfie?

Dame Googled the *School Colours* wiki Meera had told her about days before and scrolled through the character profiles one by one. Eventually, she came to one that caught her eye.

Sonoko "Sonnet" Suzuki played on the school field hockey team and was a member of the poetry club. Her favourite teacher was Ms. Lovell and her best friend was Sylvie Hart (see Cancellation Controversy). Sonnet was portrayed by Stephanie Kai.

"Stephanie Kai?" Dame said, disappointed.

But then, when she clicked on the tiny thumbnail photo of the actor, a familiar face leapt up to greet her. Of course. Stephanie Kai was a stage name.

God, how much time had Dodge spent trying to figure things like this out? How many hours had he wasted at the library, going blind on directories and microfiche? How many times had he put on rubber gloves to dig through people's trash? And now, she could do it sitting on her ass, killing time on the streetcar.

Dame texted Meera. *I might need your help with this case after all.*

A few moments later, Meera texted back. *How come?*

I think my landlord's wife is Sonnet Suzuki.

Meera filled her screen with a series of emojis Dame did not fully comprehend.

CHAPTER NINETEEN

THE NEXT DAY at work, Peggy stopped by the office.

"Dame, any chance you've returned the Atkinson blueprints to Archives?"

"Uh, no." Dame turned around in her chair. "I was going to do that this afternoon."

Peggy leaned against the door frame. "Sharon Fischer wants to take a look at them. Could I get you to run them up to her?"

"The Fish?" Dame caught Meera rolling her eyes. "That's worse than going to Archives. Couldn't we just scan them and send her an email or something?"

"Sorry, hon. She wants the real deal. You know how she is."

"Okay." Dame dragged a cardboard tube out from under her desk. "No problem."

Peggy waited and walked her to the elevator.

"How are things going with the Deputy Speaker?" Dame asked.

"Not well. Apparently, he's been seeing Alicia Patterson in Waste Management."

"Sorry, Peggy. That's really" — she cleared her throat — "shitty."

The silver-haired woman snorted. "It's probably for the best. That man didn't know devil's ivy from a Christmas cactus."

Dame smiled.

"What about you? Have you thought any more about applying for that job with the MRB?"

"A little. I wouldn't have to work alongside the Fish, would I?"

"Probably not. I think Sharon's days at the Municipal Review Board are numbered."

"Huh."

"You know, I looked into it. You'd be making almost twice as much as what you're making now."

Dame stopped and looked at Peggy. "Twice?"

"You'd get full benefits — including dental — *and*, you'd never get stuck doing private eye work again."

Dame took a deep breath. "That does sound pretty great."

"Apparently, they've been talking about designating all of West Queen West — even parts of your neighbourhood."

"Really?"

"Think of all the good we could do. The two of us working together? As a team? We could save this city from itself."

"The MRB has been making a lot of questionable decisions lately."

"If you're serious," Peggy said, "City Hall likes to fill these positions internally. But once it's posted, there'll be a lot of competition."

"So, I guess the clock is ticking."

Peggy smiled. "Isn't it always?"

WHEN DAME GOT to Sharon Fischer's office, the door was already open. The Fish was sitting at her desk, typing furiously into her computer. She barely seemed to register Dame when she knocked on the door.

"Just a moment." Her fingers clattered away at the keys for another few seconds while Dame stood, cradling the cardboard tube. Finally, Fischer looked up from the screen. "Ms. Polara," she said. "Are those the —?"

"Atkinson blueprints."

"Yes. I heard you discovered some rather thrilling history." She cleared her throat. "A heritage basement, was it?"

"Take a look for yourself." Dame held out the tube. "I wouldn't want to ruin the surprise."

"Put it on my desk, would you?" She patted the wood in front of her and turned back to her computer screen.

Dame took a deep breath and crossed the room. Fischer's office was impressively large and featured a fresh coat of Casual Khaki. Dame couldn't help but imagine what it would be like to work out of a place like this — two windows, a half-decent view of the skating pavilion — the decor was godawful, but it wouldn't be hard to redecorate.

Fischer's enormous desk was immaculate, save for a scattering of file folders that matched the beige of the room and a leather-ette day planner beside her computer. As Dame put the blueprints down, she noticed a bright turquoise business card clipped to the front of the planner. "*Anton Felski,*" it read, "*Discrete Detection.*"

Fischer stopped typing. "Was there something else?"

Dame shook her head. "Uh, no."

She made for the door and felt Fischer's eyes on her until she left the room.

IT WAS GETTING colder as Dame walked west on Queen. The sky was steely and spitting rain, and damp yellow leaves clung

desperately to their dark boughs. Her first weekly update with
Ray — the one she'd been dreading all afternoon — wasn't for
a couple hours, and Dame figured she still had enough time to
check in on Dodge.

She was thinking through reasons why someone like Sharon
Fischer might hire someone like Anton Felski, when she noticed a
young family struggling their way out of a restaurant. They were
bundled up and miserable with the weather — the baby fussing
in his father's arms, the mother dragging the empty stroller down
concrete steps. Dame smiled to herself as the little unit soldiered
out into the evening, but her smile soon faded when she recognized the familiar Expos cap.

She put her hood up over her head, but it was too late. Rachel
had already spotted her and alerted Adam, who was busy clipping
their child into the stroller. They stood there, bracing for Dame's
arrival and the inevitable confrontation. Even the cherubic infant seemed to eye her with suspicion as the length of sidewalk
between them got shorter and shorter. Dame searched the street
for a way out, but she was penned in by traffic and storefronts.
She was having trouble breathing now, her stomach churning, her
heart jackhammering. For a desperate moment, she considered
swallowing her pride and turning back the way she came. But
then, she saw a sign from above: a sign that read "*Sodapop Tattoo.*" She hung a quick left.

When Dame walked inside, the woman behind the counter
glanced at a watch strategically strapped between the artwork on
her hand and the artwork on her wrist. "Did you have an appointment?" she asked. "We don't usually do walk-ins."

Along with a number of other safe and sterile tattoo parlours,
Sodapop had cropped up a few years back to meet the growing
demand for permanent ink. But Dame remembered a time when
the location was a nameless dive that didn't card its underage

patrons — *if* those underage patrons were smart enough to sneak in by the back alley.

"Actually," Dame said. "I was hoping for more of a walk-through."

As she left the alley and turned back onto Queen, Dame could see the little family, making their way down the sidewalk in the opposite direction. Adam was pushing the stroller and Rachel kept her hand on the small of his back.

Seeing the three of them together, Dame had an acute understanding of what she'd lost. Adam was supposed to be hers. That child was supposed to be hers. And knowing they weren't, Dame never wanted to see them again. She wanted to burn them completely from her memory.

"DODGE? HAVE YOU eaten yet?" Dame stood at the doorway of her father's apartment. "I thought maybe we could order a —"

She stopped for a moment and listened. She couldn't be sure, but it sounded like someone besides her father was in the apartment. When Dame walked inside, a woman was sitting at the kitchen table across from her father. Between them were stacks of playing cards.

"Oh," Dame said. "I didn't mean to —"

Dodge looked up at his daughter. He fumbled for words that wouldn't come.

"Hello," the woman said, standing up. "I'm Fatima. From the Homecare service."

She was short and broad, and her hair was pulled back into a tidy bun. Dame adjusted her glasses. "I'm sorry. I didn't realize you worked so late."

"We don't usually. But David is quite" — she looked at Dodge — "convincing."

Dame also gave Dodge a look. "He is, is he?"

"Yes," she said. "Especially when he thinks he's winning."

"Oh well, don't let me interrupt you," Dame said. "I was just —"

"No, no," Fatima said. "I should really go home and feed my cat. He pees on the couch when I come back late."

She scooped up the cards, wrapped an elastic band around them, and left the deck on the table. "You better practice up, mister sir," she said to Dodge. "Next time, I won't go so easy on you."

A moment later, she was out the door, and Dame had taken her seat across from her father. "And here I thought I was your euchre partner."

Dodge smiled self-consciously and struggled to pronounce a word. His attempt yielded only a rumbling cough.

"I know, I know," Dame said. "Bambina."

He shook his head. "*Friend.*"

Dame nodded. "You know, another friend of yours offered me a job the other day."

Dodge gave her a quizzical look.

"There's an opening at the Municipal Review Board. I'd get to work side by side with Peggy and make some really important decisions. Apparently, the money is really good, and" — she could see something happening on Dodge's face: sadness or anger, she couldn't be sure — "the benefits are supposed to be —"

The old man stood up abruptly. He crossed to the kitchen and took a stack of coffee filters out of the cabinet. He fit one into his coffee maker.

"Dodge?"

He grabbed the can of Maxwell House on the counter and started spooning coffee into the machine.

"Dodge, if you're making some for me, I'm not —"

"*Don't.*" He turned around so quickly that some of the coffee grounds spilled onto the floor.

Dame stood up. "Don't what?"

"*Don't.*"

"Don't take the job? Why not?"

She waited patiently as Dodge filled the air with broken words.

"I'm sorry," she said at last. "I just — I don't understand what you mean."

A heavy silence hung between them. Dodge filled the coffee carafe with water and poured it into the coffee maker.

Dame looked at her watch. "Should I order us something to eat?" she said finally. "I need to get home by eight o'clock, but maybe —"

He shook his head.

"Do you want to watch a show or something?"

He shook his head again.

"Okay. Well, I guess I should hit the road, then."

There was something he wasn't telling her. Couldn't tell her. And a part of her wondered if he'd find a way to do it, before he lost his words completely.

CHAPTER TWENTY

THE PARKING GARAGE below Sunset Apartments didn't seem like a great place to store your valuables, and Dame was a little surprised that Dodge would be so lax with something he had not only named, but also used to clean and caress on a daily basis.

Her father's inexplicable funk had cleared a little when Dame asked to borrow Loretta ("*I need something for work with a decent lens*"), but when he produced the keys to his car, she was again forced to confront the very real possibility that Dodge was losing his marbles. It was only after Dame found her father's Buick — a forgettable sedan, filed neatly in its assigned spot — that she decided maybe it wasn't such a bad hiding place after all. The camera and case were in the trunk, snug inside a bogus jerry can, along with a few unused rolls of film, fake business cards, and something that looked like an old leather sunglasses case cracked with age.

Dame left the trunk open and walked around the car. Not surprisingly, two of the tires had gone flat. Technically, Dodge still had his licence, but as far as Dame knew, he hadn't climbed behind the wheel since the stroke. She wondered how much work it would take to get the old heap going again.

A couple times, Dame had thought about asking Dodge to borrow his car on a kind of permanent basis, but she realized the question would force them to acknowledge some sad truths about the old man's condition. And Dame was pretty sure neither of them were ready to have that conversation. Not yet, anyway.

She slung the camera around her neck and pocketed the film. A digital camera — even her phone — might be more practical, but there was something reassuring about the old Pentax. It was like bringing Dodge along for the ride.

Dame sifted through the rest of her father's stash. She picked up the old leather case and heard a familiar rattle inside. She stuffed it into her coat pocket, then slammed the trunk shut.

THE KID ADJUSTED *her scarf. "I told you they'd cancel school."*

"This is nothing," the detective said, a few steps ahead of her. "You know what they'd call a day like this when I was growing up?"

"Yeah. Wednesday."

She'd heard the joke before.

The sidewalks were filling up with snow and she was careful to fit her shoes into her father's bootprints. She watched the back of the detective's head. His collar was turned up, and a cap rested on his greying hair. Besides the inevitable coughing fit he'd have when they got inside, he seemed to have some sort of old man immunity against the cold.

"Do you have any work to do today?" she asked.

"Not today, partner. I was supposed to meet a client but they wimped out. Seems like the whole world's afraid of a little snow."

"Fifteen centimetres isn't 'a little snow.'"

"The way people act around here you'd think it was the Rapture."

The kid wasn't quite sure what that was, but she didn't bother asking. Already, the cold had numbed her jaw, and her words were coming out thick and stupid.

When they got to their house, the detective did a little jog up the front steps, as if the weather was finally getting to him. He took off his gloves — ludicrously thin for these temperatures — and produced his keys from his pocket.

"Here," he said, handing her a small leather case, "hold on to this for a second."

The kid stared at the thing in her hands for a moment while her father got the door open.

"Why do you have —?"

The door slammed shut on her question.

"Hey!" The kid tried the handle, but it wouldn't budge. "Come on. That's not funny."

There was no answer.

"Let me in!" She pounded on the door. "It's freezing out here!"

Snow from the eaves knocked loose and fell to the ground around her. Some stuck to the side of her mitten. Still, the door wouldn't budge.

She ran around the house but the back door was locked as well. She kicked at the metal door until the rubber tread of her winter boot left a black mark across it. A mean-spirited wind came up and found its way under her coat. Tears made her eyelashes stick together as she looked down at the little case the detective had put in her hand. She couldn't believe he was making her do this on a day like today.

The back steps were slushy with salt and foot traffic. She crouched down, took off her mitts, and opened the leather case on a clean patch of snow. Inside was a collection of slender metal instruments, like the ones laid out at her last dentist appointment. Some of the tools were homemade — fashioned from metal rake *tines, windshield wiper inserts, even from the arm of an old pair of sunglasses — but some were the real deal, and by now, she knew them by name: Deforest diamond, Bogota, gonzo hook, worm. She picked up a city rake — its slim profile like a tiny urban skyline — and put it down again.*

She pulled her scarf under her chin and squinted up at the circular lock above. She'd done this before, but not when her fingers felt like dumb stumps, and never on her own house. The kid took one of the tension wrenches and slid it into the bottom of the keyway. Keeping it in place with one finger, she got to work with a standard hook. The seven minutes she spent listening for the almost-inaudible click of the pins setting into place were a cruel purgatory.

She shed her toque and scarf in the back hallway. The air was warm and smelled of coffee. Her father came around the corner with a cup, as the kid jerked herself out of her coat and kicked her boots in his general direction.

"Less than ten minutes," he said. "Not bad."

She threw the leather case on the floor. The tools jangled out onto the linoleum.

"I figured since you weren't going to school today, you might as well learn something."

The kid stormed past her father and into the kitchen. She pulled the coffee pot off the burner but couldn't keep it steady. She put it back. The detective poured her a cup and put it on the counter.

"Did you try raking first?" he asked. "Or did you go straight to single pin picking?"

The kid took the coffee cup in two hands. "You know, Mr. Singh taught Shruti to change a tire," she said. "And Kaitlyn's dad taught her to tape up a hockey stick. That's the kind of stuff you should be showing me how to do."

He didn't say anything.

"Sometimes, I just wish you'd act like a normal dad."

"This stuff I'm showing you — it could help you." The detective coughed into his fist. "It might save your life one day."

"Not the kind of life I want to live."

The detective sipped at his coffee.

"I'm sorry," the kid said. "I don't want to be like you. I don't want to spend all my time sneaking around solving other people's problems. I want to have a normal life and a normal family. The way we were a normal family. Before."

The detective took a deep breath. "I want you to have that, too," he said, "but in the meantime, this is your life. All we've got is each other. We've got to watch each other's back."

The kid rolled her eyes. She stomped up the stairs to her room and slammed the door shut. She knew there was no point in locking it.

DAME WAS A little worried she might be late for her first weekly meeting with Ray, but she managed to beat him to the apartment by almost half an hour. When she let him in, he took off his shoes and left them by the front door. Dame was impressed. The guy's hair was even combed for once.

"Still no Dodge tonight, huh?" he said.

"Sorry."

"Well" — he shrugged — "you're the professional."

For a brief moment, Dame wondered if Ray had sent a slightly more charming twin brother in his place.

Once again, they sat together at the kitchen table facing her laptop. This time, Dame had drawn up a series of detailed notes about Aki's whereabouts over the past several days. She might have left out a few minor details — like the part where his son was nearly killed by an oncoming streetcar and the fact that Aki was secretly attending a Halloween party — but otherwise, her presentation was, as Ray had said himself, quite professional.

"So, I did a little research," Dame said. "You never told me your wife was on a TV show."

Ray grinned a little. "I'm impressed you found out about that. Her dad wouldn't let her use her real name. You know — protect the family reputation and all that."

"Has she been in contact recently with anyone who worked on *School Colours*?"

Ray shook his head. "Not that I know of. Why? Do you think that might have something to do with —"

"I just think it's interesting that she visited the high school where it was filmed. I mean, what was that? Some kind of stroll down memory lane?"

Ray shook his head. "I kind of doubt it. She never talks about that show. I even bought the series on DVD for her birthday one year, but she never wanted to watch it."

Dame nodded and looked in the direction of her bookshelf. "Did Aki ever mention an old novel that was special to her? Classic literature, maybe?"

Ray laughed a little. "No, Aki usually reads non-fiction. Autobiographies. Celebrity cookbooks. She's been really into that Michael Pollan guy lately."

"Okay. Well, I think that just about wraps things up for tonight." As she closed her laptop, Dame noticed Ray's cartoon-free fingers.

"No more Pikachu Band-Aids, huh?"

"Nope." Ray smiled. "And check out these calluses."

Dame prodded the tough skin on one of his fingers.

"You could stick pins through them and I wouldn't feel a thing," he said.

"Gross." She poked at another one. "So, does this mean you've finally mastered 'Stairway to Heaven'?"

Dame was surprised to feel Ray's fingers close around hers.

"You know," he was saying, "sometimes I think maybe you understand me better than —"

Dame pulled her hand free and stood up, knocking her chair over. She busied herself with righting it. There was a sensation like hot gravy sliding down the back of her spine.

"So, I'll contact you next Thursday with another report?" she said, a little too loudly.

"Yeah," Ray said. "Okay."

Dame stood motionless, staring at the floor tiles, and listening as Ray made his way toward the door.

"Have a good night," he said.

"Yep."

When she finally heard the door close, Dame sank back into the kitchen chair. "*Fu-uck*," she said to the empty room.

As if in response, her phone buzzed in her pocket. When she looked at it, there was a message from Aki.

Hey! You still want to go to Hugo's party on Saturday?

Dame looked at the empty chair Ray had recently vacated.

Just trying to find a sitter, she replied.

Good talking to you yesterday.

Dame felt the weight of the phone in her hand.

Yeah, she wrote. *Same here.*

She was starting to understand why Dodge hated domestics so much.

CHAPTER TWENTY-ONE

THE NEXT MORNING, Dame went into work early and made a call from the office landline. After the third ring, a young man picked up and said, "Howlett Entertainment, how may I direct your call?"

"Oh, hi." She fried her vocals a little, tried to sound younger, hipper. "Yeah, could you put me through to, uh, Hugo?"

"Is Mr. Howlett expecting your call?"

"I don't know, to be honest. I think one of my people talked to one of your people at some point? I work for *eightysomething?*"

An unimpressed silence hung on the other line.

"The YouTube channel? We profile, like, eighties TV stuff? We just hit two million subscribers. You should really check us out."

"Mr. Howlett isn't available right now, but if you'd like to leave a message —"

"Actually, if it's cool," Dame said, "I was kind of hoping to arrange an interview."

"An interview?"

"Yeah, we were thinking about doing a thing on one of his older productions, *School Colours?*"

There was a pause. Dame could hear the sound of a keyboard hard at work. "Would you mind if I put you on hold for a moment?"

The moment turned out to be a good six minutes, but when he returned, the man on the phone sounded marginally friendlier. "So, Mr. Howlett is available next Wednesday —"

"Aw, yeah. Sorry. That's not going to work for us. I've got, you know, deadlines."

More keyboard clacking. "Well, his twelve o'clock just cancelled. I could squeeze you in for lunch today. Would that work?"

"Today?" Dame tried to suppress her enthusiasm. "I guess I could make that work."

"Great. And could I get your contact information, Ms. —?"

"Highsmith," she said. "Agatha Highsmith."

Dame ended the call, and then realized she needed to do a little market research. As she sipped on her Lemon Zinger, she powered through a series of YouTube videos. She scrolled, and clicked, and found herself in a loud wasteland of gaming channels and makeup tutorials. Dame was in the middle of a video depicting teenagers trying to use a rotary phone when her colleagues walked into the office. Lewis was stone-faced. Meera collapsed into her chair. Her hair was tied up in a messy bun.

"What's wrong?"

Meera looked up at Lewis.

"Ah, shit. You haven't heard?"

"CONSTRUCTED IN 1844, *Good Shepherd was one of Toronto's first Anglican churches.*"

The little plaque was fixed to a boulder on the corner of the lot. Lewis kept reading. "*In 1977, the Monarchist League of Canada planted a Silver Jubilee Rose Garden on the property.*

While the church has undergone a number of renovations, the bell tower remains an outstanding example of Early English Gothic architecture."

"Welp." Lewis kicked at a little chunk of rubble that had found its way under the yellow tape. "Not any more it doesn't."

Dame shook her head. "How does this happen twice in one week?"

The three of them stood amid a small crowd, staring up at the remains of the west end church. Two of the pump trucks had left, but one remained, and a couple of firefighters were handling the hose. The walls of the bell tower were still standing, but the roof had collapsed, and through the open eyes of the glassless windows, Dame could see a hard blue sky.

"What do you think?" Dame asked Meera.

"The place barely survived a fire in the fifties. Only the tower and the parish hall are actually original, but none of that's salvageable now."

"Who owns it?" Lewis asked.

"The Anglicans sold it to the Neos Group about four years ago," Meera said. "They tried to turn it into condos last year, but the city wouldn't let it happen. Then they tried to sell it and couldn't find a buyer."

"So, Neos burned it down for the insurance money," Lewis decided.

"I don't know," Dame said. "Doesn't it seem a little weird that two heritage buildings owned by two different developers would burn down in one week?"

"Here's another interesting fact," Meera said. "The church has a list of their former donors on its website. One of their biggest contributors was a guy named Dr. Ichiro Miyamoto."

"Think he's related to Aki Miyamoto?"

"Could be."

There was a sound like someone bowled a strike, and Dame looked up in time to see the bricks of the tower collapsing. One of the cops on crowd control took it as a sign.

"Okay, people!" he shouted at everyone and no one. "We're going to need you to move along. Let the firefighters do their job." The cop was baggy-eyed and looked too old for the crisp enthusiasm of his uniform.

"We should probably get back to the office," Meera said.

"You guys go ahead." Dame looked back up at the church. "I'm going to take a poke around."

GOOD SHEPHERD WAS built on a corner lot, but when she arrived at the back of the parish hall, Dame was surprised to see how little damage there was. The brick of the rear wall looked sturdy and unscorched. The wind had carried most of the soot and debris in the opposite direction, and from where she stood, she could even make out a little grass, flat and brutalized by the heat of the fire and the early cold of the weather. In that little patch of brown, she saw something: a cigarette butt with blue-green maple leaves above the filter. A Dominion cigarette. She stared at it for a moment, her fingers catching and releasing the yellow tape that stretched and zagged in the wind. She didn't notice Carol January until she was almost right beside her.

"They used gasoline, didn't they?" Dame said.

"How can you tell?"

"Saw some footage of the fire online. Yellow flame and white smoke. Always a dead giveaway."

"Pretty observant" — Carol took out a pack of Player's and lit one — "for a City Hall employee."

"I'm willing to bet you found traces of gas at Loyalist Collegiate, too."

The Fire Marshal shrugged. "Doesn't mean much. Gasoline is a pretty common accelerant."

Dame shook her head. "Peter Dinsdale used paraffin. Raymond Lee Oyler used a Marlboro. John Orr — the 'Pillow Pyro' — used bedding. They figured he set nearly two thousand fires that way."

"I'm familiar with John Orr, Dame. What's your point?"

"My point is, guys like this usually have some kind of tell."

"Guys like what?"

"Serial arsonists."

"Two fires in one week is a coincidence, not a pattern. We don't even know if they're connected."

"Then why are you here? Sharon Fischer on your ass again?"

"Actually," Carol said, scratching the corner of her eye, "Fischer contacted the office this morning and tried to convince us to drop the investigation."

"Drop it?"

"Said it was a waste of taxpayers' money. She called right after the news about Good Shepherd broke."

"What'd you say?"

"Well, we can't drop it now. There's too much evidence."

"So, you *do* think it's arson."

Carol nodded. "Uh-huh."

"And you think Fischer's involved somehow?"

"I'm starting to think you do." Carol took another drag and squinted at Dame. "You know, our security cameras have footage of someone trespassing at that old high school Monday night." She let the smoke hang in her mouth a moment before she breathed it out. "You wouldn't happen to know anything about that, would you?"

"Couldn't make out his face?"

"Her face. And no. Too blurry."

"You guys can't 'zoom in and enhance'?" Dame framed the

imaginary footage with her thumbs and forefingers. "You know, like they do on CSI?"

Carol shook her head.

"Seems like you might need some better security cameras."

"Seems like." Carol flicked her cigarette into the street beside them. She shoved her hand into the pocket of her old firefighter's coat and pulled out what looked to be a business card. "Here," she said, handing it to Dame. "That's my direct number. If you have any more bright ideas about doing my job, call me instead. In the meantime, I want you to stay away from burning buildings." The tall woman bent over and put her face in Dame's. Smoke seemed to leak from the pores of her skin. "I get that you're as smart as Dodge. Just don't be as reckless as he was, okay?" She stood up to her full height. "Next time, we might have those good cameras."

"CSI cameras?"

"Uh-huh."

Dame started to walk away, but the Fire Marshal called out to her. "Polycarbonate," she said.

Dame paused. "Polycarbonate?"

"Kind of plastic. Usually used in construction and car parts. They found significant traces of it near the point of origin at Loyalist Collegiate."

"Okay?"

"Thought it might be from the jerry can, but they make those out of high density polyethylene. You got any thoughts?"

"Polycarbonate." Dame said the word again and shook her head. "No. Sorry."

But when she started walking again, she moved a little faster.

CHAPTER TWENTY-TWO

"CAN I GIVE you a hand with that?" Peggy asked Dame.

"I'm okay. Thanks."

"That's quite a load you're carrying."

"Incident reports" — she nodded her head toward the cardboard box in her arms — "for designated structures impacted by arson and vandalism."

Peggy frowned through her bifocals. "Don't we file those electronically now?"

"We do. I just wanted to cross-reference some older stuff."

"Well, I'm sure you know what you're doing. It's a shame about that lovely old church, isn't it?"

"I know. And so weird this happened twice in one week."

Peggy nodded and started to turn away, but stopped. "Before I forget — they're about to post that MRB job. Is your CV all up to date?"

Dame's last visit with Dodge came back to her: *Don't.*

"You know, I thought about it, Peggy, and it's just more responsibility than I'm ready for right now."

"Are you sure, hon? Might be another couple years before a

chance like this comes up again. And think about how much fun we could have working together."

Don't.

"Yeah. I'm happy where I am right now."

Peggy was quiet for a moment. "Well, I suppose you know best." She forced a smile to her face. "So, how's the big detective case coming?"

The box grew heavier in Dame's hands. "Uh, a little more complicated than I thought it would be."

"Your father always said those domestic cases were so messy."

"He wasn't wrong."

"Just be careful, hon." Peggy started walking off in the opposite direction. "Don't forget what happened to your poor mother."

Dame hurried on. Her arms ached and the box felt like it weighed several tonnes. When she got to the Heritage office, she finally dropped the thing on her desk.

"Yikes," Meera said. "What's this all about?"

"1992 incident reports."

"For what?"

"Give me a minute ..."

Dame flipped through the files until she found what she was looking for. She opened the folder, riffled through the papers, and then slowly ran her finger down to the bottom of the page. "I *knew* it."

"Knew what?"

"Carol January said they found significant traces of polycarbonate at Loyalist Collegiate."

"And?"

"Back in '92, they ruled that what happened at the Sainte-Marie was arson, because they found what was left of a five-gallon water cooler jug. Someone had filled it with gasoline and used it to set the fire."

Meera stared at her and shrugged.

"Water cooler jugs are *made* of polycarbonate."

"Couldn't that just be a coincidence?"

"Yep." Dame pulled her phone out of her hip pocket and checked the time. "But coincidence has a bad habit of turning into pattern."

AN HOUR LATER, Dame and Meera sat parked in the Jeep, a block up from a Salvadoran restaurant in Koreatown.

"All right." Meera crossed her arms. "What's the plan?"

Dame looked at her friend. "I'm going to have lunch with Hugo Howlett. When I'm done, you're going to drive us back to work."

"Okay, but do you need me to do anything? Like, maybe I could come inside and create a diversion?"

"Why would you do that?"

"I don't know. What if I just came inside and ordered some tacos?"

"Why would you —"

"Because I'm hungry. I'm skipping lunch for this."

"No. I need you to stay here and wait for me."

"So, that's it? I'm just your chauffeur?"

"Look, you don't have to do this if you don't want to."

Meera looked past Dame. "Well, what if I see something suspicious?"

"What could you possibly see that would be suspicious? It's a busy street in broad daylight."

"I don't know. Those two people over there are acting pretty suspicious."

Dame turned around in the passenger seat. Outside Lotsa Tacos, she could make out a man and a woman hunched in a heated
exchange. When she looked back, Meera was staring at the couple through an enormous pair of binoculars.

"Great," Dame said. "Now *we* look suspicious."

"That guy's really familiar."

"Why do you even have those?"

"Lewis went through a brief birdwatching phase." She adjusted
a dial. "That's Hugo Howlett over there. I recognize him from his
Wikipedia page."

"When did Lewis start birdwatching?"

"Last summer."

"Why did he quit?"

"He decided birds are too ostentatious." Meera took a sudden
breath. "Holy shit! Dame, that's Sylvie!"

"Who's Sylvie?"

"Here" — Meera handed her the binoculars — "take a look."

Dame put her glasses on her head and looked through the lenses.
It was definitely Howlett. He was talking to a vaguely familiar
woman with short blonde hair.

"She looks so different with that dye job. And all those tattoos,"
Meera said.

"Okay, who am I supposed to be looking at?"

"Sylvie. Sylvie Hart. You know, as in *Sonnet* and *Sylvie?*"
Meera pulled her phone out of her pocket and searched up the
School Colours wiki. "See?"

Dame put the binoculars down and looked at the screen.

"There's Sonnet. And there's the love of her life, Sylvie Hart
— *a.k.a.* Charlotte Pierce — *a.k.a.* the woman standing across the
street, acting suspicious."

Dame took the phone out of Meera's hand and held it closer
to her face.

"And you just wanted me to be your *chauffeur*," Meera grumbled.

The image was old but clear. On the front steps of the high school sat two teenagers. One of them grew up to be Ray Hobart's wife, but the other —

Dame looked through the binoculars again. "Jesus." The outline of a small deer was visible on the back of Sylvie's neck. "That's the woman I chased out of Loyalist Collegiate."

CHAPTER TWENTY-THREE

"PLEASE DON'T TELL me you broke into an active crime scene," Meera said, "because that's some super illegal bullshit."

Dame started rolling down her window.

"Whatever happened to 'operating within the confines of the law'?" Meera asked.

"Well, that's really for licensed investigators. I have the advantage of being decidedly unlicensed. Now shush. I'm trying to hear what they're saying."

Howlett was murmuring something inaudible, and Dame watched as the blonde turned on a heel and stormed down the sidewalk.

"Guess she won't be joining you for lunch," Meera said.

"Guess not."

She watched Howlett go inside the restaurant.

"Okay," Dame said, getting out of the jeep. "Wish me luck."

"If it's all the same" — Meera crossed her arms — "I'm going to wish myself tacos."

"YOU MUST BE Agatha."

Howlett stood up when Dame approached his table. "Please, sit down."

Even in late October, the temperature in Lotsa Tacos was uncomfortably warm. Dame had been here plenty of times — the food was good, the *cervezas* cold — but she was a little surprised that someone like Howlett wanted to meet in a place like this. The guy was in his early fifties. He was fit, clean, and well manicured. His clothes quietly acknowledged they cost more than Dame's rent, and whatever subtle cologne he was wearing was now her new favourite smell. She thought of long-haired, gangly Ray, sliding his callused hand over hers. If Aki was trading up for Howlett, it wasn't hard to see why.

"I was thinking we could start with a couple margaritas," he said. "They're really good here, and I don't know about you, but I could use a drink."

Dame was happy to oblige, and almost by telepathic command, a waiter brought them their menus and took their drink orders.

"Oh, and you *have* to try the *pupusas*," Hugo continued. "Get them with *chicharrónes*. They're amazing."

Dame took out her phone. "Hugo, would you mind if I recorded this?"

"Oh God, as long as I don't have to listen to it. I can't stand the sound of my own voice."

As the waiter delivered two icy margaritas, Dame pressed the appropriate buttons on her phone and laid it on the table. "So. *School Colours*."

Howlett sipped his drink. "I'm tickled that *eightysomething* wants to feature my first project. I thought you mostly reviewed American programs."

"We try to feature shows that have some sort of cultural cachet," Dame-as-Agatha bullshitted, "and shows that have a loyal fan base. *School Colours* has both."

By the time the food arrived, Dame had all but convinced herself that reviewing forgotten Canadian television on YouTube might actually be a legitimate source of income.

"But what exactly do your viewers want to know about *School Colours*?" Howlett asked.

Dame bit into the recommended *pupusa* and chewed thoughtfully.

"Well, from what I've seen, the Sonnet and Sylvie narrative seems to have the most currency, especially with the whole unresolved love story."

"You know, those two characters —" Howlett poked at his enchiladas with a fork. "When we found Charlotte and Akiko, I tell you, we thought we struck gold. They were beautiful, and their *chemistry*, it was just —" Howlett shook his head. "It was pretty clear that they should be the heart of that show."

In any interview — Dodge once explained to Dame — there's a turning point. Some kind of opening. A weakness in the perimeter fence. When you found that opening, you slipped in and brought your most direct question with you.

"Is there any truth to the rumour that they were the reason the show was cancelled?"

"Well ..." Howlett looked down at Dame's phone. "Could we turn that thing off for a sec?"

Bingo. Dame tapped the red button.

"The thing about Charlotte and Aki," he said, "was that after a while, they weren't really acting. It was pretty obvious. I mean, *everyone* knew."

Dame took that in for a moment. "So, why did I have to turn off my phone if '*everyone*' knew'?"

"Because the one person who *didn't* know was Aki's father, Dr. Miyamoto. He was pretty old school. Very religious."

A little bell rang in Dame's brain.

"When he found out, he threatened to have me charged with corruption of a minor. And he had some high-priced lawyers who would've done it. Things were a little different back then." He put a forkful of enchilada in his mouth and chewed. "In the end, we agreed to let her out of her contract."

"And then you got cancelled."

Howlett washed down his food with more margarita. "Some people want to make like it was a big conspiracy, but the truth is, the show just wasn't getting a lot of traction back then. Plus, we blew half our first season budget on Maestro Fresh Wes."

"What happened to Aki?"

He looked up from his food. "You know, you're pretty interested in a story that's off the record."

"What can I say? I'm a big fan."

"Fair enough." He dabbed at his mouth with the paper napkin. "She met some guy her parents liked — I think he was going to school to be an engineer or something."

"Do you ever see her anymore?"

Howlett hesitated. "We keep in touch."

"That's it?"

"Well" — the television producer leaned over the table — "this is also *definitely* off the record, but we've been in talks with the CBC about filming a new *School Colours* series. A where-are-they-now kind of thing. Nothing's finalized, but I've managed to get most of the old gang on board."

"Most?"

"I've had some trouble convincing everyone."

"Like Sonnet Suzuki?"

"Aki was a little ambivalent at first. I think the idea of a reunion brought up a lot of complicated feelings for her. But she's on board, now. Some other parties are still a bit" — he took a breath — "*reluctant*. Let's just say I'm still working on it."

Dame changed course. "I heard that the school where you filmed the show burned down last week. That must've been a bummer."

"Yeah." He sighed. "It really was."

"Seems like the end of an era."

"Maybe." Howlett drained the rest of his drink. "Or, maybe it's just the start of a new one."

AS DAME MADE her way back toward the Jeep with a bag of tacos in her fist, someone fell in step beside her.

"Well, hello again." Anton Felski's turquoise satin jacket made a swishing sound as he walked. "Strange how we keep crossing paths, isn't it?"

Dame stopped. "Yeah. It's almost like you're following me."

"Following you? Well, someone's a little self-centered, aren't they? The world doesn't revolve around you, sunshine."

"And yet, here you are."

"If I was following you, I'd be doing a pretty lousy job of it, wouldn't I? Wasn't that Dodge's Rule Number One? *Don't get caught*?"

"That's Rule Number Three. Rule Number One is, *Don't get too close*."

"My mistake." Felski took an exaggerated step away from her.

"You're working for the Fish, aren't you?"

"The Fish?"

"Sharon Fischer. She works for City Hall. I saw your 'classy' business card on her desk."

Felski shrugged. "Afraid I can't breach client confidentiality, Dame. You know how it is."

"But you could tell me if you weren't working for her, couldn't you?"

"Let's just say I'm doing some surveillance work for Ms. Fischer."

"And you just happened to be in the neighbourhood?"

Felski shrugged. "I just *happened* to look in the window of this fine taco establishment and notice you having lunch with the same handsome man Aki Miyamoto had dinner with a couple weeks back. Now, if you want to talk coincidence, that's a pretty big one."

"Seems like there's a lot of that going around lately."

"Listen sunshine, if you're looking to catch Hobart's wife cheating, it seems like you're taking the long way around."

"I can't break client confidentiality either, Felski."

"Well, maybe I'm wrong," he said, walking past her. "Or maybe, you're not quite sure what you're looking for anymore."

UNDER THE FLUORESCENT lights of the City Hall parking garage, Meera climbed out of her Jeep. "So that guy really used to work for your dad?"

"Felski?" Dame slammed the door behind her. "Yeah, they worked together for a couple years."

"He seems too sketchy for someone like Dodge."

"You should see some of the other guys in the business. There was this one guy they called 'The Widower.' He kept a bunch of black widows as pets."

"What happened to him?"

"They found him dead in his apartment."

"Spider bite?"

Dame shook her head. "Non-Hodgkin's lymphoma. It was really sad."

"Now that you're a private investigator, does that mean you're going to start having a bunch of weirdo associates?"

"Nope." Dame smiled. "Just you."

Meera ignored her and groped around in the paper bag. "Ooh, Jarritos." She took the bottle out and gave it a closer look. "They didn't have mandarin?"

"You're welcome."

"I'm just saying — by now, you should probably know what flavour of Jarritos I prefer."

"Come on," Dame said. "We're already late."

As they walked through the lot, Meera dug out a shredded pork number.

"You can't wait 'til we get inside?" Dame asked.

"I'm starving," Meera mumbled through a mouthful of taco. She chewed and swallowed. "So, is Sonnet sleeping with her old producer or what?"

"Something's going on between those two, but I don't think it's sex."

"Do you think Howlett burned down Loyalist Collegiate?"

"I don't know. I don't think so. There could be some kind of rental insurance angle I'm not seeing, but he just seems too sentimental for that kind of thing. You were right about Dr. Miyamoto, though. I'm pretty sure he's Aki's father."

"So, Aki's linked to the school and the church."

Dame nodded. "And, you were also right about the *School Colours* reunion. They're apparently in talks with the CBC."

"I *knew* it!"

"That's off the record, though."

"What record?"

As they got closer to the elevator, the doors opened and two figures walked out. Both of them unfortunately familiar.

"Shit," Dame said under her breath. "We should've taken the stairs."

CHAPTER TWENTY-FOUR

"MS. POLARA. AND Ms. Banerjee. Enjoying an extended lunch break, are we?"

Sharon Fischer made her way toward Dame and Meera. The man walking beside her seemed to possess the particular kind of confidence that comes from inherited wealth.

"I thought you'd be paddling around Lake Couchiching by now," Dame said.

The woman smiled what passed for her smile. "I'm just on my way now. It's a shame you couldn't join us."

"There's always next year."

Fischer gestured to the man beside her. "I'm sure you know Phillip Marinetti."

The man was dressed in a bright orange jacket and exuded the hale heartiness of a cross-country runner. If it wasn't for the crow's feet around his eyes and the crest of thick white hair that swooped back from his forehead, he might've been mistaken for someone twenty years his junior.

"We've met."

Marinetti smiled and raised his eyebrows. "I'm sorry, you'll have to refresh my memory."

"Phil, you remember Dame Polara," Fischer said. "She works in the Heritage Planning department."

"Of course." Marinetti's blue eyes brightened in recognition. "David Polara's daughter. Your father's a very brave man."

"He wouldn't have to be so brave if developers didn't burn down their own buildings."

Meera took a bite of her taco.

"Listen, Dame." Marinetti cleared his throat. "I still feel awful about what happened with the Sainte-Marie Hotel — to your father, to that poor little boy — but it's been more than twenty years. And you have to know by now that they weren't the only victims."

"Can't say I've got a lot of sympathy for Marinetti Developments."

"I'm not talking about lost revenue, Dame," Marinetti said. "I'm talking about lost opportunity. That old derelict could've been replaced by affordable, energy-efficient housing for hundreds of people."

"That 'old derelict' is a cultural landmark. It's a part of our history."

"And I'm sure all that will make a fascinating coffee table book someday, but you have to be realistic. It's been years, and that old hotel is well beyond repair."

"But that's only because you —"

"Look Dame, we're not talking about Buckingham Palace here. Heritage can keep me tied up in red tape as long as they want, but one way or another, the Sainte-Marie will have to come down. Now, if you'll excuse me, I've got a two o'clock in Liberty Village."

Marinetti and Fischer walked past Dame. Their steps echoed across the parking garage.

"THAT FUCKING ASSHOLE." Dame slammed her backpack down on her desk.

"Come on," Meera said, catching up with her. "Can we please not get into this again?"

"Get into *what*?"

"Hey" — Meera held up her palms — "I don't like the guy either. But he's a rich developer and you're never going to beat him. Besides" — she took a deep breath — "maybe he's got a point."

"A *'point'*?"

"Look, I know how much the Sainte-Marie means to you, but we can't save it. And that neighbourhood — your neighbourhood — could really use some more affordable housing."

"So now you agree with him."

"Just think about it for a second. I mean, you've got a good job working for the city and *you* can barely make rent. What about other people? People just scraping by? Where are they supposed to live?"

"That piece of shit started a fire that ruined my dad's health and killed a little boy. Now you're taking his side?"

"I'm not 'taking his side,' I just —"

"How can you stand there and —"

Behind them, someone cleared her throat. "Could I offer anyone a Portuguese egg tart?"

Meera and Dame turned toward the door. Peggy was walking into the office with a small box in her hands.

"Go on," she said. "I grabbed half a dozen from that little place on Ossington."

Sheepishly, they each picked a tart out of the box. As they took their time chewing, Peggy put the rest of the baked goods down on Meera's desk.

"I hate to say it, Dame, but I think you're wrong."

Startled, Dame looked at Peggy.

"Do you know why they could never pin that fire on Phil Marinetti?" She leaned against Dame's desk.

"Because rich people have really good lawyers?"

"No. Because he didn't do it."

A shell of laughter burst from Dame's mouth. Tiny bits of pastry went flying across the room.

"Phillip Marinetti is a lot of things, Dame — greedy, dishonest, corrupt — but he's not stupid. Think about it. Before that hotel caught fire, Marinetti was already under tons of scrutiny for trying to have a well-known historical building demolished. You might be too young to remember, but I'm not. There were protestors and newspaper articles. Your mother even wrote a huge piece about it for the *Star* — Marinetti would've known that even a whiff of foul play on his part would've landed him in heaps of trouble."

Dame stared hard at the floor.

"Listen, I know you want someone to blame for everything that happened — to you, to Dodge, to that little boy — but Marinetti's just not your man." She put her hand on Dame's shoulder. "You've got a lot of history with that old hotel, but people can't live in museums. And if some developer wants to turn it into affordable housing, I say we let him."

Dame shook her head in disbelief. "I thought we were supposed to '*celebrate the past to awaken the future.*'"

"We are. But we also have to survive the present, don't we?"

Dame didn't say anything.

"Well, I'm sure you're both very busy," Peggy said, smiling. "And, I have a philodendron that isn't going to water itself."

She left the room, and for more than a minute, Dame and Meera didn't say anything. Dame's phone buzzed, but she ignored it and sat down at her desk.

Meera picked up the box of tarts and then put them down again. A funny look came over her face. "Chocolate-covered raisins."

In spite of herself, Dame snorted. "Sweet on the outside, and then *bam*." She looked up at Meera and sighed. "Look, I'm sorry. You know what I'm like. I get ahold of something, and I have trouble letting it go."

"It's okay." Meera smiled.

Dame's phone buzzed a second time.

"Jesus. When did you get so popular?"

"Probably just my creep of a landlord again." Dame pulled the device out of her pocket.

But when she looked at her phone it wasn't Ray. Or Aki, for that matter. It wasn't even the phone company trying to upsell her on a new data package she didn't need.

"It's Gus Morrow."

"The firefighter?"

Dame read the messages aloud.

Dinner tonight? asked the first.

The usual alleyways and crime scenes are all booked up. Alessio's at 7pm?

"Alessio's?" Meera said. "That's a big commitment. What with the bread basket, and drinks before, maybe dessert after — you're looking at a good two hours. What if he turns out to be really boring?"

"I'll skip dessert."

"What if he turns out to be really interesting?" Meera raised an eyebrow.

"We'll get dessert to go."

"So? What are you going to say?"

Dame stood up and walked over to the box of pastries. "I better tell him to make it eight o'clock. I have to work late tonight."

"On a Friday? To do what?"

She tossed Meera the last tart. "Some super illegal bullshit."

CHAPTER TWENTY-FIVE

"DID YOU HEAR that?" Meera whispered.

"Hear what?" Dame whispered back.

Meera killed the flashlight. Dame sighed and did the same. In the shadows of Sharon Fischer's office, the two women listened and waited.

After about ten seconds, Meera turned her flashlight back on. "I hate this," she hissed. "You're a bad influence, you know that?"

Dame turned her own light on and opened the top drawer of a filing cabinet. "You're the one who insisted on coming."

Earlier that afternoon, when Dame had taken the elevator down six floors to case the Municipal Review Board offices, she was amazed at how empty the place already was. It seemed as though a lot of MRB employees had started their weekend early.

Now, at almost seven o'clock, the place was a ghost town. Custodians had been short-staffed all month, and security was mostly concentrated where the mayor hung his chain of office on the second floor of the rotunda. Still, it paid to be cautious. And quiet.

"I figured the door would be locked, and that would be it," Meera whispered. "I didn't think you'd pull some James Bond break-and-enter kit out of your ass."

Dame shushed her.

"I can't help it. I'm nervous. I talk when I'm nervous."

Meera twisted her hair up into a bun, and then made her way over to Fischer's massive desk. "What are we even looking for, anyway?"

"I'm not sure."

Dodge used to warn her about taking unnecessary risks on a hunch, but a hunch was all Dame really had. If the two arson cases were somehow connected, Fischer's fingerprints were on them just as much as Aki Miyamoto's.

Dame scanned the room with her flashlight. Seeing it again, it was hard to imagine that this was someone's day-to-day workspace. It looked like one of those offices you'd find in a swanky hotel suite. The smooth laminate, the pastel watercolours, the ergonomic office chair — the room was scoured of personality.

"Check it out." Meera reached into the wastepaper basket and produced an empty carton of plain yogurt. "Everything about this woman is boring."

"Not everything." Dame pulled out a file labelled "*Planning 1990–2003*." She shone her light on the papers inside. "Did you know Fischer used to work for Heritage?"

"Really? Weird."

"Years ago." Dame turned a page. "She even pushed to have the Sainte-Marie Hotel designated when Marinetti tried to demolish it."

"Also weird."

Dame returned the file and eased the cabinet drawer shut. "Did you look in her desk?"

"Not yet, I'm just — oh my *God*."

"What?" Dame hurried over to where Meera stood.

"Do you see how *cute* her son is in this picture? How old is he? Five? Six? He's adorable!"

Dame shook her head.

"I feel like I've seen him before. Has she ever brought him into work?"

"Meera, Sharon Fischer is pushing sixty. That kid's probably older than we are, now." She picked up a teddy bear from a shelf behind the desk. Dead eyes stared out from its smooth beige fur. "Can you imagine the Fish as someone's mother?" Dame shuddered and put the bear back down.

Meera opened one of the drawers and rifled through it. "Man" — she held up a small black tube of lipstick — "even her makeup is no-name, generic stuff."

"Come on, Meera." Dame shone the flashlight at her friend. "Stay focused."

"I can't even tell what shade this is." Meera popped off the top and twisted the base, but instead of a bevelled red edge, the tube ended in a square metal plug.

"What is that?" Dame asked.

Meera handed the small cylinder to her. "Looks like some kind of flash drive."

Just then, someone rattled the knob on the office door.

Dame looked at Meera. They snapped off their lights and crouched behind Fischer's desk. Dame slid the fake lipstick into her pocket. The doorknob twisted again, back and forth. She could hear Meera take a deep breath and hold it.

There was a gentle tapping on the door. In the narrow glass panel beside it, a face appeared, cupped by two hands. "Meera? Dame?"

Meera exhaled. "Oh, for fuck's sake."

"You told Lewis?"

"Hey, I have no secrets from my husband."

Meera stood up from behind the desk and turned on her flashlight. She crossed the room and opened the door.

Lewis came in, breathless and sweaty. "Oh my God, you guys —"

"*Shhh!*" they shushed him.

He put his hands on his knees, tried to catch his breath. "I ran into this —"

"*Shhh!*" they shushed him again.

"I ran into this security guard on the way up," he whispered. "I think she recognized me from our floor. She said, 'You sure are working late.' So I said, '*Yes, and* — I can't go home until I file a report.'"

"Good work, Lewis," Meera said. "Way to use your improv skills."

"Did you find anything incriminating?" Lewis asked.

"I'm not sure," Dame said. "I'm not sure there's really anything to find."

"Maybe we should call it then, before that Pinkerton walks by," Meera said.

Dame agreed.

As they rode the elevator up to their floor, Meera slouched against the mirrored wall. "Well, that was both terrifying and useless."

"Maybe," Dame said. She reached into the pocket of her jeans and pulled out the flash drive. "Maybe not."

"You stole her lipstick thingie?"

"Sure. Why not?"

"Because it's *illegal*. That's why not."

"So is breaking and entering."

The door to the elevator opened and they all stepped out and started walking back to Heritage.

"Think about it," Dame said. "Everything in that office was crazy organized, right? I mean, she sorted her paper clips by size *and* colour."

"So?"

"So, you found this with all her makeup. Why would Fischer keep a flash drive with her makeup?"

"Maybe she just forgot what it was," Meera said. "It fooled me."

"Maybe." Dame scrutinized the device between her thumb and forefinger. "Or maybe she was hiding it for a reason."

CHAPTER TWENTY-SIX

AS DAME HURRIED down the sidewalk to meet Gus Morrow, she was surprised to feel a familiar surge of cold pass through her body. When she looked out onto the street, she saw it. The white Chevy. It cruised past her like a slow-moving shark, and Dame found herself wondering exactly how it got those ugly dents in the bumper. She watched the car until it took a left and disappeared out of sight.

When she finally reached the restaurant, Dame checked her phone again and realized she'd missed two calls and a text message from Gus.

Can you call me when you get this?

She knew it couldn't be good news. And sure enough, when he answered his phone, she heard screaming on the other end.

"Is everything okay?" she asked.

"Yeah. Well, actually, no."

"Who's screaming like that?"

"Uh, those would be the screams of children," he said. "But don't worry, they're happy screams."

"They don't sound happy. They sound terrified. Where are you?"

"Well, that's why I called. One of the guys at my station got sick and I had to pick up his shift. I tried to call earlier, but I couldn't get through."

"You're not" — *couldn't be* — "at a fire, are you?"

Gus laughed. "Typically, we don't answer the phone when we're fighting fires."

"So where —?"

"Listen, I'd still really like to see you. Is there any way you'd come here? I promise I'll have dinner ready by the time you arrive."

"Well, maybe. But at some point, you'll have to tell me where 'here' is."

"Right. We're up in Weston. On Elrose and Wilson. Think you could find it?"

"I guess," Dame said. "If I have any trouble, I'll just follow the sounds of screaming children."

WHEN DAME ARRIVED, she realized that the address Gus had given her wasn't for a house, or a fire station. As she stepped out of the cab, she found herself on the perimeter of a sinister carnival. Rubber skeletons and Styrofoam tombstones decorated a small asphalt parking lot. Parents stood around and ate food over paper plates. A horde of relatively unsupervised tweens strolled past her, shout-speaking profane emphatics (Oh my *God*! What the *fuck*?). And in the centre of it all stood the burnt-out husk of a detached two-storey warehouse. A corpse of a building.

She found Gus in full fire regalia, turning hot dogs on an enormous barbecue.

"Hey!" he said.

"Nice place you got here."

"Usually" — he pointed a pair of tongs over one shoulder — "we use this structure for search and rescue training. You know, smoke, gas-fed booby traps, that kind of thing. But right now, there's something way scarier inside."

As if on cue, a recorded cackle echoed out of the building behind him.

"You invited me to a haunted house?"

Gus shrugged. "We run this thing every year. Proceeds go to help kids with muscular dystrophy. It's pretty popular."

"I can see that. So, why are you wearing all your gear?"

"Part of the whole shtick. And, you know, the kids kind of like it."

God, he was cute.

"So" — he pointed the tongs toward the barbecue — "you hungry?"

"Starved. What's on the menu?"

"Well, today's special is a hot dog with your choice of ketchup or mustard. On tap we have a variety of beverages. Actually" — he looked at a plastic cooler beside his feet — "it looks like we're down to Canada Dry."

"I'll take a dog with the works," Dame said, "and your finest ginger ale."

"Excellent choice."

A lineup had materialized behind her, so once Dame had her food, she moved a few feet away and watched the firefighter do his thing. He chatted with the kids and joked with the adults. When a flash of flame jumped up from the grill, he pretend-threatened it with a nearby extinguisher. Everyone laughed.

Dame made short work of the dog and had just cracked into her pop when the crowd cleared. She took a slurp and walked back over. "So, this works out pretty well for you, doesn't it?"

Gus looked confused. "What do you mean?"

"This last-minute change of venue? You get to save a few

bucks on pasta, show off your charity work, plus, you get to wear the uniform, which I'm sure some girls are kind of into."

"Oh yeah? Are you into it?"

"Listen, the longer you stand behind that barbecue, the more you look like a fry cook playing dress-up."

"Guess I better hurry up and turn it off, then." He reached down and twisted the propane nozzle. "How about I give you the grand tour?"

More screams sounded through a first-floor window.

"Dinner *and* a show." Dame took a final swig of the ginger ale, then set it down. "You really know how to show a girl a good time."

She started walking toward the warehouse and Gus caught up. He led her past a handful of civilians waiting in line. At the front, a grim-looking firefighter stood with his brawny arms crossed and a service radio humming. Behind him, a heavy black curtain hung in the door frame.

Gus took off his helmet and coat and handed it to the man. "Hey, Rick? Could you give us a head start on the next group?"

Rick nodded and turned to Dame. "You look after him in there, ma'am. Gus scares easy."

"Is that so?" She looked back at Gus, and then pushed her way through the curtain.

For the most part, the place was furnished with the usual fare. The walls of the hallway were painted black and lit with strobes and jack-o'-lanterns. The sound was amplified as they moved through the first antechamber: chainsaws, screams, howls. Occasionally, a ghoulish volunteer would open a door and take a half-hearted swipe at them with a plastic axe. Overall, there didn't seem to be any real theme. Dame spotted a mummy, a werewolf, a Dracula. It was a monster mash-up of Halloween classics. Only the smell was authentic. Dame had spent enough time in burnt-out buildings to know that the carcinogenic stink usually meant death of one kind or another.

They moved slowly, and soon the group behind them caught up. A dozen or so kids pushed past, screaming their way into the hilarious horror. For a moment, Dame thought she saw a familiar face — a curly-haired little boy — moving through the crowd. In an instant, he was gone.

"You okay?" Gus put his hand on her arm after they'd triggered a mechanical zombie to sit up and moan at no one in particular.

"Yeah." She smiled up at him. "I'm good."

And she was. Although, she had to admit that any game this poor guy had was strictly junior high. In a way, it was kind of adorable. Kyle Harris had tried the same thing on her when she was fifteen, except instead of suspenders and boots and a haunted house, it was a varsity jacket and a midnight showing of *I Know What You Did Last Summer*.

When they reached a flight of metal steps, Gus stopped. "There's an exit here if you want to leave. It's supposed to be a little more intense upstairs."

Dame took his hand and pulled him toward her. "I'm not the one who scares easy." She had to stand on her tiptoes to kiss him. It was the first time in over a year that she kissed someone. And the first time in more than seven years that she kissed someone without a beard. Why hadn't she made Adam shave that awful thing off?

The stairs were all caution signs — safety first — but when they arrived at the second floor, Dame found herself in a grimy hospital wing, with flickering fluorescent lights and demented surgeons manhandling the bloody coils of their vivisected amputees.

"Jesus," Dame said. "This is worse than St. Mike's."

"Our platoon chief designed this part. He used to be a paramedic."

They walked on, past beds full of writhing blankets and surgeries gone wrong. A doctor in bloodstained scrubs carried a glistening fist of human heart that pulsed and squirted. In one room, they walked through a maze of gently swinging body bags.

"This is genuinely creepy," Dame said.

"Told you."

At the end of the hall, a woman dressed in a pristine nurse's uniform stood motionless and stared at them.

"That's Sheila from the One Thirty-One," he whispered. "She's really good. Never breaks character. Watch." Gus waved his arm in the air. "Hey, Sheila!"

The woman said nothing and continued to stare. Then, slowly, she beckoned them to her. As they walked down the hall, Dame heard an unsettling noise — the sound of a baby crying. Softly at first, and then louder as they got closer. Nurse Sheila motioned toward a blue hospital partition.

"I think we're supposed to open it," Gus said.

"Uh, I'm not so sure —"

But before she could stop him, the firefighter pulled the curtain back. Behind it was an antique bassinet, and when Dame looked inside, she stopped breathing. A monstrous child reached toward her with disfigured purple arms.

"*Maa-maa* …" it wailed.

"Fuck this," Dame said. "I'm out."

She pushed past Gus and Sheila and ran back down the hallway, almost knocking over the wannabe cardiologist and his tray of red muscle. She was halfway down the stairs when she heard Gus calling after her. *Dame?* She weaved through the parents and children who jumped and cowered like she was part of the act. She ignored Rick, the firefighter-turned-bouncer, who asked, *Ma'am? Everything all right?*

No, she thought. Things were decidedly not all right.

CHAPTER TWENTY-SEVEN

DAME WALKED FOR three blocks, her phone buzzing in her pocket, until she had the wherewithal to look for a street sign. She found herself in a desolate commercial neighbourhood, surrounded by furniture outlets and offices for personal injury lawyers.

It was quiet and — unlike so much of the city — seemingly void of pedestrians. Dame leaned against the fence of a used car lot and called a cab, praying to the gods of credit that there was enough money on her card to cover it. As she waited, she scrolled through messages from Gus that were sweet with worry:

Are you okay? What happened?

I'm so sorry if I did something to upset you.

I can't find you. Can you please text me back and let me know you're safe?

Finally, Dame replied. *I'm okay. Sorry about that. Good night.*

She wanted to add, *I'll call you tomorrow.* Or even, *Next time, let's actually go to Alessio's.* But she wasn't sure if she would call him. She wasn't sure if she wanted there to be a next time. She was starting to feel like maybe she was all out of next times when it came to this kind of thing.

She'd been so stupid to think she could go on a date like a normal person. Stupid to think she wasn't still just a hash of unresolved feelings and hormones: a thirty-six-year-old divorcee trying to subsidize a geriatric pregnancy by playing private investigator. Who would swipe right on that profile?

The cold had made its way through her threadbare coat, and Dame realized she wasn't exactly dressed for bailing on a date in the middle of nowhere. She waited under the lonely fluorescence while occasional traffic swished by and stretched her shadow across the sidewalk. Eventually, she heard a car coming closer. Dame pocketed her phone, but when she stood up, she didn't see a cab pulling over to the curb. Instead, she saw the white Chevrolet Caprice. Stopped in the middle of the road. The impassive black of its windshield still obscuring the driver.

Dame's chest filled with ice. For a moment, she wasn't sure what to do, but when she heard the wet growl of the engine, the answer came to her in an instant.

Run.

She bolted down the sidewalk. Almost immediately, the clap of her shoes was swallowed up by the sound of screeching rubber. Dame could hear the car's suspension take the concrete curb and feel its yellow eyes square on her back. Her whole body felt like it was made of glass.

She took a hard right through a parking lot, cut across an empty street, and found herself in an alley between a squat Korean church and a hardware store. For a few beautiful seconds, she thought she'd lost the car, but her heart sank when the narrow corridor was suddenly bathed in its cruel, relentless light.

The old police cruiser moved slowly now, filling the laneway. Dame had made a mistake and she knew it. Bottlenecked between the two buildings, she would never make the exit in time. She stumbled back a step and looked over her shoulder. There were no back doors. No low windows. Just a few recycling bins, and — *oh God* — she'd only have one chance to get this right.

The Chevy made the first move, its tires spinning on the pavement's grit. Dame turned and hurtled toward the first blue bin. She grabbed it by the handle and — against every natural instinct in her body — dragged it toward the oncoming car. She stopped, scrambled on top of the teetering thing — *Jesus fuck* — and reached her hands above her head.

As the white car tore through the belly of the bin, Dame clutched at the concrete sill of the second-storey window above her. She pulled her legs up to her chest and hung suspended for a moment as plastic, metal, and cardboard showered the alley below. Dame had just enough time to watch the white car fishtail out onto the next street before she lost her grip and fell to earth. Her ankle gave out when she hit the pavement and she landed hard on her hip bone. She lay there, cursing at the night sky, while bottles and cans rolled and clattered around her.

Despite the fact that her heart pounded against her rib cage, all she could think about was her high school track coach. The day she cut Dame from the team, Mrs. Yanchus had offered her one hard consolation: *Some people just aren't built for speed.* A 1989 Chevrolet Caprice 9C1 police model, on the other hand, had a fuel-injected 350 cubic-inch small-block V8 under the hood and, despite being a few decades old, could probably still do zero to sixty in about ten seconds. If the driver had really wanted her dead, she'd already be a stain on the laneway.

Dame pushed herself to her feet. Somebody was trying to frighten her. And she had to admit, they were doing a pretty good job of it.

CHAPTER TWENTY-EIGHT

MORNING WAS A slow start. Even after she got out of bed, Dame wore her comforter over her shoulders and shuffled around the apartment drinking a mug of tea she wished was a cup of coffee. Her ankle was already feeling better, but a fist-sized bruise had started to flower on her hip.

She had trouble remembering how she got home. After the attack, she limped around the city for what felt like hours, numb with cold, flashing with terror every time she saw a white car. Finally, she had a vague recollection of riding in the back of a strange-smelling cab, whose driver told her that life wasn't so bad and she should really smile more.

When she finished her tea, Dame texted Dodge to see if he wanted to go out for lunch. His succinct response was: *Can't. Movies with Fatima.*

It wasn't long before Dame found herself standing and staring at the cardboard boxes stacked up on her back porch. Most of them weren't even labelled. When she left her husband the year before, she hadn't been able to throw anything away, but she also couldn't bring herself to write out words like "*Wedding*" or "*Adam*" or "*Baby*" in something as enduring as permanent marker. Now, the little room seemed like a poorly organized evidence locker of failure.

As memories of the night before fermented in her brain like bad *kombucha*, Dame wished she could box them away, too. The firefighter. The haunted house. The white Chevrolet. If she could, she'd give them each their own unmarked cardboard grave.

Why was the white car following her? Who was trying to scare her off? Did the Fish somehow know about last night's break and enter? She remembered the little card clipped to Fischer's day planner. How was Anton Felski involved in all of this?

Dame moved to the bedroom and found her jeans in a puddle of denim on the floor. She went through the pockets and teased out the one and only thing she had taken from Fischer's office: the lipstick flash drive. In the living room, she plunked down on the couch and slid the little mechanism into the side of her laptop. A window popped up, and when she clicked on it, a list of files appeared. Moments later, she picked up her phone and made a call.

"Meera?" Dame was pacing the hardwood.

"Hey! How'd it go last night?"

She told her everything.

"Jesus, Dame. Maybe it's time to call the police."

"I don't even know what I would tell them." Dame took a breath. "Listen, you know that flash drive you found in Fischer's desk?"

"You don't think what happened last night was because —"

"I don't know," Dame said. "But there's a bunch of files on it — site assessments for heritage properties."

"Well, it's Fischer's job to know about that stuff, right? It's not really surprising she'd keep files on it."

"Right, but check out which buildings she was researching:

Loyalist Collegiate, Good Shepherd, the Atkinson Theatre" —
Dame paused — "and the Sainte-Marie Hotel."

"So?"

"So, three-quarters of those properties are toast. Two as of
last week."

"You think it's some kind of arsonist to-do list?"

"I don't know. But there's one file I can't open. Looks like
some kind of video, but it's password protected."

"Weird."

"Yeah, but the weirdest part is how the file is labelled: 'A.M.'"

"'A.M.,'" Meera considered. "Anne Murray? Alanis Morissette?"

"Yeah, or Aki Miyamoto."

"You think Sonnet Suzuki is some kind of firebug?"

"All I know is that she and Howlett are up to something.
Something she's keeping from her husband." Dame thought for a
moment. "Hey, what are you doing tonight?"

"Usual Halloween fare. Hand out candy then fall asleep on the
couch while Lewis rewatches *Monster Squad*. Why?"

"You want to help me crash a party instead?"

JUST FOUND A *sitter!* Dame texted Aki. *Are we still on for tonight?*

By the time Dame got out of the shower, Aki had responded.

*Yes! 33 Mill Street. I'm heading over around 9:00 after trick-
or-treating.*

Great! she wrote. *Meet you there!*

Dame realized her alter ego, Nancy, used a lot of exclamation
marks.

Aki saw her punctuation and raised her a happy-face emoji.
*Just buzz Hugo Howlett's suite. Someone will let you in. And
don't forget your costume!*

A costume. Right. Seeing as though she couldn't be both Nancy the Newly-Single Mom and Agatha the Social Media Influencer at the same time, she was definitely going to need a good one. And Dame had just the thing.

"REALLY?" MEERA SAID. "*That's* what you're wearing?"

Dame stepped out of Meera's bathroom and did a little twirl in the hallway.

"It's a classic." Her voice was barely muffled by the cheap thread count. "Plus, no one will know who I am."

Meera shook her head. "You are *not* going to some swanky costume party in a stained bedsheet with eye holes."

"I'm a scary ghost."

"You're an insult to Halloween. You can't be seen in that."

"That's kind of the point," Dame pulled the sheet off her head. "But I suppose you have a better idea?"

Meera looked her friend up and down. She walked in a slow circle around her. "Come with me."

Dame followed Meera down the hall of her Leslieville duplex and into the spare-bedroom-turned-office. Lewis sat behind a desktop, squinting at the screen.

"I'm not having much luck with this flash drive password so far. You wouldn't happen to know Fischer's birthday, would you? Or if she has any children? Or pets?"

"Sorry, Lewis," Dame said. "I know she has a son, but I don't know his name."

"I'll keep trying." His fingers started working again at the keyboard. "I've got a few more tricks up my sleeve."

Dame didn't have the heart to tell him that she'd already tried typing in every personal detail she'd gathered on Fischer — lipstick brands, disappointing handbags, corrupt property developers. The truth was, Dame just hadn't been able to dig up a lot of dirt on the woman.

While Lewis gently hacked, Meera was engaged in a full-frontal assault. She scraped and tore her way into the depths of the closet, throwing assorted garments and accessories onto the carpet. Eventually, she re-emerged, pushing a cardboard box across the floor with her foot.

"Man, I used to love Halloween. Until I married that guy." She gestured toward her husband. "Turns out boring is contagious."

Lewis looked up from his screen. "Hey, I'm committing indictable cybercrimes as we speak. I'm easily the most exciting person in this room."

Meera turned to Dame. "Let's go over our options." She put a thoughtful fist to her chin and surveyed the mess on the floor. "What to wear to a TV producer's Halloween party? It's got to be funny, referential, maybe *slightly* ironic —"

"— and actually disguise who I am. I don't want anybody at that party knowing I was there."

"Right." Meera crouched down and rummaged around in the box. "So, what if you went as" — she stood up with a furry brown tail and a black bandit's mask — "Conrad the Raccoon?"

"Who?"

"Remember? In July? There was that dead raccoon on the corner of Yonge and Church and it took the city, like, fourteen hours to pick it up. People created a memorial for it and everything?"

"Its name was 'Conrad'?"

"Spray-paint rings around the tail, buy yourself a few sympathy roses, and you're good to go."

Dame considered the potential outfit. "I don't know. I think people will still recognize me."

"Okay then … what about this one?" She held up a plastic panda face. "You could go as Er Shun!"

"Who?"

"Er Shun! The pregnant panda? People love her. You could wear black tights and stick a soccer ball under your —"

Dame raised an eyebrow.

"Oh," Meera said. "Guess not."

Dame crouched down and poked through the pile. Cat ears. Slightly squashed pirate hat. Feather boa. Wonder Woman tights. She sighed. "I don't know if any of this is going to work."

Meera nudged the costumes with her toe. "Hmm." A light went on behind her eyes. "Hold on a sec. I'll be right back."

As his wife left the room, Lewis brought the flash drive over to Dame. "Sorry," he said. "No luck. You should probably put this somewhere safe, though."

Dame pocketed the little device as Meera came stumbling into the room with another, even larger cardboard box.

"I almost forgot I had these," she said. "I've been saving them for a special occasion."

She put the box down and picked at the tape, ripping it off in long strips. Finally, she pulled open the tabs and, not without a little reverence, coaxed the costumes from the box. The heads came out first, like someone had guillotined a small, forgotten part of Ontario's pop culture. Then the rest came in greens and browns, yellows and greys. The 1970s made a weird, plushy flesh.

"What the hell are those?" Dame said.

"Don't you remember this show?"

"I was more of a *Read All About It* kind of girl."

"My mom used to tape TVOntario for my older brother. It's the first thing I remember watching as a kid. When I found these on eBay a couple years ago, I couldn't pass them up. I think they're original. They were probably stolen from some CBC archival warehouse."

She handed Dame one of the enormous heads. Dame lowered it onto her shoulders.

"Smells like wet dog in here." Dame's voice bounced around inside.

"Yeah," Meera said, "but they're funny, referential, ironic —"

"I can't see shit in this thing."

"And no one can see you. Plus" — Meera fitted herself with the second head — "there's one for me, too."

Lewis stepped back and assessed the two of them. "You guys look like idiots."

"I know," Meera said, her voice down a well. "It's perfect."

CHAPTER TWENTY-NINE

WHEN HUGO HOWLETT opened the door to his condo, he was confronted with the blank stares of two enormous woodland creatures. The shorter of the two was a grey beaver dressed in a yellow plaid vest and matching cap. The taller was a chocolate-coloured moose with antlers that barely cleared the door frame. It wore a green football jersey with a large *M* emblazoned across the front and a Pentax K1000 35 mm SLR around its neck.

"Oh, wow," Howlett said, taking a step back. "It's the Cucumber Club!"

A woman dressed as Elvira, Mistress of the Dark materialized beside him. "What's the 'Cucumber Club'?"

"You don't know The Children's Underground Club of United Moose and Beaver for Enthusiastic Reporters?"

The woman shook her enormous hairdo.

"From the show *Cucumber*? It was classic children's programming. John Candy was on it. Martin Short. Jeff Healey."

Elvira gave the two newcomers an unimpressed once-over, then disappeared back into the party.

"You guys look fantastic."

Sporting a pale three-piece suit and a large bandage taped to his nose, Howlett was doing a solid impersonation of Jack Nicholson in *Chinatown*. "Who's under there? Walter and Ezra?"

The animals shook their heavy heads.

"Frankie and Nico?"

Again, it was a no.

He grinned. "You're not going to tell me, are you?"

The Cucumber Club offered a collective shrug.

"I love it. Come on in and make yourself at home. There's a bar set up just over there. Have a great time" — he winked — "*whoever* you are ..."

They watched their host cross the living room to someone dressed as Where's Waldo. Howlett gestured back toward them. Waldo looked and laughed.

Beaver slugged Moose's shoulder and pointed at the red-and-white-striped adventurer. "That's Ford Kelsey!" she said. "And — *ohmygod* — over there? Beetlejuice eating the canapé? That's Yvonne Rogers. She got killed by a drunk driver in episode seven: 'End of the Road'!"

"Okay, Meera," Moose said. "Keep it together."

"Sorry. It was a really emotional episode."

Dame took a step forward into the party and got a sense of things: the polished hardwood beneath their feet, the sleek mid-century furniture in the living room, the yards of Calacatta marble in the kitchen. Every surface was suffused with the warm glow of money.

"So, what do we do now?" Meera asked.

"We look for Aki."

The condo was stuffed with costumed revellers: Freddy Krueger worked his razor glove around a craft beer. A giant pizza was eating a tiny slider. For a moment, Dame thought the two men in white shirts and pink bow ties were dressed up as caterers, until she realized they actually were caterers. The music got louder. Conversations swelled and climaxed in bursts of laughter.

"There she is," Dame said. "By the big painting."

Standing alone in front of an enormous slab of abstract expressionism was a woman dressed in a gold-sequined coat and top hat. *Rocky Horror's* Columbia.

"Looks like she's behaving herself so far," Dame said.

"Well, I'm dying under this thing. You want to get some air?"

"You go ahead. I'm going to snoop around a bit."

"Okay. Just don't get us thrown out before I can try those smoked salmon rolls."

"I'll do my best."

Dame worked her way around the apartment feeling anonymous and avoidable in her ridiculous outfit. In her head she could hear Dodge pontificating: *People keep their secrets in bedrooms and bathrooms.* So, when the bathroom yielded nothing of interest but Rogaine and a Michelle Obama prayer candle, Dame moved on to the primary bedroom.

It was empty when she found it. She stepped inside and closed the door behind her. Low lit with bedside lamps, it was surprisingly large. A framed movie poster of *Jules et Jim* hung above a king-sized bed, and a deep, double-doored closet filed away tidy rows of shirts and sport coats. Outside the room's floor-to-ceiling windows, the city sparkled like a handful of diamonds someone tossed off the balcony.

Dame hoisted the moose head and put it on the foot of the bed. She wiped a slick of forehead sweat on her fuzzy sleeve and opened the drawer of the nightstand. Watch, tie clips, a novel on the go — nothing out of the ordinary. When she opened its symmetrical mate, she discovered a stack of *Sight & Sounds* and a little zip-lock of weed.

Conversation flared up outside and Dame heard a hand on the knob. She dashed across to the closet and left the doors open a crack — just wide enough to see that she'd managed to forget the moose head on Howlett's bedspread.

"*Shit*," she whispered.

She was about to jump out and grab it, but the door swung open, and into the room walked Hugo Howlett and Ray Hobart's wife.

From the closet, Dame watched as Aki closed the door against the noise of the party. Howlett put his drink down on the night-stand and picked up the moose mask. He sat down on the edge of his massive bed and arranged the thing in his lap so he could gaze into its vacant, googly eyes. "Looks like somebody lost their head."

Dame tried to control her breathing. There was a wild jangling in her chest. She watched as Howlett carefully pulled the ban-dage off his nose and then dropped the moose head over his own. "How do I look?"

Aki laughed and sat down beside him. "Terrible. And you smell like wet dog."

Howlett took the mask off and placed it on the bed. "I wonder if it's the original. I mean, there can't be much of a market for TVOntario Halloween costumes, right?"

"Probably not," Aki said, taking off her sparkling top hat, "but I bet they could move a few hundred units of Casey and Finnegan."

Howlett snapped his fingers. "Next year, I should go as Sam Crenshaw from *Today's Special*. You could be Muffy Mouse."

"No one would get it." Her smile faded a little. "Have you ... heard anything?"

Howlett shook his head and put his arm around Aki. "I'm sorry. No."

Dame wasn't exactly sure what was happening, but just to be safe, she brought her father's camera up to her eye and found the two figures in its viewfinder. As she pushed the silver button, she hoped the dull thud of the party outside would mask the shutter's click. When Aki put her head on Howlett's shoulder, Dame advanced the film and took a second picture. When Howlett kissed the top of Aki's head, Dame took a third.

"She's not coming, is she?"

For an impossible moment, Dame thought they were talking about her.

"No. I don't think so."

Aki stood up and walked to the window. "You should probably get out there, you know. Make your big announcement."

"It can wait a minute." He fixed the bandage to his nose and then leaned back on the bed. "You know it wasn't your fault, right? You were just a kid. You didn't have any choice."

Aki kept her eyes fixed on the window. "I know."

"One of these days, Charlotte's going to figure that out, too."

"Maybe." Aki cleared her throat. "Why don't you go ahead? I'll be right out."

"You sure?" Howlett asked.

"Yeah. Just give me a minute."

Howlett pushed himself off the bed and made his way out of the room. For a few seconds, Aki stood at the window, like she was waiting for someone out there. She turned and examined Dame's ridiculous moose head, running a finger over its felt. Frowning, she looked around the room. Eventually, her eyes stopped on the closet door.

She started walking toward it, and Dame felt her guts turn to water.

"Hey!" An enormous grey beaver was standing at the bedroom's entrance, her voice muffled under the costume. "I think Don Johnson or whoever is about to make a toast."

"Who — who are you under there?" Aki asked.

The beaver cocked her head. "Who are *any* of us, really?"

Aki rolled her eyes. She fixed her top hat in place and walked out of the room.

Meera closed the door behind her. She took off the beaver head and held it under her arm. "You can come out now."

The closet door creaked open. "Jesus. That was close. How did you know I was in here?"

"Well, I looked everywhere else for you. So, deduction? I guess?"

"Nice work, Sherlock."

Meera smiled. "Find anything interesting?"

"Yeah, but we should probably amscray. I'll tell you all about it once we get out of here."

In the living room, Moose and Beaver could see that everyone was gathered around Howlett.

"... and I know," he was saying, "that for a lot of you, the loss of Loyalist Collegiate was a real blow. But, I have some good news."

Dame and Meera walked past, nice and easy, and paused at the door to listen.

"I'm happy to announce that — despite a few minor hurdles — the CBC has agreed to air eleven brand new episodes of *School Colours* featuring the original cast!"

The room erupted with cheers. Meera opened the door.

"Who's directing?" someone shouted.

"When do we get to see a script?"

As the partygoers plied Howlett with questions, Dame took one last look around the room. Everyone was lit up and laughing with the possibility of real work. Everyone except Columbia from *The Rocky Horror Picture Show,* who once again stood alone, staring into her drink.

CHAPTER THIRTY

"I COULDN'T GET a single hors d'oeuvre under this thing," Meera said, taking off the enormous head. "Lewis better save me some peanut butter cups. Or Mars bars. If I come back to a handful of Kraft Caramels, I'm going to be pissed."

Dame unmasked as well. The night air felt good in her damp hair. They climbed into Meera's jeep and put the costume heads in the back seat. Dame put her father's camera in its case.

"So?" Meera said. "What did you find out?"

"She's not having an affair."

"Why do you sound so disappointed?"

Dame sighed. "She's not sleeping with anyone, but it's still kind of" — Dodge's word came out of her mouth again — "messy."

Meera shrugged. "Sometimes the truth is messy."

"To be honest, I think she's hung up on her old co-star."

"Wait" — Meera's eyes glittered — "*Sonnet* is still in love with *Sylvie*? This might be the best Halloween ever."

"Yeah well, I'm not sure how to tell Ray that his wife's cheating on him with a memory."

"What did your landlord want?" Meera asked. "Something concrete, right? Something he could use in court?"

"Yeah."

"Do you have something concrete?"

"I guess." Dame looked down at her father's camera and thought of the image she just captured on its film: Aki and Howlett, embracing on a bed. It wasn't exactly the truth, but it could work. "We still don't know why Aki was hanging around Loyalist Collegiate. Or, why it went up in flames. And I sure as shit don't know why some asshole is chasing me around town in an old cop car."

"Well, maybe this is your chance to leave all that behind. Get while the getting's good. Show your landlord the photos, tell him you won't be returning your key anytime soon, and *boom*, mission accomplished."

"Yeah. I guess you're probably right."

"You've got to learn to let things go." She gave her friend a little punch on her fuzzy shoulder. "Chalk this one up as a win."

Dame sighed. "Okay, but Nancy should probably text Aki first, though." She switched her phone back on. "Let her know she's not going to make it to the party."

"What are you going to tell her?"

Dame started tapping on the screen. "Sitter bailed. Crying face emoji."

A moment later, the phone pulsed in her hand and Dame looked down, expecting to see a response from Aki. Instead, she saw a message from someone else. "Huh."

"What's up?"

"It's Gus. He wants me to come over for a drink."

"And?"

"I don't know. I mean, by the time I get home and change —"

"So, don't change. Just go. It's Halloween. Trick-or-treat."

Dame put the phone down and drew a little smiley face in the fog of the passenger window.

"Look," Meera said. "It's been over a year since you and Adam split up. I really think —"

"Yeah, I've heard this lecture before. I need to get out there. Meet new people. Start living my life."

"Actually, tonight?" Meera cleared her throat. "I think you just need to get laid."

GUS LAUGHED WHEN he opened the door to his apartment. "Who are you supposed to be?"

Dame shrugged.

Gus snapped his fingers. "You're that moose. From the kid's show."

"You guessed it." Dame eased the head off. "I'm that moose."

"You want to come in for a drink?"

"I don't know. You got something besides Canada Dry?"

"I'll see what I can do."

Dame put her backpack down and looked around while Gus worked on beverages. The condo was tiny compared to Howlett's, but uncluttered enough as to not feel claustrophobic. She was surprised a little that it didn't stink like stale cigarettes. She didn't even see an ashtray. The place was furnished with the same Ikea stuff she'd seen a hundred times before: the Poäng chair, the Hovslund rug. The pictures in their Ribbas seemed hung less for decoration and more to offset the stark whiteness of the condo walls.

"It's not much to look at," Gus said over the refrigerator door. "I spend more time at the station than I do here."

He sliced into an orange and she watched him as he worked. He didn't wear a ring or a watch. He wore jeans, but they weren't his favourites. They fit him just fine — as far as Dame was concerned — but the denim was stiff and didn't move with him. His shirt was untucked, but had the lines to suggest it was fresh out of the drawer. He was carefully casual.

"Here you go." He crossed the room and delivered the drink.

"Tequila Sunrise," she said. "Fancy."

"Mind if we take these out on the balcony? I'm trying not to smoke inside."

Dame shrugged her moosey shoulders. "Luckily, I'm already wearing a winter coat."

Gus was on the nineteenth floor. Up there, the view was different than Howlett's. The other buildings stood closer, interrupting the city in long dark shadows. Dame heard the scrape of a match and the hungry suck of its fire. She watched him light a Dominion Filter King and replace the matchbook in his sweater pocket.

"So, no big plans for tonight?" Dame asked.

He shook his head and let a lungful of smoke out into the sky. "Just finished my shift a couple hours ago. I got lucky this year. Halloween is usually a mess."

"Did you have to work that big fire on Thursday?"

"At the church? No. They didn't need me for that one. What did you get up to tonight?"

"I was at some party," she said. "Wasn't exactly my scene, so I bailed."

"You do that sometimes, don't you?"

"Yeah. Sorry." Dame put two gloved hands on the balcony rail and turned to look out at the city. "Look, maybe I should tell you — I was married before. It didn't exactly work out." She took in a breath of cool air. "A lot of things in my life haven't worked out the way I thought they would."

She felt him standing next to her.

"You know," he said, "I don't think anyone makes it to thirty without some kind of baggage, Dame."

"Probably not."

"Are you planning on bailing tonight?"

"We'll just have to wait and see." She turned back toward the city and pointed out into the night. "Did you know they built Toronto's first skyscraper right there?"

"The Temple Building."

Dame looked at him, a little impressed.

"My mom's a bit of an architecture buff."

"Huh. Did she tell you it used to be the tallest building in the British Empire?"

"Yep." Gus took a drag. "All twelve storeys of it."

"It would've been beautiful," Dame said, undeterred. "Red brick and grey stone like Old City Hall. But they knocked it down and put up those monstrosities." She motioned toward a pair of boxy monoliths.

"Hey," Gus said, moving closer, "just because something's new doesn't necessarily mean it's bad." He pulled Dame toward him, wrapped one arm around her waist, and kissed her. There was a good four inches of fabric between them.

"Maybe I'll go back inside," she said. "Slip into something a little less Bullwinkle."

IN HIS BATHROOM, the toilet seat was up. And while a couple stray pubes curled on the edge of the bowl, there was no yellow ring, and she was happy to see he knew how to hang a roll of toilet paper.

The moose suit wasn't exactly designed for bathroom breaks, so Dame had to climb out of the entire thing to pee. Under the costume, she was sporting an old Deadly Snakes T-shirt and a pair of Meera's athletic shorts. Under that? She wished she'd had the foresight to put on underwear that was a little less worn and a little less beige. She wondered if she even owned nice underwear anymore.

In front of the mirror, Dame smoothed her hair. The humidity inside the mask had not done her any favours, but Gus didn't seem to mind. So, okay. She could do this. But first.

Dame's reflection fell away and she opened the medicine cabinet. Shaving cream. Deodorant. Toothpaste. Dental floss. And pills. No valaciclovir, no azithromycin, no cipro — only Advil and Tylenol. She took out one of the little bottles and gave it a closer look.

"Hey, Dame?" Gus's voice was on the other side of the door.

In her hand, the pills rattled like a maraca.

"Yeah?"

"Do you want me to make you another drink?"

"Uh, sure."

A few moments later, Dame walked out into the kitchen in her t-shirt and shorts.

"Hey, where'd that moose go?" Gus handed her a fresh glass.

"Why? Are you one of those guys who's into mascots?"

Gus smiled. "No, this is definitely better. You kind of look like you got lost on the way to phys. ed. class."

"Oh" — Dame took a pull of her drink — "so, you're one of those guys who are into coeds."

"No! Jesus." Gus scratched the back of his head. "I just meant —"

Dame put down her glass. "Relax," she said. "Why don't you show me the one room I haven't seen?"

IT WAS A little cluttered, and there was a pile of half-folded laundry on his bed, but otherwise, no real concerns. No muscle car calendars, or *Star Wars* models, or pictures of other women on his nightstand. No terrarium full of giant snakes or spiders.

Gus walked in and started gathering up the clothes on his bed. "Sorry about the mess."

"I've seen worse."

Dame shut the door behind her and crossed the room. She kissed him up against the wall until he dropped his armload of clean sweaters and T-shirts. She tasted the smoke on his breath and felt him hard against her. Her fingers found the top button of his shirt.

For a moment he broke away, breathless. "I didn't think — I don't have any —"

"It's okay." She kissed him again.

Soon, his hands were on the small of her back and then fumbling with her bra strap.

"This one's a bit tricky," she said. But it wasn't really. Why did guys always have so much trouble with this part? She reached behind her, and a moment later, the T-shirt and ugly bra were on the floor of his room.

It felt good to be touched. To want someone just for the sake of wanting him. During those last couple years with Adam, sex was just a means to an end, something they'd schedule on her ovulation calendar. And then, it wasn't even that. It was something he did with someone else.

Gus was sliding her shorts over her hips, down her legs, kissing her belly.

"This doesn't seem fair," she said, pulling him back up. "You still have all your clothes on."

She unbuttoned his shirt and slid it off his shoulders. She expected the carved marble of his firefighter's physique, but in the glow of the city lights, she saw something else. The skin of his left shoulder was mottled pink and red, a relief map of trauma.

Dame traced the scars with her fingers. "What happened?"

"There was a fire." He moved her hand away and kissed it. "Years ago."

"Does it hurt?"

"No. But look, if this is too —"

Dame kissed the words out of his mouth. She pushed him backward on the bed and he landed in the clean laundry. He picked up a sock in one hand and tossed it at her. "I was almost done folding this stuff."

Dame climbed onto the bed and straddled him. "Never start something you can't finish."

CHAPTER THIRTY-ONE

SHE LAY THERE for a little while. Despite the uneven terrain of buttons and seams pressing into her skin, she didn't want to move. Not a muscle. It had been a long time since she felt this good.

Gus sat up against the headboard. "Mind if I smoke?"

"God no."

He reached into his nightstand and pulled out a glass ashtray and a pack of cigarettes. A moment later, lazy grey tendrils made their way toward the ceiling.

"One of these days, I'll get around to quitting."

"Took my dad a few runs at it," Dame said. "I think he mostly stopped so I wouldn't nag him anymore."

"I wish someone had made my dad quit," Gus said.

"Is that how —?" Dame stopped herself from asking the question.

"Pretty much," he answered anyway. "He'd had this cough for a while, but no one thought much of it. By the time he went to the doctor, it was stage four lung cancer. Couple months later he was gone."

"A couple *months*?"

"Just a few days shy of my sixteenth birthday."

"That's awful."

"I was at school when it happened, so I never really got to — you know." Gus took another drag. "They called me down to the office, and I *knew*. I was pretty messed up for a while. Did a lot of stupid stuff. God" — he shook his head — "my poor mom. I was so angry at her. Just for being alive when he wasn't."

Dame was quiet for a moment. "My mom was killed in a hit and run when I was eleven."

"Jesus. I'm so sorry."

"They never caught the guy who did it. Some people — well, my dad mostly — thought it was intentional. Apparently, the car didn't even stop."

Dame pulled the blanket up a little. All of a sudden, she felt very cold.

"You okay?" Gus put his arm around her.

"Yeah." She smiled. "I mean, no. It's never okay, is it?"

Gus shook his head. "But, why would anyone want to …?" It was his turn to leave a question unfinished.

"I don't know. My mom was smart. Really smart. And kind of a badass. She worked for the *Toronto Star* and wrote lots of controversial op-ed stuff." Dame sat up. "She did this exposé on Conrad Black, once. Apparently, he called her a 'left-wing rabble rouser' on *The National*. She was always in the middle of one controversy or another. I think maybe she was onto something — something big — before she died."

"So, you think it was political?"

She sighed. "I don't know what I think anymore. I just miss her."

"Is she the one that came up with the name 'Dame'?"

"No, that was my dad. He likes all those old detective movies. '*I knew the dame was trouble when she walked in*' — that kind of thing. I think Rosie was still woozy from the epidural when she agreed to that one."

"I figured it was just a nickname."

"Nope. A name like mine kind of guarantees you never get a nickname."

"My dad always called me by my full name — Augustus."

"Augustus Morrow. Very fancy."

"No one really calls me that, now."

"Not even your mom?"

Gus grinned. "My mom always called me 'Goose.'"

"Goose?" Dame cackled. "Like the guy who dies in *Top Gun*? I am *definitely* going to call you that from now on."

"Please don't."

"Oh, *Goose*, could you tell me what time it is?"

Gus shook his head.

"*Goose*, could you get me something to drink? I'm a little thirsty."

"Okay." Gus stood up. "If I make you another drink, will you stop calling me that?"

"I'll consider it ..." she lowered her voice, "*Goose*."

Dame watched his naked form leave the room. She fell asleep before he came back.

DAME'S *CUCUMBER* COSTUME might've made for a particularly embarrassing walk of shame that morning, but luckily, Gus was a good guy. He didn't hurry her out. Made her some huevos rancheros. Even dropped her off right outside her door.

"Did you want to come in for a bit?" Dame asked, as his truck idled on the street.

"Can't today," he said, "but next time for sure, okay?"

When she got inside her apartment, she slid her camera bag off her shoulder and dialled her landlord. Ray's phone went straight to voicemail.

"I've got something," she said in her message. "Give me a call."

Dame took the camera out of its case and rewound the film. She popped open the back cover and dug out the yellow cylinder inside. She tossed it in the air and caught it in her fist.

Granted, the pictures of Aki and Howlett were misleading, but Ray would have enough evidence to accuse Aki of adultery, and Dame would be able to keep the apartment. It didn't feel good, but investigation work — Dame reminded herself — rarely did.

After a quick shower, Dame got dressed, pocketed the film, and headed out into the world. There was a little privately owned place her father used to use to get film developed. Dame hoped that in this age of digital photography and chain stores, it was still in business.

She hung a left on Queen and walked a few blocks when she noticed a familiar woman wandering out of a nail salon.

Fuck. It was Rachel Suarez.

Dame hunched her shoulders, kept her eyes on the sidewalk, and prayed Rachel wouldn't notice her as she walked past. These prayers, like so many others, were not answered.

"Hey!" Rachel called out in her syrupy sweet voice.

Dame kept walking.

"Hey," the voice continued, "hey, come on. Hold up for just a second."

Dame started walking faster.

"Okay, fine. I'll walk with you." Rachel caught up and kept pace beside her. "And don't think for a minute about running away, again. I've got spin lessons three days a week, and my instructor? Alphonse? He says I've got the best speed and endurance in the group. He thinks I should be in his advanced class."

"Are you fucking him, too?" Dame asked through gritted teeth.

"Alphonse?" Rachel smiled. "Are you kidding? Besides, I'm still a bit of a mess down there. I still pee when I laugh sometimes. Happens to a lot of new moms, apparently."

"I wouldn't know."

"Oh, for sure. I had to wear an adult diaper for three weeks after I had Luka."

Luka. Adam had campaigned for that name, but it just reminded Dame of the depressing Suzanne Vega song. Now she would find the name depressing in a whole new way.

"Shouldn't you be looking after Luka, now?" Dame kept her legs moving, but she was starting to feel a little winded. Rachel seemed perfectly content at their current speed.

"He's with my brother. I just needed a little alone time."

"Well, don't let me keep you from that."

Rachel frowned. "Look, Dame. We should talk."

"There's nothing to talk about."

"You can't just avoid me all the time."

"I don't see why not. It's a pretty big city."

"We were friends, Dame. Good friends. You looked out for me in high school. You were like a big sister to me."

"Yeah, and you repaid me by fucking my husband."

"Oh, so what?" Rachel said.

Dame stopped, flabbergasted. "*So what?* You ruined my life and that's all you've got to say? 'So what'?"

Rachel shrugged. "You were going to leave him, anyway."

"*What?* What are you talking about?"

"He told me, Dame. How you two were barely speaking. How you wouldn't sleep in the same bed with him."

"But that was just —"

"You blamed him when you couldn't get pregnant. You thought it was his fault."

"That's not true at all."

They stood there, facing off in the middle of the sidewalk, pedestrians moving around them.

"Seems like maybe we do have something to talk about," Rachel said. "How about you give me a call sometime. My number hasn't changed."

"Yeah, but unfortunately" — Dame saw an opening in the traffic and jogged out into the street — "neither have you."

CHAPTER THIRTY-TWO

A BELL RANG when Dame walked into Cosmo's Cameras. The tiny store was permeated with the vinegary smell of stop bath and jammed full of Nikons, Canons, and Pentaxes. Dusty frames hung on the wall, showcasing photos of fake families gone blue with age.

"Well, look who finally decided to pay me a visit," said an unusually high voice.

"Hey, Cosmo. Long time no see."

In fact, she barely could see the little man at all. He sat tucked away behind the counter, working at a desk littered with camera guts, his glasses perched in his thick white hair.

"So, this guy's getting arrested by a lady cop," the man said, still squinting at the equipment. "She tells him, 'Listen buddy, anything you say will be held against you.' So, the guy turns to her and says —"

"Boobs," Dame finished.

Cosmo let loose with a high-pitched giggle. "You've heard that one before."

"You need some new material, Coz."

"Why mess with what works?" He put down the disembowelled camera and turned toward Dame. "So, what brings you by?"

She held out a little roll of Kodak between her thumb and forefinger. "Need to get some film developed."

"Film, huh? You working for your old man again?"

"Not exactly."

"But should I assume this film is of a" — he raised an eyebrow — "*sensitive* nature?"

"Kind of" — Dame handed the little roll across the counter — "but I wouldn't get your hopes up if I were you."

"I'm seventy-three years old, Dame. I haven't been able to get my hopes up since 2012. Which reminds me, why can't women parallel park?"

"Because men keep telling them that *this*" — she put her hands in front of her and measured out the length of a thimble — "is what seven inches looks like."

"You know that one, too?"

"Listen," Dame said, "there's only a few pictures, so —"

"You want me to do it right away?"

"Could you?"

"Sure." He looked at his watch. "How about you come back in an hour or so? I'm going to close up a little early today."

"Thanks, Coz." She started toward the door.

"Hey, wait," he said. "Why do women belong in the kitchen?"

Dame smiled weakly. "Because they're full of milk and eggs."

The old man drummed a rimshot on the counter, and Dame pushed her way through the door. Above her, the lonely bell rang one more time.

THE DETECTIVE WAS *sitting at the kitchen table drinking red wine out of a little juice glass. He was dressed in his housecoat, and a cigarette dangled between his fingers.*

"I thought you quit," the kid said, sitting down at the table.

"I did quit." He crushed the cigarette into the ashtray. "Look, here I am, quitting again."

"Why are you still up? It's late."

The detective coughed into his fist and cleared his throat. "What do you see?"

She pushed the smelly ashtray to the other side of the table. "I see my father. Smoking in the kitchen when he should be in bed."

"Do you see the calendar on the wall behind your father's head?"

The kid looked past the detective. It was Rosie's birthday.

"You know," he said, "your mother and I went back and forth for a long time about having kids." He took another sip of his wine. "This job is mostly waiting and watching, but every once in a while —"

"— it's dangerous."

The detective nodded.

"Like when you broke your femur chasing down that pick-pocket?"

"I was in Toronto General for a week. Your mother was furious."

"Yeah" — the kid smiled — "but I also remember that she stopped by the hospital every day and brought you cannoli from Georgio's."

"Yeah," he said. "Those were good."

They were quiet for a moment. Eventually, the detective cleared his throat. "When you were born, I used to worry what your mom would do if — you know — something happened to me." A sad smile flickered across his face. "I never thought it would be the other way around."

The kid reached across the table and squeezed her father's hand.

"You think I would've figured it out sooner," he said. "All the gumshoes in those books wind up alone, don't they?"

"Don't worry, partner," she said, still holding on to his hand. "I'll watch your back."

"Well, good" — he cleared his throat — "because I need a little help Friday night."

"With what?"

"Skip trace. Someone owes my client some money. I have a pretty good idea where she's hiding out. I just need" — he mimed the clicking of a camera with his fingers — "evidence."

The kid slumped back in her chair. "Another surveillance job?"

The detective nodded.

"Why can't we ever do anything fun? Like solve a murder? Or foil a jewel heist?"

"Do you happen to know any jewel thieves currently planning a heist?"

The kid shook her head.

"Yeah. Me neither."

"The Weatherhead Case was interesting. Why can't we do more like that?"

"Cases like that don't come around that often. Unfortunately, the same can't be said about our hydro bill."

"Could I at least work Loretta this time?"

"Sorry," he said. "Official detectives only."

She sighed. "So, where is this place, anyway?"

"It's an old hotel called the Sainte-Marie." He finished off the wine and put his little glass on the table. "Just a few blocks east of here."

CHAPTER THIRTY-THREE

DODGE STILL HADN'T answered her texts by the time Dame reached Jameson Avenue. These days, she was a little leery about making unannounced visits. Now that Dodge had a "friend," she didn't want to walk in on the two of them getting friendly.

But as she made her way down the familiar block, the temperature seemed to drop twenty degrees. Dame stopped. Just outside her father's building, the Chevrolet Caprice was waiting like a terrible white spider. The bubbling black tint of the back window watched her with a hundred blank eyes. She took a step closer and the car pulled away from Sunset Apartments and disappeared into the traffic ahead. For a moment, Dame felt flushed with relief, but as she looked up to the bank of windows on the sixth floor, an awful possibility seized her.

Dodge.

Dame shook herself from a frozen horror and ran for the front door. When she got to the elevator, she stabbed the button repeatedly with her finger. When it didn't come, she leapt up six flights of stairs and flew down the hallway.

"Dodge!" She pounded on the locked door while she fumbled for her key. "Dodge! Are you in there?"

The latch rattled and the door came open a crack.

"Dodge?"

He seemed to be in one piece. But then, what was that car doing here? And why did the driver tear off when they saw her? Where were they going?

Dame took a step back and tried to catch her breath. "I'm sorry, I thought —" But still, there was something wrong. She could smell it. "Wait, have you been *smoking*?"

Dodge cast a guilty glance at the floor. He opened the door the rest of the way. The skin revealed by his undershirt looked like the ruined surface of some uninhabitable planet. Inside, she could hear the television blaring. The sink was full of unwashed dishes, and the counter was littered with empty soup cans, their sharp metal tops open like switchblades. On the kitchen table stood a heaping ashtray.

"Jesus, Dodge. What happened?"

She walked past her father into the living room, picked up the remote, and muted the television. Grey-suited Matlock continued arguing his case in silence. Dame looked around. A bunch of old photos had been spread out on the carpet.

Dodge put his hands in his pockets, and then got down to the work of communication.

Sometimes, listening to Dodge was like listening to someone speak a foreign language. It was as if he forgot that the sounds coming out of his mouth weren't quite words, and he carried on with the same inflection and intonation he always had, telling a story that only made sense to himself. A soft fluttering of non-words. This time, he got stuck on one consonant for what seemed like forever. Finally, "*F-Fatima.*"

"What about Fatima?"

He didn't try again. He just jerked his thumb over his shoulder to indicate that she was gone.

Dame sighed. "I'm sorry, Dodge. I know you liked her."

They were both silent for a moment. Dame crouched down and picked one of the photos up off the floor. It was a picture of her mother in her late twenties, standing outside the cottage they used to rent every year at Paint Lake, a toddler-sized Dame in her arms. She picked up another. In this one, Rosie was camera shy, her face turning away, the sun flashing off her glasses.

"Is this why Fatima's gone?"

She looked up at her father. With one hand, he rubbed at the scars on the other. "N-*no.*"

Dodge shambled toward his bedroom and Dame followed. The air inside was still and sour, and she wondered when her father had last washed his sheets.

"If she left because you're a lousy housekeeper, I don't think there was much hope to begin with."

Dodge shook his head and flicked on the light. Dame's heart sank.

"Oh no," she said. "Not this again."

A cardboard box lay on its side, the spill of its contents covering a good portion of the floor. The mirror above the dresser was gone and replaced by an enormous corkboard, pinned with photographs, sticky notes, receipts, and maps.

"Dodge, I thought we were past all this. The doctor said it wasn't good for you to fixate."

The old man opened his mouth to speak, but then thought better of it. Dame stepped carefully over the pile of folders and documents on the ground and took a closer look at the board. The black headline of a yellow newspaper clipping screamed out at her: "*Woman Dies Following Hit and Run in West End.*"

"I get it," she told her father. "It would be easier if there was some kind of reason. Some kind of logic to all of this."

Dodge crossed his arms and leaned against the door frame.

"But you know as well as I do that sometimes there isn't an explanation. Sometimes, shit just happens. Good people die for no good reason."

The old man looked unconvinced.

"Besides" — Dame pointed at a picture of Rosie on the board — "she wouldn't want you to spend the rest of your life obsessing over case files, right? She hated it when you worked too much."

He nodded his head, just a little.

"Let's put all this away then, okay? You go open some windows, and I'll start cleaning up."

When Dodge left the room, Dame called Meera.

"Hey. I need a little help. Could you go to Cosmo's on Queen and pick up some photos for me? They're the ones from last night."

"Sorry," Meera said. "I've got hot yoga in exactly thirty-six minutes."

"Shit. I can't really leave Dodge right now."

"Could I send Lewis?" Meera offered. "You'd be doing him a favour. He's been watching zombie movies all morning and let me tell you: life is starting to imitate art."

"Okay," Dame said. "I'll let Cosmo know he's coming. Tell him to put them in my mailbox. And please tell him to hurry. Shop closes in less than an hour."

She ended the call and crouched down to sort through the mess that cluttered the floorboards. There were heaps of old files, unrelated to her mother's accident. Most of it was loose papers, news clippings, and battered folders stuffed with ancient minutiae. There were files that dated back to the Princess Margaret Hospital scandal and the old Sherbrooke case. Dame recognized one thick and particularly abused-looking folder as the file on Jill Weatherhead, a case that mystified her father for months.

By chance, she also came across a few pieces of brittle mimeo-
graph that read "*Anton Felski: Psychological Profile.*" She folded
them up and shoved them into her back pocket. They would make
for some interesting reading later on.

Dame surveyed the chaos. How had Dodge ever functioned
without a secretary? It was clear he needed an Effie Perine to
organize his files, bandage his wounds, and bring him the occasional whiskey.

It would've taken hours to organize the mess, so instead, she
shovelled it all back into the big cardboard box. She stood up,
dusting her hands, and stepped over to examine Dodge's evidence
board. Dame was disheartened to find she could make little sense
of it. Among the dead-end clues were a scrawled number on a
dirty napkin, a hand-drawn map of an intersection, and a car
wash receipt. Some of the stuff he'd pinned up there didn't
make any sense at all. Like, why was there a copy of the peti-
tion to protect the Sainte-Marie Hotel? And why was there an
old photo of Rosie and Peggy sitting at a picnic table, hoisting
cans of beer?

Maybe it wasn't just the clues that were mixed up. Maybe the
old guy really was losing it.

One by one, Dame unpinned the scraps of paper and photos
and tossed them in the box as well. When she got to the jaundiced
news article, she stopped and took a deep breath.

"*Woman Dies Following Hit and Run in West End,*" she read
again.

When it happened, Dodge had done his best to shield her from
any media coverage. As an adult, she thought about searching for
the story online, but something always prevented her. Now here it
was. Right in front of her face.

"*A thirty-six-year-old woman is dead after she was struck at a crosswalk at the corner of Bloor Street and Lansdowne Avenue Thursday night."*

Her breath caught in her chest. She never knew exactly where it happened. God, how many times had she crossed the street right there without knowing? Tears blurred her vision and she wiped them away.

"The vehicle was travelling eastbound on Bloor and subsequently fled the scene. Toronto police are searching for the driver of a late model white Chevrolet Caprice. Anyone with information is asked to contact —"

Dame stopped.

She read the description again: *"white Chevrolet Caprice."*

In the warmth of the small room, a terrible coldness crept through her body.

Couldn't be.

When she looked up, Dodge was standing in the doorway. His eyes were full of concern.

IT TOOK DAME the better part of the afternoon to help her father tidy his apartment. She washed dishes, emptied ashtrays, and dumped wine bottles into the recycling.

"You know, I could take that old box of files with me," Dame told her father. "Throw it in the recycling on my way home."

Dodge seemed to consider the offer for a moment, but then shook his head.

"Suit yourself. Are you still going to want these?" She held out a half-finished pack of Du Mauriers she'd found on top of the fridge.

Dodge shook his head again, and Dame threw them in the trash.

"Couldn't find any Dominions?"

The old man shook his head again.

"Yeah," she said, still looking at the discarded package, "you don't see a lot of people smoking them anymore."

She was deep in the crisper assessing a flaccid carrot when Cosmo's joke came back to her. "Hey, why do women belong in the kitchen?" She closed the refrigerator door and tossed the carrot into the garbage under the sink.

Dodge was standing in the front hall, a funny look on his face. "*How-how-house?*"

"Not the house. The kitchen."

"*How's your case?*"

Dame looked at her father for a moment. "You know?"

Dodge pointed at himself. "*Detective.*"

She hauled the bag of garbage from underneath the kitchen sink. It was heavy with vegetable muck. "The case is fine, I guess. It's just a little —"

"*M-messy?*"

She tried to tie the plastic bag shut, but her hands were slippery with grime.

"Yeah. It's messy."

The old man looked at her and frowned. "*Be c-careful.*"

THE STREET LIGHTS were on by the time Dame turned down O'Hara, putting the pale grey sky out of its misery. As she walked up the sidewalk, she could see that her front door was once again ajar.

In all fairness, she had to admit that her landlord had acted with reasonable restraint in the past couple days. And she couldn't blame him for wanting to know the truth. She had once felt the same way. But still, she would be glad when this was all over.

"Ray?" She stomped up the front steps. "Look, I don't know how many times I have to tell you —"

She saw the blood first. Dark red. Almost black. And then she saw where it was coming from. Lewis lay sprawled across the front hall. He wasn't moving.

CHAPTER THIRTY-FOUR

THE SOUND OF the siren was distant, but getting closer. Dame sat on the floor of her front hall and hugged her knees to her chest. She hadn't bothered to close the door, and the cold was creeping in like a stray nosing for food.

Beside her, Lewis was still unconscious. He was breathing, but his left eye was swollen shut and his face was ugly with colour. The 911 dispatcher had told her to stay on the line, but all she wanted to do was hang up and call Meera.

Around her was the evidence of frenzy. Furniture overturned. Couch cushions gutted. Picture frames splintered and jewelled with broken glass. Her laptop had been pried open and smashed. Its keys littered the floor in a deranged alphabet.

At first glance, it looked like nothing had been taken. The 42-inch Sony flat screen was still on the wall. Even Dodge's Pentax — still worth a few bucks — sat untouched on the kitchen table. In fact, as far as Dame could tell, there was only one thing she couldn't account for: the pictures of Aki and Howlett.

She turned and looked at Lewis. His mouth hung open, and a low groan crawled out of it. She ran her fingers into his pockets. Keys. Wallet. Phone. Dirty tissues. She unzipped his coat and searched around inside. Nothing. She pulled the zipper back up and gingerly brushed a lock of hair off his forehead. Dame got to her feet and adjusted her glasses. She walked out onto the front step and tried her mailbox. The photos weren't in there, either.

She tried to rewind the scene in her head. Lewis didn't have a key to her place, which meant the door had to be open when he came by. He must've surprised whoever was inside and gotten himself clobbered in the process. But why would someone take the photos and nothing else?

Dame walked back inside and sat beside her friend. She watched the rise and fall of his breathing. Put a hand on his arm.

Why had someone done this to him? What wasn't she seeing?

Slowly, she stood up again. She closed her eyes, took a deep breath. Outside, the sirens were still getting louder. Tires hissed over the rain-slick asphalt. Sunday night voices floated on the air. She took a step forward. Broken glass and Cheerios crunched under her boot. The hardwood creaked.

Dame stopped.

She opened her eyes and crouched down. With the tips of her fingers, she pried up the loose floorboard Ray never got around to fixing. Underneath, right where she'd left it, was Sharon Fischer's flash drive.

THE PARAMEDICS BURST in wearing fluorescent jackets and snapping plastic gloves up their wrists. They swarmed Lewis, stabilized his neck and head. *When did you find him? Does he have any medical conditions? Has he taken any medication today?* On the wall, the red and white light of the ambulance shimmered like stained glass. Dame paced as the paramedics worked. Every minute seemed unending.

Airway is patent. Putting the C-collar in place.

A decade passed.

Breathing's at twenty. Blood pressure's one-thirty-four over eighty-six.

A century.

Sats are ninety-eight. Pulse is one hundred and five.

A Bronze Age.

Orbital bone looks fractured. Okay, let's lift him up. On three ...

Now that she could, Dame picked up her phone and ended the 911 call. Immediately, she made another.

"Meera?" she said. "Something's happened. Lewis is hurt. I had to call an ambulance."

Dame expected another barrage of questions, but Meera only had one. "Where are they taking him?"

She told her and Meera hung up.

THE POLICE ARRIVED just as they were packing Lewis into the back of the ambulance. She had wanted to go inside and grab her bottle of mezcal, but they wouldn't let her. Instead, she waited in the front yard, leaning empty-handed against its one tree. Her front window bled light into the darkness of the yard and framed the uniformed figures who searched her apartment. Dame had the strange feeling she was watching some kind of stage production set in her own house.

Eventually, an officer approached her, notebook in hand. He was about her age and had a kind face, or at the very least, a face that was trained to be kind in these situations.

"Scary stuff, isn't it?" he said to her.

Dame nodded.

"Is this your apartment?"

"Yeah."

"And the injured party was … your husband?"

Dame shook her head. "My friend's husband."

He looked at her and then wrote something down in his note-book. "Does your friend know her husband was visiting you?"

She swallowed a little laugh. "Yeah."

"What was he doing here?"

"Just stopping by."

He looked at her again, and Dame could see him putting the narrative together in his head. Testing her story for holes. As he kept on with his questions, Dame marvelled at the many-headed police machine. There was the cop interviewing her, the cop taking pictures of her front door, the cop interviewing her neighbour. So many cops. What good was a private investigator next to this shining hydra?

"Any chance you saw who did this?"

"They were already gone."

"Any security features we should know about? Alarm systems? Cameras?"

She shook her head.

"Do you know if they took anything?"

Dame put her hands in her pocket. "Not that I could tell."

"Can you think of any reason why someone would want to break into your apartment?"

Her fingers found the flash drive in her pocket and closed around it. "No."

The cop looked back at the house. "Well, it's possible that this was an attempted robbery, and your friend just showed up at the wrong time. Hopefully, he's okay. And hopefully, your insurance will cover the damage."

"Hopefully."

"Weird though" — the cop tapped the notebook with his pen — "they had time to trash the place, *and* do a number on your friend, but they didn't take anything."

"Yeah," she said. "That is weird."

HALF AN HOUR later, Dame found Meera sitting in the ER waiting room. She was holding an empty coffee cup in her hands and her hair was up in a bun. A few seats down, a grey-haired man sat with his leg straight out in front of him. He gripped the sides of his chair and sweat beaded on his face.

Meera smiled a little when she saw Dame. She looked down at the coffee cup in her hands as if she just noticed it was there, then put it down by her feet. Dame sat in the chair beside her and held her hand.

"They're doing a CT scan," Meera said. "To see if there's —"

She didn't finish her sentence.

"I'm sure he'll be okay," Dame said.

For a moment, neither of them said anything.

"He used to drive me home," she said, staring out at the bank of chairs across from them. "Did I ever tell you that? When I first started working at City Hall. I didn't have a car back then, and he offered to drive me. I was living with my parents in Etobicoke, and he said it was on his way. I didn't find out for months that he lived in Little Italy. He must've driven an extra hour, every single day." She sighed. "He always did have a lousy sense of direction."

"I think he knew what he was doing."

"That first time I brought him home, my dad didn't crack a smile once. My mom and I made this really good chicken *karahi*, but my dad wouldn't touch it. Just asked Lewis all these questions: Where did he grow up? What did his parents do? What school did he go to?" Meera sniffed a little and sat up straighter.

"And Lewis, he just took it like a champ. Answered all his questions. Plus, he ate two helpings of chicken."

She put her face in her hands. Dame rubbed her back. A woman in blue scrubs hurried past them carrying a clipboard. After a little while, Meera dug a Kleenex out of her pocket and blew her nose. "This is all my fault."

"What are you talking about?"

"It was supposed to be me, but I sent him instead."

"Meera" — Dame levelled a look at her — "Lewis caught some asshole breaking into my apartment. Don't blame yourself."

Meera took a deep, shuddering breath. "Did they take anything?"

"I'm not sure."

"What do you mean?"

Dame looked down at the floor. "Do you know if Lewis picked up the photos from Cosmo's?"

"Yeah," she said. "He texted me right after he got them. Why?"

"They weren't there when I — you know — found him."

The old man with the wonky leg cleared his throat.

"Who would want those pictures?" Meera asked. "I mean, you don't think Hugo Howlett did this to Lewis, do you?"

"No," Dame said. "I don't. But whoever did it tore my apartment to shreds. I think they were looking for something."

"What?"

Dame reached into the pocket of her jeans and pulled out the lipstick flash drive. "Something they didn't find."

Recognition dawned on Meera's face. "But how —?"

"Maybe someone saw us sneaking around the office that night and told Fischer. Maybe she put two and two together. I don't know. But it's the only thing that makes any sense to me."

"So" — Meera's eyes stayed locked on the flash drive — "what did you tell the police?"

"About what?"

"About *that*." She pointed at the little device in Dame's hand. "About Sharon Fischer and strange white cars and whatever else."

"Nothing."

"Nothing?"

"What am I supposed to say? That we broke into our colleague's office and stole a secret flash drive? That maybe she hired someone to steal it back?" Dame scrutinized the device between her forefinger and thumb. "I just wish we could see what's on that video file. Maybe if I could get into Fischer's office, again. Look around a little more ..."

"Do you even hear yourself?"

Meera was staring at her in disbelief. Her eyes were ringed with dark circles.

"We're in a hospital. Lewis might have brain damage, and you" — she squinted at Dame — "you still want to play detective?"

"Meera, you were the one who said I should do this."

"I know. And you did it. It's done. But all this —?" She looked around the waiting room. "This isn't your job, Dame. This is way out of your league. Whoever did this to Lewis is still out there. You *have* to talk to the police."

Dame didn't say anything.

"What if they come after me next time?" Meera asked. "Or you? Who's going to look after Dodge if you get hurt?"

Dame looked at the flash drive. "Maybe Dodge knows someone who's good with computers. Maybe I could —"

"Dodge is almost seventy!"

The man beside them adjusted his leg and grunted quietly.

"The guy can barely work his flip phone. Jesus, Dame, he doesn't know anything about *computers*." She sighed. "This world you think you're living in — all this Humphrey Bogart cloak and dagger bullshit — it doesn't exist, okay?"

Dame was quiet for a few moments. She sat hunched in her chair, rubbing the back of her neck with her hand. "I *know* Fischer's hiding something. If I could just —"

"Okay. No." Meera held up one hand. A barrier between them. "I can't do this right now. I think maybe you should go."

"Meera, I'm just —"

"Please, Dame." She stared at the floor. "Just go. I don't want you here."

"I'm not going to leave you here alone."

"I'm not alone," Meera said. "I have Lewis."

CHAPTER THIRTY-FIVE

IT WAS ALMOST nine o'clock by the time Dame left the hospital. She caught the streetcar and got off at Dunn Avenue. Outside the Dollarama, Mrs. Carnegie was still on the sidewalk, guarding her little library. Dame noticed that *Nate the Great* was back on the blanket.

"Are you all finished with that one, Mrs. C.?"

"*Think I read them little kid's books?*" She pulled hard on her cigarette and was instantly gripped by a coughing fit. She brought her hand to her mouth, and when the attack subsided, she wiped a slug's trail of mucus across the front of her coat.

"*You're Polara's girl?*"

"Yeah."

"*You tell him something for me, okay?*"

"Of course."

"*You tell Polara he shouldn't have gone to all that trouble.*"

"It was no trouble," Dame started. "He was only —"

"*No, you tell him*" — she took another long drag on her cigarette — "*he should've left me there. He should've left me with my little boy.*"

"I KNOW THIS *place.*"

As they pulled up to the curb, the kid squinted through the windshield. "It's been abandoned for years," she said. "What kind of person lives in an abandoned hotel?"

Beside her, the detective turned off the engine. "The kind of person that owes my client money."

The kid adjusted her glasses and leaned over the driver's side to get a better look. From across Queen Street, the dark windows of the hotel stared out into the night like the compound eye of some giant insect.

"Well, if she's living in there, I don't think your client's getting paid anytime soon."

"You're spilling coffee," the detective said. "Come on, we're trying to keep a low profile."

She eased back into her seat, switched on the radio, and started scrolling through a noisy carnival of chatter and song.

The detective put his hand on the knob and turned down the volume. "Low profile."

They sat there, listening to the radio murmur. Steam twisted up from their Styrofoam cups and wove its way through the shadows of the car's interior.

The kid took a sip of her coffee. "God, these things are so boring," she said. "Why couldn't I just stay home tonight?"

"Because we watch each other's back. That's what we do. Besides" — he pulled the lens cap from his camera — "I thought you could be on Loretta tonight."

She put her coffee down in the cup holder. "Really?"

He held up the camera in the small darkness between them. "Did you read the file?"

"Five foot three, one hundred and sixty pounds, brown hair, grey eyes," she recited. "Forty-three, but looks a lot older in the photo. No visible scars or tattoos. Last seen wearing a blue windbreaker."

"Okay then, partner" — he put the camera in her hands — "what do you see?"

For a long while, the kid sat pointing the lens at the old hotel, scrutinizing everyone who walked through her crosshairs — drunks, suits, students — everyone tricked out in their Friday night best. Most of the action was heading east, leaving her neighbourhood for some place better.

Eventually, she noticed something unusual through the viewfinder. A teenager, just a few years older than she was, came stumbling out of the alley between the hotel and the pawn shop next door. His shirt was in tatters, and his eyes were wild. With shaking hands, he lit a cigarette. He looked once over his shoulder before hurrying down the sidewalk.

"Hey," she said, "somebody just —"

But before she could finish, the kid heard the unoiled squawk of the driver side door opening. When she turned around in her seat, the detective was outside the car.

"Stay here," he said.

"Are you taking a leak?"

"Stay here!" He slammed the door shut and jogged across the street.

"That's not very low profile," she muttered to herself.

The kid watched the detective walk into the alley and disappear behind the old hotel. For a few minutes, she waited for him to come strolling back — hands in his pockets, grinning sheepishly — but what came instead were white tentacles of smoke, creeping out of the darkness, wrapping themselves around the base of the building. She looked up and saw that the hotel's once-black windows were now lit from within by a strange flicker.

She put the camera down on the seat and stepped out onto the pavement. Cars were starting to slow, and people were looking up and pointing. She could hear it now: the ominous pop and crackle, the eerie whistling. Inside, something exploded in a blue and yellow spiral, and the glass from a main floor window shattered and fell. People nearby pulled each other away from the burgeoning chaos. The kid leaned back and put her palms against the cool steel of the car. There was no sign of the detective.

A full minute passed before she spotted him — climbing through the broken window, appearing out of the smoke like he just performed some ridiculous magic trick. A woman lay slumped over his shoulder, and close behind him, a man and another woman followed, unsteady on their feet. The gathering crowd parted to let them through. There was a confused babbling. A few people cheered. The detective lowered the woman down onto the sidewalk, and despite all the soot, the kid recognized her face from the file photo. She looked unconscious, but then, as the detective rested her head against the concrete, her hand snaked out and grabbed his wrist. She pulled him closer and said something to him. He stood up and looked back at the burning hotel.

"No!" the kid shouted, the plaintive syllable cutting into the confusion.

A few heads turned, but the detective didn't seem to hear. As he started making his way toward the broken window, the fire reached for him with sudden, grasping fingers. Someone in the crowd shrieked. The detective shielded his face with his arms. He took a couple steps back and then hurried down the narrow alley beside the building.

Even before she got to the other side of the street, the kid could feel the temperature change. No one stopped her when she broke through the crowd and followed the detective into the alley. As she turned the corner of the building, she saw him squeeze through a boarded-up back entrance. She stopped short and stepped away from the unforgiving heat. In the distance, she could hear sirens.

The kid called out the detective's name. For the longest minute of her thirteen years, she stood there, staring into the horrible orange mouth, waiting for an answer. Waiting for her father to perform his magic trick one more time. She called his name again. When the minute passed and he didn't reappear, she knew what she had to do.

The kid took off her glasses, folded them into her pocket, and climbed inside the Sainte-Marie Hotel.

CHAPTER THIRTY-SIX

FOR THE FIRST time in a while, Dame found herself walking into Lath & Plaster, a dimly lit, well-stocked hole in the wall where no one would bother her. She ordered a shot of mezcal and sat down at the bar. The air was a comforting stink of old beer and — despite a decade of anti-smoking regulations — old cigarettes. Behind the liquor bottles, a warped antique mirror reflected her image. She held up her glass to the strange Dame. *Here's looking at you, kid.*

As the bartender poured her another, she turned her attention to the flat screen mounted on the wall. CP24 was cycling through the news, the banner near the bottom of the screen boiling it down into digestible bites: *"Trudeau Picks His New Cabinet." "A Mass Shooting in Colorado Springs." "Kansas City Takes the World Series Lead."*

"You want to start a tab?" the bartender asked.

Dame shook her head. "Think I'm going to head out after this one."

But as she put the glass to her lips, something orange flickered on the screen. She put the drink back down on the bar and slid off the stool. On the television, lights flashed and a powerful jet of water arched through the sky. She took a step closer. A moment later, the scrolling chyron confirmed what Dame was already seeing. The Atkinson Theatre was on fire.

She looked back at the bartender. "Maybe I'll start that tab after all."

DAME HAD BEEN knocking for a full minute when Gus finally opened the door. His hair was wet and dark, and he was only wearing a towel.

"Well, that explains why you wouldn't answer my texts." Dame pushed past him into the apartment. "God, who has a shower at" — she checked her watch — "one o'clock in the morning?"

"Shift workers." Gus closed the door. "My sleep schedule's still messed up."

"Well, that works out well for me." She stepped closer to him and hooked a finger where the towel cinched at his waist. "You're all nice and clean."

"So, let me guess," he said. "You just happened to be in the neighbourhood."

Dame shook her head and pulled him toward her. "I was nowhere near your neighbourhood." She kissed him on the mouth. "In fact, I came from a completely different neighbourhood."

The firefighter smiled. "Was there a bar in this completely different neighbourhood?"

Dame wrinkled her nose. "Obviously. There's a bar in every completely different neighbourhood."

She tried to kiss him again, but he stopped her.

"Hey, just — hold on. Is everything okay?"

"Well, let's see" — Dame stumbled back a step and counted out her trouble on three fingers — "my friend's in the hospital. The Atkinson Theatre burned down. And I'm too afraid to sleep in my own apartment tonight. So, no. Everything is decidedly not okay."

"Wait. Who's in the hospital? And why are you —"

She put a finger to his mouth. "Long, long story." Dame walked past him into the living room. There was a crumpled pack of Dominions on the coffee table. "You smoking inside again? Smells like smoke in here."

"Could I make you some tea?" Gus moved into the kitchen and took a mug out of the cupboard. "I've got orange pekoe, Earl Grey, and that stuff with the tiger on the box."

Dame walked over to him. She took the cup out of his hand and put it on the counter. "I don't really want any tea right now."

He tucked a strand of hair behind her ear. "Could you at least tell me what happened?"

"I don't really want to talk right now, either." She took his hand and led him to the bedroom.

DAME WOKE UP the next morning breathing the salt and smoke of the firefighter's skin. The first grey efforts of dawn were breaking through the window, and in the pale light she could make out the strange, corrugated flesh of his shoulder. She resisted the urge to reach out and smooth it with her fingers. For a moment, she let herself think of Jamie Carnegie. But just for a moment.

She sat up and fumbled for a glass of water on the nightstand. The full hangover hadn't arrived quite yet, but it was definitely in the mail.

Gus shifted under the blankets, and then turned over to face her. He squinted at the glowing alarm clock. "It's still early."

"I know." She kept her voice morning-quiet. "But I should get going."

"Are you sure?" He sat up beside her.

"There's a couple of things I need to do before work." She swung her legs over the side of the bed. In the sunless gloom, she realized just how naked she was.

"I thought maybe we could go get some breakfast," Gus said. "There's this place on Richmond that makes really good eggs Benedict."

"Sorry." She gathered up her underwear and T-shirt from the floor. "Going to have to take a rain check."

"You've said that before."

She kissed him on the cheek and left the room.

The overhead lights in the small, windowless bathroom seemed impossibly bright and she squinted at herself in the mirror. She looked pale, and the slow thump in her brain was already starting to pick up speed. Dame washed her face and squirted some of Gus's toothpaste on her finger.

"Could I at least make you something to eat?" he said through the door.

She spat into the sink. "I'm good."

"I've got granola, grapefruit, toast. I think I might've missed the window on this avocado ..."

Dame shimmied into her jeans, clipped her bra behind her back, and pulled her T-shirt over her head. When she left the bathroom, Gus was puttering around the kitchen in his underwear. He had the kettle going and was opening a bag of bread.

"I'm not really hungry. But thanks, though." She looked at her phone. "Shoot. I should get going."

"Is this —" Gus started. "Is this all there is?"

"What do you mean?"

"I mean, is this all you want? Because I thought maybe this was going to be — I don't know — something more. But whenever we're together it seems like you've got somewhere else you'd rather be."

Dame frowned. "It's a little more complicated than that."

"Look" — Gus sighed — "I know you've got some baggage. I've got baggage, too. I thought that's why this might work."

"Could we maybe talk about this later? Now's not really the best time."

"Okay. Sure." Gus nodded his head, but he wouldn't meet her eye.

DAME'S BRAIN WAS pounding by the time she started down O'Hara, and the Advil she'd swiped from Gus's medicine cabinet wasn't doing whatever good it was supposed to do. When she got to her place, she walked up the front steps and opened the door. Sooner or later, Ray was going to have to change these locks. She wondered if she'd still be living here by the time he did it.

"Hello?" she called out.

There was no answer, but it didn't make her feel any better. She stepped into the front hall. Lewis's blood had dried in small, dark continents on the hardwood.

In the morning quiet, she surveyed the violence. Her shabby credenza — the one she'd bought with Adam when they'd first moved in together — was turned over, one of its legs snapped and splintered. All over the floor, books lay with their covers open like wounded birds. Dame picked up Aki's copy of *Wuthering Heights* and dusted it off. She put it back on top of the bookshelf.

Surprisingly, the kitchen wasn't in bad shape. There were a few broken cups and dishes, but with all the fragile things in the cupboards, Dame figured it could've been a lot worse. But then, as she crossed the linoleum, she accidentally kicked something with her toe and sent it skittering.

She picked up a small shard of orange ceramic. "They got you, too, huh?"

The little tiger had been smashed open, its body in pieces across the floor. Dame picked up a few of the fragments and set them on the kitchen table.

The back porch was a disaster. In the pile of debris that carpeted the little room, the first thing that caught her eye was her wedding album. It was hideous — all white leather and rose gold inlay. Adam's mother had given it to them as a gift, but somehow, Dame had become its caretaker. Some of the photos had already slipped loose and Dame gathered them up and shoved them back between the covers. She caught a glimpse of her bridal party: Adam cinched up in his tux, the white circus of her wedding dress. Meera and Lewis, just recently married themselves. Six young, optimistic people, dressed in clothes they'd never wear again, caught in a conversation that never really happened. The moment was so acutely invented.

And there was Rachel. Even in the unflattering bridesmaid's dress, her old friend couldn't help but look beautiful. All smiles. The youngest of their gang. Had she wanted Adam even then? Had Adam wanted her?

Half an hour before the ceremony, Rachel had held back her hair while Dame tried not to puke on her wedding dress.

It's just nerves, Dame said after, touching up her lipstick in the bathroom mirror.

You sure about that? Rachel said. *First comes love, then comes marriage, then comes —*

Let's not get ahead of ourselves.

God, I'm so jealous. Rachel offered her a piece of gum. *I so want what you have.*

Dame hurled the book across the room.

CHAPTER THIRTY-SEVEN

WHEN DAME GOT to City Hall, her friends' absence seemed to manifest itself in every inch of the office. It was too cold. Too still. Her fingers on the keyboard were too loud. Worse, when she opened her email, she found a message from the last person she wanted to hear from.

Ms. Polara, it read. *Please see me in my office. Tomorrow at 5 pm.*

Sharon Fischer had marked the message as urgent, but Dame wasn't really sure what the rush was. The Atkinson hearing would inevitably be cancelled and all that was left now was the avalanche of paperwork. Unless, of course — a dark thrill ran through her — there was another reason why the Fish was summoning her.

Dame took the lipstick-looking flash drive out of her pocket and turned it over in her fingers. She began pulling all the necessary files on the Atkinson, but soon, she found herself digging up everything she could, not only on the old theatre, but on the high school, the church, and the hotel. The four heritage sites listed on Fischer's flash drive. There had to be something that linked those places.

For the better part of the morning, Dame scoured the internet and the City Hall databases for titles, contracts, insurance agreements, permits, news articles. She researched the developers that owned them — Okusha, Titun, Neos, Marinetti — and tried her best to tie them together. But in the end, it was futile. She couldn't find the common denominator. Finally, a thought occurred to her and she dialled a number.

"January," the voice said on the other end.

"Carol — you get anything back from the lab about Good Shepherd?"

"Uh-huh."

"Did they find any traces of polycarbonate?"

"Near the point of origin. Why? Something you want to share with the class?"

"What about the Atkinson Theatre?"

"Jesus, Dame. It hasn't even been twenty-four hours. The whitecoats don't work that fast."

"They do when they know what they're looking for."

"Okay, yeah. They found polycarbonate there, too."

"That's three for three. Still think it's coincidence?"

"Maybe. Polycarbonate's in a lot of stuff." The Fire Marshal sighed. "Look, Dame. You've got good instincts. And I know you've got some personal stake in all this, but I'm going to ask you again to leave this alone and let me do my job. I mean it. Let it go." Carol ended the call.

If polycarbonate was batting a thousand, then whoever set the fire at Loyalist Collegiate probably set the other fires as well. And maybe not just the ones that happened this past week. Four different properties owned by four different developers. Why would one person want to burn them all down? She inserted the flash drive into the USB port of her desktop. Once again, she stared at the video file, the *A* and the *M* searing her retinas.

It had to be the missing piece of the puzzle, but there was nothing she could do to access it. Maybe Meera and Carol were right.

Maybe it was time to stop pretending and let the professionals handle this.

"Dame?"

Peggy appeared at the door, carrying a mug of tea. "English Breakfast with milk and honey. Thought it might help."

"Thank you." Dame pulled the flash drive out of her computer and slid it into her pocket.

Peggy put the tea down on Dame's desk. "To be honest, I'm kind of surprised you're even here today."

"I just figured with the Atkinson and everything" — she took the cup in her hands and blew steam off its surface — "someone better come in and mind the store."

"Well, that's very thoughtful" — Peggy leaned against Dame's desk — "but God, this awful business with poor Lewis. And I heard whoever did it turned your apartment upside down. Did they take anything?"

"No, not really."

"What were they looking for?"

The flash drive dug into Dame's thigh. "I'm not really sure."

"Did it have anything to do with that woman you were investigating?"

"I think maybe —" she blinked and the letters *A* and *M* flashed across the back of her eyelids "— maybe it did."

Peggy was quiet for a moment, and then unexpectedly, she slapped the top of the desk. Tea slopped over the side of Dame's mug. "*Dammit.* I warned you that something like this would happen."

As Dame dabbed up the mess with a couple Kleenexes, Peggy took a deep breath. She seemed to regain her composure, but Dame could feel an undercurrent of anger buzzing below her words.

"I'm sorry, but all this snooping around business has never done you or your family any good. And now, it's put your friend in the hospital." She shook her head. "One day you're going to have to learn that your choices don't just affect you. They affect the people around you, too. The people you care about."

Dame nodded.

"You know, you're lucky your mother isn't alive to see this. She'd be sick with worry."

"I know." Dame's voice seemed small and far away.

"And, to be perfectly honest, I'm not sure how you'll ever make this right with Meera."

Dame's guts swirled with guilt. "Did you talk to her today?"

"About an hour ago. She was very upset. They still haven't told her what the prognosis is." Peggy sighed. "You know, maybe it would be best if you just took the rest of the day off, okay?"

Dame could feel the tears welling in her eyes and fought them back. "Okay, Peggy."

"Go home and get some sleep." She stood up and gave Dame a sad smile. "Maybe tomorrow you'll figure out a way to put this all behind you." She turned and left the room.

Dame leaned back in her chair and rubbed her eyes. They felt like two smouldering craters. Peggy was right. She'd made a mess of things, just like she always did. There was nothing left to do but hope tomorrow was a better day.

AS THE QUEEN car rumbled down its track, Dame leaned her head against the window. She watched the restaurants, the shops, the homes of the city rush past her. She looked at all the architecture — Romanesque, Second Empire, Edwardian — how much of it would soon be cold glass and steel? How much of it had already been lost?

She thought of the Wesley Building, a massive rendering of Neo-Gothic architecture that once served as a Methodist publishing house. When Allan Waters bought the property for his media empire in 1985, he could have demolished the place. Instead, he restored it and turned it into one of the West End's most iconic modern landmarks: the CHUM-City Building. Why didn't more developers follow his lead? Why did people have to raze the past when they could stand on the shoulders of giants?

When the streetcar got close to the Dufferin Street Bridge, she pulled the yellow cord. She got out, crossed the street, and looked up at the structure in front of her.

Despite its scorched bricks and crumbling terracotta, the Sainte-Marie Hotel was still impressive. For a few moments, Dame stood on the sidewalk and admired its arched windows, recessed entrances, and muscular columns. Originally, the central tower had ended in a storey-high cupola, but it had to be removed after the fire. A lot of things had been lost in that fire.

She took the narrow alley between the hotel and the pawnbroker next door, which led to the back entrance of the building. Dame had visited the old hotel a handful of times and knew just which boards to pry loose. Inside, the smell was a layered reek: fading carcinogens, urine, the slow menace of mould. Somewhere a pigeon cooed and fluttered. The afternoon sun filtered in through the ruined roof, giving the main floor the appearance of a vast atrium. The light revealed grey rubble and dusty, bright wires. To one side, the remains of an ornate steel elevator stood like a blackened birdcage.

Always, there was the evidence of recent exploration — mickey bottles, cigarette butts, fresh epithets dripping down the wall — but Dame knew better than most the dangers of these exploits. The old building was alive with decay. Once, she had put her boot through the boards before she realized the whole southwest corner of the floor had finally succumbed to rot. She'd been lucky not to fall through to the unforgiving concrete below.

In a way, the place had the quality of an old photograph, blurred around the edges. She could almost see what the Sainte-Marie might have been. The lobby over there. The bar and ballroom further along. She could see other things too, if she let herself. Things she spent most days trying to keep locked inside her head.

"You haven't been around for a while."

The little boy sat on the sill of a boarded-up window. One pyjama-clad leg hung over the side, swinging back and forth like the pendulum of a clock.

"I know," Dame said. "I'm sorry."

He lowered himself down off the window. "Did you forget about me?"

"No," Dame said. "I didn't forget."

The boy surveyed the ruined interior. "Do you think my mom forgot? She never comes here, anymore. Only you."

"I think she's forgotten a lot of things," Dame said, "but she hasn't forgotten about you."

He looked up at her. "I don't really remember what she looks like anymore. Do you remember what your mom looked like?"

"Sometimes." Dame wiped tears away with the back of her hand. "Not always."

"Do you think maybe one day you'll forget about me?"

Dame shook her head.

"Do you think one day you'll stop coming here? Like, when you have a little kid of your own?"

"I don't know."

"Is that why you want one so badly? So you can finally get rid of me?"

"I don't know."

"But you know why I'm here though, don't you?"

"Yes." Dame sniffed and nodded her head. "You're here because of me."

CHAPTER THIRTY-EIGHT

WHEN SHE MADE her way back through the narrow alleyway and onto Queen Street, there was someone waiting for her.

"So, this is where it all happened, huh?"

Anton Felski stood on the sidewalk, his ear muffs clamped to his skull. He put his hands on his hips and framed his swollen belly. "Ol' Dodge braved the flames and rescued a handful of junkies." He shook his head. "Too bad about that little boy, though. Guess you can't win 'em all ..."

Dame's head started to pulse again. "Why are you still following me?"

"How about this" — he put a cigarette in his mouth and tried to light it, but the green Bic only sputtered and sparked — "you tell me all of your secrets and I'll tell you mine."

"Forget it, Felski."

"Look, I just thought I'd stop and be collegial. See what kind of luck you and Dodge had with that domestic."

The pulse started to pound. "That's none of your business."

"Well see, it *was* my business, until you stole it from me." Felski finally got his cigarette lit. "Come to think of it, you're getting pretty good at stealing things, aren't you, Dame?"

Her head dull-thudded like a drum. "I don't know what you're talking about."

"I think you know exactly what I'm talking about." Felski took a step toward her. "And I think that, maybe this time, you've bitten off a little more than you can chew. So as a professional courtesy, I'm going to make a suggestion."

"Can't wait to hear it."

"Walk away, Dame. Walk away from all of this."

Dame shook her head. "You know, I've been hearing that a lot, lately."

"It's good advice."

"You know what Dodge used to say when someone told him to walk away?"

"No. What did the Great Dodge Polara say when someone told him to walk away?"

"He knew he was getting close."

"Sounds like something he'd say." Felski sighed. "The truth is though, Dame, some people just don't know what's good for them" — he conjured a loogie in his throat and spat it on the ground between them — "even when it hits them right over the head."

He shoved his hands into his pockets. "Speaking of which, send my regards to your friend Lewis. I heard he had a little accident."

Dame's fingers curled into fists.

"Sounds like maybe you and your pals need to be more careful." Felski turned and made his way down the sidewalk.

BY THE TIME Dame got home, all she wanted to do was lock the door, crawl under the covers, and go to sleep. But when she walked into her little kitchen, she realized she wasn't alone.

"Where have you been?" Ray was sitting at her kitchen table, drinking her El Silencio.

"Jesus Christ." Dame switched on the light. "Are you trying to give me a heart attack?"

Ray stood up and steadied himself against the chair. His long hair was dishevelled and he was drunk. "You leave me a message saying you've got 'something' and then you don't answer any of my calls?"

"I got robbed, Ray." Dame swung a gesture around the room. "My friend was assaulted. Does any of that ring a bell? The cops may have mentioned it, you being the landlord and all."

"I don't —" Ray swatted at the air between them. "I don't care about all that. Just tell me what's going on. Tell me the truth."

Dame took a glass out of the cupboard and emptied the rest of the bottle into it.

"You want to know the truth, Ray? The truth is, I don't have any evidence that your wife is cheating on you."

He stared at her, uncomprehending.

"The truth is, she's *not* cheating on you." She took a slug of the mezcal. "Not the way you think, anyway."

"What's that supposed to mean?"

"It means you don't know who your wife is, Ray. You never did."

"You're full of shit." He took a step backward. "Your father didn't have anything to do with this case, did he?"

Dame shook her head.

"You're even worse than Anton Felski, you know that?"

Ray stumbled out of the kitchen. She heard him zip up his coat in the front entrance. "Deal's off," he said. "I'm not paying you another dime. And you've got forty-eight days left to vacate the premises. Feel free to consult your precious Landlord-Tenant Act."

Dame expected to hear the door slam, but true to form, Ray didn't even bother to close it. She waited for a minute and then gently pushed it shut herself. In the silence that followed her landlord's departure, she felt an unexpected finality. For a moment, she was reminded of her last argument with Adam before they split for good. There had been other arguments, times when she screamed and wept and threw things, but this one had been quiet and cold. A polite disagreement between two people completely resigned to their own separate fates. She couldn't even remember what they argued about.

Dame walked back into her ruined kitchen and sighed, knowing full well she'd never be able to sleep surrounded by this kind of chaos. She dug a broom out of the closet and got down to it. She hung up the shirts that sprawled on her bedroom floor like chalk outlines. She threw out the trampled papers, the broken picture frames, the crushed lampshade. When she got as far as the back porch, the little room was freezing, and the floor was carpeted with the contents of boxes she'd been too afraid to open. The prospect of reorganizing all those ancient artifacts was exhausting. Dame picked up the white leather wedding album and then dropped it back onto the pile. The hell with it.

She grabbed garbage bags from under her sink and started stuffing them full. The wedding mementos went first — photographs, invitation mock-ups, the tiny idiots who once stood together on top of that mountainous cake — gone. The Adam ephemera was next — postcards, movie tickets, the little notes he'd written her when they were first together — also gone. And then there was the baby stuff. Ovulation charts. *What to Expect When You're Expecting*. Her first positive pregnancy test. She hesitated for a moment. Then, it too was gone.

She managed to shove the whole of it into six garbage bags. A bag for every year she'd spent with Adam. More bags than would fit into the bins outside, but fuck that, too. The raccoons could have their way with it for all she cared.

First comes love, then comes marriage — the grotesque nursery rhyme squirmed in her brain.

Standing there, staring at the trash heap of her former life, she knew she was done with it all. And not just Adam and Rachel. She was done with the West End Fertility Clinic. Done with needles and cold metal tools inside her body. Done with the endless waiting room her world had somehow become.

When she came back inside, Dame saw the copy of *Wuthering Heights* she'd left on top of her bookshelf. She grabbed it and started to take it to the trash as well, but something made her stop. Instead, she flipped to the back page and pulled the library card out of its little pocket. Aki's signature was the slow, careful work of a child, and Dame understood that whatever this book had once meant, it wasn't her place to throw it away.

Dame sat down on a blanket in the empty spare room and opened the novel to its first chapter. She laughed a little when she realized it was a story about a bad landlord.

CHAPTER THIRTY-NINE

WHATEVER SLEEP DAME got that night didn't make her feel any better. She woke up before her alarm and shuffled through a lukewarm shower and a cold bowl of cereal. She was dreading work. It would be full of people she didn't want to see and missing all the people she did want to see. It was still early by the time she pulled on her boots and coat, and she knew that, before she made another trip to the Clamshell, there was something else she should do.

When she arrived at the hospital, the room smelled of chemical cleaners and something a little too human. Somewhere, the beep of a heart monitor kept a steady pulse. Meera was in the corner, conked out in a chair that — even by hospital standards — looked wildly uncomfortable.

"I'm not really sure how she's doing that," a voice said. "At home, she needs, like, four or five pillows to fall asleep. Minimum."

"Jesus, Lewis." Dame's eyes stung with tears. "Is that you under there?"

He was sitting up in bed. His head was wrapped in bandages and there was a patch of gauze over his left eye. What she could see of his face barely looked like him at all.

"Yep. Me and five milligrams of morphine." He pointed at his
IV. "The drugs in this place are pretty great."

She sat down on the edge of his bed and sniffed. "I'm so sorry.
About all of this."

"Hey, you weren't the one who did this to me." He paused.
"I mean, unless you were. I really don't remember all that much."

Dame managed a little smile. "I brought you some breakfast."

She reached into her backpack and took out a small pastry
box.

"Oh, wow." His one visible eye widened. "Cannoli?"

Dame nodded.

"From Georgio's?"

She nodded again and put the box on his lap. Lewis lifted the
lid and then immediately filled his mouth with fried dough and
ricotta.

"God," he said, still chewing. "That's almost worth having
my head bashed in." He offered the box to Dame, but she shook
her head.

"So" — Lewis swallowed his food — "I guess you already
know about the Atkinson."

"Yeah."

"I heard it on the radio yesterday. Thought I was having another weird morphine dream."

"This is all starting to feel like one."

From the chair, Meera muttered something incomprehensible,
then started snoring.

"She's pretty furious with me," Dame said.

"Well, fury is kind of Meera's go-to emotion."

"She thinks I should let the police handle it from here."

Lewis shrugged. "She's got a point. I mean, this isn't exactly
what you signed up for, is it?"

"You agree with her?"

"Come on, Dame. When do I ever agree with Meera?" He tried to sit up a little more and winced. "Look, it might just be the morphine and pastries talking, but you're the only person I know who could make sense of this mess. And if there's a chance you could get the guy who did *this*" — he drew an invisible circle around his face — "I say you take it."

"I don't know. All I seem to do is make things worse."

"Well, whatever you do, just be careful, okay? I don't want Meera mad at me, too." He took another bite of cannoli.

WHEN DAME FINALLY got to work that morning, her meeting with Sharon Fischer hung over her head like bad weather. Alone in the office, she slogged through the Atkinson paperwork, ate her reheated lunch, and obsessively watched her phone for a message from Meera that never came. Even Peggy seemed to steer clear of her. She didn't suddenly materialize in the office with pastries or pie or even a few kind words to improve Dame's mood.

At lunch, she texted Gus. *Hey! Can I see you tonight?*

Can't, he wrote back. *Already have dinner plans.*

I could stop by after …?

Sorry, he replied.

What about later this week?

She watched the indicator dots bubble across her screen for a moment and then disappear. Dame waited a minute, then two, then five. An hour later, there was still no word. As the day limped forward, her brain invented a hundred perfectly credible reasons why Gus hadn't responded. None of which she could bring herself to believe.

AT FIVE O'CLOCK, Dame took the elevator six floors down to the Municipal Review Board. Fischer's door was open when she got there, and the woman was straightening little things on her desk — lamp, picture frame, blotter. In the remaining daylight, the office maintained its dull austerity.

"I hope it isn't too much of an inconvenience to stay late, Ms. Polara," she said. "I understand this must be a challenging time for you."

"It's fine."

"Please. Come in and shut the door."

Dame did as she was told.

Fischer gestured toward the chair opposite her desk, and they both sat down.

"I often do my best work this time of day." Fischer looked out the window. "It's quiet. And there are fewer interruptions." She smoothed her skirt along her thighs. "I often work on Sundays, as well. I know there are those who believe it should be a day of rest, but I find putting in a few hours on a Sunday to be incredibly restorative. It prepares me for the challenges of the week ahead, and allows me to rest easy at night."

"Sounds like you've really nailed that work-life balance."

"Yes, well, you can imagine my frustration then, when I returned to my office this past weekend to find my filing cabinet disordered and my personal photographs askew."

It was becoming pretty clear that this meeting wasn't about the Atkinson Theatre. "Maybe you should have a word with the cleaning staff."

"Unfortunately, I suspect it was someone with more sinister motivations. It seems a rather important piece of technology is now missing from my desk drawer. A USB drive containing some particularly sensitive information."

"That's too bad. Did you check the lost and found?"

"No, Ms. Polara, I haven't checked the lost and found. In fact, I'm quite confident that *you* broke into my office and stole the drive."

Dame played it cool. "I'm sorry, Sharon, but I don't know anything about that."

Fischer stood up. "I have no intention to debate what you know and don't know." She walked across the office and opened her door. "Instead, I've arranged for someone else to discuss the matter with you, on the off-chance you might be more forthcoming with him than you would be with me."

Anton Felski stepped into the room. The pastel satin of his Dolphins jacket looked cartoonish against the dull-coloured paint.

"I believe you're both already acquainted?" Fischer said.

"We go way back" — Felski smiled — "don't we, sunshine?"

Dame frowned.

"I'm going to leave you two alone." She nodded to Felski. "Oh, and Ms. Polara?" The Fish pointed toward a long cardboard tube leaning against the wall. "When you're finished, be a dear and return the Atkinson blueprints to Archives. I believe they're still signed out in your name, and to be honest" — a shark's grin spread across her face — "I really can't stand the place."

Fischer shut the door behind her and Dame stood up to face Felski. His ear muffs were around his collar and his head looked strangely narrow without them.

"Well, here we are," he said, "just a couple of old pals working for the city."

"Nope," Dame said, moving to get past Felski. "Whatever this is, I'm not doing it."

"Easy, there. Slow down." Felski stood in her way.

"Or else what? You'll put me in the hospital? Like you put Lewis in the hospital?"

"Hey, I just want to have a conversation. No need to get riled up."

Dame stood still, her fists clenching and unclenching.

Felski continued, "I wanted to compliment you on these." He half unzipped his jacket and removed an envelope. From it, he slid out a black-and-white photo: Howlett and Aki. "This is good work. I mean — not exactly a money shot — but you got them both on the bed, at least."

"Those are mine."

"Mine. Yours. That kind of thing never really seemed to bother you before, did it?" He slid out another picture and admired it. "I imagine our friend Ray Hobart would be willing to pay a few extra bucks for these. Way I see it, he still owes me a little severance pay."

He put the photos back into his jacket. "Secondly, our mutual acquaintance — Ms. Anal-Retentive there — she really wants her doohickey back."

"I don't know what you're talking about."

"Be smart, Dame. You think someone that uptight wouldn't be running a nanny cam in her office twenty-four seven?"

She scanned the room and looked at the dead-eyed teddy bear. *Fuck.* How could she have been so stupid?

"So, here's what we're going to do," Felski continued. "I'm going to give you one day to cough up the doohickey, otherwise, I'm going to have to come look for it, understand?"

Dame shook her head. "Uh-uh. No way."

"Now, I'm guessing it's not at your apartment, because — as you're probably aware — I had myself a poke around the other day. But, if for some reason you can't produce it by tomorrow, I'm going to have to assume it's at your old man's place. From what I gather, he still lives in that shithole over on Jameson, doesn't he?"

"You stay away from him."

"Now, I know poor Dodge is suffering from some kind of" —
he tapped his temple — "mental deficiency these days. Think I'll
have to jog his memory a little? Help him remember where you
put it?"

"If you touch him, I swear to fucking Christ —"

"Hey, hey," Felski soothed. "Don't get all excited. Just be a
good girl and give back what doesn't belong to you. Then we can
put all of this ugliness behind us."

Dame's eyes ached.

"Look, I'll make you a deal," Felski said. "You bring me the
doohickey and I won't touch a hair on your old man's head. And
just to prove I'm not such a bad guy, I'll even throw in the photos
of Hobart's wife and Mr. Producer Man. How about it? Tit for
tat. Everybody wins."

Dame took a deep breath. "Where?"

Felski walked past Dame and fingered the objects on Fischer's
desk. "How about the City Coffee on Queen West. You won't
even have to leave the comfort of your own neighbourhood."

"When?"

"Let's say tomorrow. Seven o'clock? We can skip the dinner
rush." He picked up a picture in a frame. "And I imagine you'll
be smart enough to come alone."

Felski looked down at the framed picture in his hands. "Good
lookin' kid she's got." He handed it to Dame as he made his way
toward the door. "Must've been adopted."

For almost a full minute, she stood alone in the centre of the
room, wanting desperately to smash everything to pieces. When
she finally got a handle on herself, she looked down at the picture
of Fischer's son.

Felski was right. The kid was cute. But more than that, he
was familiar. She adjusted her glasses. The picture was an ele-
mentary school photo, and Dame could tell by the kid's haircut

and fluorescent T-shirt that it was more than thirty years old. The frame itself was a little unusual, especially for Fischer's office. Dame would've expected something plain and modern, but instead, it was a folksy piece of maple with a swan carved into the right-hand corner of the wood.

No. Not a swan.

A goose.

Dame's eyes went wide. She picked up the blueprints and walked out of Fischer's office as quickly as she could.

CHAPTER FORTY

"OKAY, OKAY." MEERA opened up her front door. "I can hear you. You don't have to break the thing down."

"Hey," Dame said.

"Hey."

"Listen, I — I need to use your computer."

"Are you kidding me?" Meera took a step back. "I thought maybe you'd come over to apologize, or —"

"I'm sorry," Dame said. "Really. I didn't want either of you to get mixed up in any of this. It was a mistake. But right now, I really need to use your computer."

"Use your own computer." Meera started to close the door.

"I can't. The guy who put your husband in the hospital smashed it to pieces."

Meera sighed and shook her head. "You've got ten minutes."

Dame stepped inside and headed down the hall toward the spare bedroom. She sat down behind the desktop.

Meera stood watching her. "What are you even trying to do?"

Dame held the flash drive up between her finger and thumb, then slid it into the USB port.

"You've been through all the files on that thing a million times."

Dame nodded. "All except for one."

"Right, because it's password protected."

Dame moved the mouse around on its pad and clicked it a couple times. "I hate this computer," she said. "Where's the —?"

Meera took a deep breath. "Just get out of my chair."

She stood up and Meera took her place at the keyboard.

Dame cleared her throat. "How's Lewis?"

"Oh, so suddenly you give a shit." Meera stared at the screen for a moment. "They're keeping him for one more night, but there's no permanent damage."

"Meera, I —"

"He told me that you came to see him."

Dame nodded. "He said I should try and make sense of things."

"Making sense of things won't change the fact that Lewis looks like he went ten rounds with Georges St-Pierre."

"I took him for granted," Dame said. "I took you both for granted. And I'm sorry."

"Don't let it happen again, okay?"

"Okay."

"All right, so" — Meera clicked on a few things — "I've got the list of files up here. What do you want me to do?"

Dame paced on the other side of the desk. "Click on the one labelled 'A.M.'"

"All right." Meera navigated the mouse. "It says, '*File A.M.mov is password protected. Please enter the password below.*' What now?"

"Type in G–O–O–S–E."

"Goose?" Meera said. "Like the guy who dies in *Top Gun*?"

Dame nodded and kept pacing.

Meera's fingers moved across the keyboard. She was quiet for a moment, and then, "Huh. It worked."

"It did?" Dame came around the desk to see. "What is it?"

"Not sure. It's playing, but nothing's happening. Looks like old black-and-white security footage. Outside a store or something."

Dame squinted at the screen. "Timestamp says July 10, 1992."

"So?"

There was a strange feeling in Dame's chest, a poisonous cloud of dread expanding in her lungs. "That's the night the Sainte-Marie caught fire."

"Someone's coming," Meera said.

It was a man. A boy, really, but broad-shouldered and tall. His face was partially obscured by the hood of his jacket. And he was carrying something heavy.

"What's that in his hand?"

Dame already knew the answer. "It's a water cooler jug."

The boy put the container on the ground and stood there for a minute, finishing his cigarette. When he was done, he reached into his jacket and pulled out a small crowbar. He worked at the same boards Dame had snuck through so many times, and then he heaved the jug off the ground and disappeared inside the hotel.

A minute of nothing went by. Then two. Then three. The little numbers on the bottom of the screen were the only evidence that time was moving forward.

"Maybe we should skip ahead," Meera said. "We could probably — hey, wait … do you see that?"

The first tendrils of smoke crept out of the back door. They grew thicker and darker, a malevolent grey octopus reaching up toward the sky.

"Oh shit —"

Meera's eyes flitted back and forth. Dame held her breath.

The boy came hurtling out of the building. He was on fire. So bright that it temporarily blinded the camera's eye. He shimmied out of his jacket and stamped out the flames. Gingerly, his fingers tested the raw skin of his shoulder. His face, still partially obscured by shadow, finally turned toward the camera.

Meera stood up out of her chair. She covered her mouth with her hands.

Dame reached over and paused the footage. On the screen was the frozen image of a young man who just realized he was being filmed. He was skinnier, his hair was cut differently, but nevertheless, there was no mistaking those eyes. Even in black and white, Dame could tell they were bright green.

"It's him, isn't it?" Meera asked.

Dame nodded, still staring at the screen.

The initials AM didn't stand for "Anne Murray" or "Alanis Morissette" or even "Aki Miyamoto." They stood for Sharon Fischer's son, Augustus Morrow.

CHAPTER FORTY-ONE

ALL THE WAY home, the pieces came together in Dame's head like she was watching something shatter in reverse. The squashed Dominion cigarette outside Good Shepherd. The smell of smoke in his apartment after the Atkinson burned down. The scars on his shoulder.

There was a fire. Years ago.

Meera parked outside Dame's apartment. "You going to be okay staying here?"

"Yeah."

Meera cleared her throat. "He did them all, didn't he? Loyalist Collegiate, Good Shepherd, the Atkinson ..."

Dame fiddled with the vent. "I think so."

"Why?"

"I think maybe he was trying to protect himself. And his mother."

"What do you mean?"

"Someone must've been using that security footage to blackmail Fischer. Someone who wanted all those heritage buildings green-lit for demolition. And when it looked like she wouldn't be able to cut through the red tape, Fischer must have warned Gus —"

"— and Gus took care of it himself."

Dame nodded.

"So, who was blackmailing her?"

"If I knew that, maybe I could do something." Dame leaned back in her seat. "God, why didn't I see it before?"

"Because you wanted him to be a good person," Meera said. "You didn't listen to your instincts because you didn't like what they were telling you."

Dame saw the old ghost of a smiley face in the passenger window's fog. She smeared it into nothing with the side of her fist.

"Look, Dame. No one sees the whole picture. Not even you."

They sat in silence for a moment.

"Are you going to call the police?" Meera asked.

Dame shook her head. "If I do, Felski's going to put Dodge in a hospital bed next to Lewis."

"So, what *are* you going to do?"

"I need to figure out who's blackmailing Fischer. But first, I'm going to try and make something right."

THE FOLLOWING DAY, Dame and Meera took an early lunch and drove to Kensington Market. Meera found a decent parking spot on Augusta, and they climbed out of the Jeep.

"What time is Lewis coming home today?" Dame asked.

"He has to see the doctor one more time around three o'clock. He's got a mild concussion, so they're not going to let him watch TV for a while." She looked around the neighbourhood. "Thought I might head over to Ponyboy Vinyl while you do your thing. See if I can find some old George Carlin records. I figure Lewis could use a little comedy."

Dame slung her backpack over one shoulder. "I think maybe we all could."

"Hey" — Meera gestured at the gaudy-looking bakery across the street — "any chance you could get me an autograph?"

Dame smiled and shook her head. "Not likely."

INSIDE THE BRICKERY, the air was delicious with the smell of coffee and Dame's whole body ached for it. Lunchtime customers were already starting to crowd the place, and when Dame got to the front of the line, the beefy-armed woman at the register looked at her with weary expectation.

"It's Val, right?" Dame asked.

"Yep." The woman clearly had no memory of Dame or the two Boston cream donuts she'd purchased. "What can I get you?"

"Is Aki around?"

"She is, but she's pretty busy right now."

Dame heard the door open again behind her and sensed the impatience of the people in line. "Could I talk to her? It's kind of important."

Val sighed. "She's in the back. Come around the counter and just head through there. First door on your left."

Dame followed the directions and found herself in the little heart of the bakery. It was hot, hotter than it had been a week ago when they sat and drank bourbon. In the centre of the room, twin fires crackled in their brick ovens. Aki was kneading dough on the stainless steel table.

"Seems a little late to be starting a new batch," Dame said.

"This is for tomorrow. A good baker's always one step ahead." Aki kept working the pale mass.

"How was the Halloween party?"

"It was okay. Nice to get a little break from the routine."

Dame looked around the room. "Doesn't seem like such a bad routine."

Aki shrugged. "I didn't always want to be a baker. When I was a kid, I thought I was going to be an actor. I played Dorothy in a grade six production of *The Wizard of Oz*, and when I was twelve, my mom helped me land a speaking part in a Shreddies commercial."

"That's cool," Dame said.

"Yeah." Aki turned and folded the dough, then continued to push at it with the heel of her hand. "And then, I got a part on a TV show — nothing you'd remember — but it was exciting." She looked at Dame. "Kind of weird though, right? Pretending to be someone you're not?"

A spasm of guilt worked through Dame's guts.

"On the show, I had to act like I was in love with someone. I mean, I was fifteen, and I'd never been in love with anybody. But after a while" — Aki shrugged — "it was easy. I didn't have to pretend anymore." She pinched some flour from a plastic container and sprinkled it over the table. "That all ended, of course. And a few years later I got" — she paused — "a new acting job. And I've been pretending ever since."

"I'm sorry," Dame said.

"Me too." Aki slammed another hunk of dough down onto the steel. "So, were you the beaver at Hugo's party?"

Shit.

"No," Dame said. "The moose."

"The photographer. Right. Has Ray seen the pictures?"

"No."

"Is he going to?"

"Not if I can help it. To be honest, Ray kind of fired me."

"He fired you?" Aki put her hands on her hips and looked Dame up and down. "What a weird job you must have. How exactly does one get into your line of work?"

"I've spent most of my life trying to stay out of it."

"So, what do you want now? An exit interview?"

Dame slid her backpack off her shoulder and reached inside. "I brought you something."

"A parting gift," Aki said. "How thoughtful."

Dame held out the old copy of *Wuthering Heights* and watched Aki's eyes dilate.

"Where did you find that?"

"Loyalist Collegiate. It's yours, isn't it?"

"Well, technically, it belongs to the Toronto Public Library." The baker wiped her hands on her apron and reached for the book. She flipped through the first few pages, then skipped to the back. She slid the card out of its pocket.

"This is what you were looking for, right?" Dame asked. "Last week, when I followed you to the school?"

Aki nodded. "Hugo was renting the place. Trying to figure out how to use it as a location. He gave me a key, but when it all burned down, I thought —" She cleared her throat. "Thank you."

"Your friend was looking for it, too."

"My friend?"

"Charlotte Pierce. She was there when I went back to the school, but when I tried to talk to her, she disappeared."

Aki stared at the book. "Charlotte was looking for this?"

"I just couldn't figure out why it's so important. Is it the story? I mean, I finally sat down and read the thing — tragic figure, haunted by lost love —"

"Yeah." Aki gripped the book with both hands. "I couldn't really get into it, either."

Without sentiment, she tore the pages from the cover. Dame stepped back in surprise. From behind the binding, Aki teased out a strip of glossy paper. She held it under the light. "There was always a lot of footage of Sonnet and Sylvie," she said. "But this was the only real evidence of Aki and Charlotte."

She held the strip up so Dame could see. On it were photo booth pictures of two young women — kids, really — posturing for the camera. They were smiling and laughing. In the last photo, they were looking at each other.

"A couple days after we took these, my dad found a bunch of letters from Charlotte in my room. He destroyed them and told me I was going to have to leave the show. He said I wouldn't be able to see her anymore."

"So, you hid the photos away," Dame said.

"We did it together. Sort of like a time capsule. She thought maybe one day we'd come back together and find them again." A faint smile moved across her face.

"Charlotte didn't know you were leaving."

"I didn't know how to say goodbye," she said. "And I haven't seen her since."

"Ray hired me because he thought you were having an affair."

Aki laughed. It was a short, bitter burst. "That's rich. Ray's been screwing around on me since Hank was born. He probably tried something with you, didn't he?"

Dame was quiet for a moment. "He said he needed evidence to use against you in court. He said your family had money and that you were going to take him for all he's worth."

Aki placed the photos between the pages of the mangled *Wuthering Heights*. She put the book on the back counter. "My father doesn't believe in divorce. He wouldn't give me a red cent. The truth is, Ray just wants what most men want."

"What's that?"

Aki started working another piece of dough. "The biggest piece of the pie."

CHAPTER FORTY-TWO

MEERA WAS ALREADY waiting in the Jeep when Dame got back from the bakery.

"I got Richard Pryor, George Carlin, and Gilda Radner. That should keep him busy for a while."

Dame climbed into the passenger seat and shut the door. "You're a good wife, you know that?"

"Damn right I am."

"Do you think —" Dame took a breath. "Do you think you guys will ever have kids?"

"Are you joking? I clearly have my hands full looking after Lewis."

"Sometimes I wonder why I even want a kid. When people ask me, I usually say something about family or — I don't know — trying to bring something good into the world. But the truth is, there's no logical explanation. It's just something I want."

"You don't have to know why you want something to want it. Your feelings aren't supposed to be logical. That's why they're feelings."

Dame stared at some dead leaves by her feet. "I guess."

"Oh, by the way, I got this for you."

She passed a record across to Dame. It was an old beat-up copy of *New Skin for the Old Ceremony*.

"That was your mom's favourite, right?"

Dame smiled. "Yeah. I haven't listened to it in ages. Thank you." She reached across the Jeep and gave her friend a hug. "I'll show Peggy when we get back. She loves Leonard Cohen."

Meera put the key in the ignition. "And then? What's your plan?"

"Well, first I need to tell Mrs. Stephanopoulos that she can't slap vinyl all over her limestone, and then I need to make sure Mr. Beaumont can't tear down his two-hundred-year-old porch to put in some kind of hot tub cabana thing."

"No, I mean ... after work."

"I have to return the Atkinson blueprints to Archives, and then I have to meet with" — Dame felt guilty just saying the name — "Anton Felski."

A darkness passed over Meera's eyes. She gripped the steering wheel with two hands.

"I know what you're going to say," Dame said, "and you're right. That guy should be rotting in a jail cell."

Meera shook her head. "This whole thing reminds me of that episode of *School Colours* when Jamal gives Darren Masterson his lunch money and then Darren pounds the crap out of him anyway."

"Meera ..."

"But then, Jamal is elected student council president and Darren gets chlamydia, so really, in the end —"

"*Meera.*"

"I guess what I'm saying is — do you really have to do this?"

Dame thought of Dodge, coughing and shuffling around the apartment in his ratty old undershirt.

Don't worry, partner. I'll watch your back.

"Yeah," she said. "I'm sure."

DAME COULDN'T SAY just what it was about the City of Toronto Archives that was so acutely unpleasant. Certainly, parking was a challenge, but even as a pedestrian, there was always something about the place that set her teeth on edge. It might have been the building's quiet, bureaucratic menace, or the labyrinthine stacks that inevitably made her feel like a lost child in a department store. It might have been the fact that every floor smelled inexplicably like vegetable soup. But Dame suspected that the primary reason for her dislike was an administrator named Allen Gourley.

Dame didn't know what Gourley's official title was, but at some point, he seemed to have appointed himself CEO of Making Everyone's Life More Difficult. An anemic-looking man, bald and pale as a three-week-old dog turd, Gourley seemed to revel in his role as gatekeeper and took a particular pleasure in limiting people's access to vital information.

When Dame walked into the broth-stinking foyer and made her way toward the circulation desk, she was relieved to see that Gourley wasn't behind it. Instead, there was a somewhat harried-looking woman hunched over her computer.

"Hi," Dame said, sliding the cardboard tube across the desk. "I'm just returning some blueprints."

The woman looked up from her work. "Oh. Sure thing."

She opened a drawer beside her and slid a piece of paper and a pen across the desk. "I'm just going to get you to fill this out."

Yet another thing Dame despised about Archives was the fact that you couldn't even use the bathroom without filling out a form first. As she put pen to paper, Dame heard a brittle voice beside her.

"Lee-ee," it said, extending the woman's name from one syllable to two, "have you finished cataloguing those bylaw amendments?"

"Not yet, Allen."

Dame looked up and saw a man running an agitated hand over his hairless scalp.

"I thought we agreed you were going to do that this morning."

"I was, but" — the woman behind the desk lowered her voice — "we've had a lot of visitors today."

Gourley met Dame's gaze and pushed an unpleasant smile onto his face. He turned back to Lee. "Well, when you're done, I need you to bring all those photo boxes in the office down to the stacks, okay? I don't want to be here all night."

As he walked away, Lee breathed an audible sigh of relief, and Dame was struck by an idea.

"So, you keep a record of who borrows materials *and* who returns them, right?"

The woman looked up from her screen and raised an eyebrow. "This is Archives. All we do is keep records."

Dame cleared her throat. "Right, so, this is kind of embarrassing, but I was supposed to return a few other blueprints for my boss today, and I couldn't find them. Could you tell me if they've been returned already?"

"Well" — the woman seemed to think for a moment — "if you know the file number, I could probably —"

"See, that's just it. I'm not a hundred per cent sure which blueprints they were. Is there any way I could just take a look at everything my boss brought back this week?"

Lee sucked a little air through her teeth. "If you want to access information about a City Hall employee, you'd have to file a Freedom of Information Request. And then in a couple weeks —"

"A couple weeks?" Dame leaned over the desk and kept her voice quiet. "Listen, I just started at the MRB and my boss already seems a little ... *demanding*. Is there anything you could do to help me out?"

Lee looked across the foyer to where Gourley was straightening a framed picture on the wall. "What's your boss's name?"

"Sharon Fischer."

"Fischer?" The woman gave her a sympathetic look. "Let me see what I can find."

Her fingers went to the keys again and then she clicked on something with her mouse. "Okay, here's all of Sharon Fischer's activity from the last thirty days." The woman angled the screen toward Dame. "It looks like she returned three blueprints earlier this week: a high school, a church —"

"— and a hotel?"

"Yep. You got it."

"*Thank* you. You're a life saver. And — sorry, just to make sure — were those blueprints she took out herself, or —?"

"Uh, nope." Lee tapped the monitor. "Says here someone else was kind enough to do that for her."

Dame squinted at the name on the screen. "That doesn't make any sense."

"What doesn't?"

"Sorry," Dame said. "It's nothing. Just … thinking out loud."

But it wasn't nothing. It was very much something. And as Dame left Archives and walked out into the constant blur of Toronto, she looked at her city as if for the very first time: hundreds of years of history, made of stone, steel, wood, and concrete. How long could it all last?

What Dame knew now, what she was carrying around in her fragile, impermanent skull, placed her squarely between the clashing rocks of yesterday and tomorrow. And if she wasn't careful, the truth of it would crush her.

CHAPTER FORTY-THREE

TEN YEARS EARLIER, when the Skyview Restaurant was gutted and turned into a City Coffee that looked like every other City Coffee in Ontario, Dame had been outraged. She'd avoided the place since it opened and was now a little surprised to see that in the last decade, the franchise had developed its own bleak patina. The floors were grey with pre-winter muck, and a few of the tiles were missing. The display cases were full of dried-out donuts and shrivelled croissants. In fact, the whole place smelled more of industrial cleaner than it did of coffee or baked goods. There was no trace of the old Skyview in here. The place had been hollowed out, and it had stayed hollow.

It was just before seven o'clock, and only a few of the seats were occupied.

Dame took a table facing the door, just as a teenage boy wearing his beige City Coffee uniform materialized from the back, wiping his hands on the sides of his pants. On his chin, acne and the first sprouts of facial hair were fighting out a territorial dispute.

"You can't stay if you don't order something," he said.

Dame stood up. She walked over to the counter and slid a toonie across its surface. "Orange pekoe."

The boy fished a limp tea bag out of a cardboard carton and dropped it into a paper cup. He filled the cup with hot water from a dispenser.

"Milk or sugar?"

Dame shook her head.

He fixed a plastic lid to the top of the cup, and then looked at the coin on the counter.

"It's $2.40."

Dame reached back into her pocket and dropped a clattering handful of nickels and dimes. "Keep the change."

She sat back down on the plastic chair and put her tea on the table. Behind the counter, the cashier started restocking the cups.

"Fancy meeting you here." Felski walked toward her, pulling his ear muffs down to his collar.

"Let's just get this over with."

"Sure, but" — he pointed up at the menu board — "when in Rome ..."

Dame watched Felski head over to the counter. Her stomach was squirming; her bowels, untrustworthy. She wanted to be on the other side of this. As he started talking to the teen cashier, she heard the door open and the sound of the city pour inside. Dollar Sixty-Five walked in, looked around the coffee shop, and started petitioning the closest customers for bus fare.

"Sir?" The teenager's voice was flat with weary authority. "I've told you before — you can't do that in here."

Dollar Sixty-Five held up his palms in mock surrender but nevertheless made his way to another table. Felski returned with a steaming coffee, working the plastic lid off the cup. He sighed. "They never give you enough cream in this place ..."

"Sir?" the teenager said again. "You can't —"

Suddenly, Dollar Sixty-Five was at their table. "Hey," he said, stumbling into Felski, "could I borrow —"

"*Jesus!*" Dame jumped up from her seat. Felski's scalding coffee had spilled all over her thighs. She tried to brush the hot liquid from her jeans.

"You little —" Felski gave the beggar a shove and he fell hard on the floor. "Who's going to pay for this now?" He held up his dripping, half-empty cup. "You?"

The cashier helped Dollar Sixty-Five to his feet and escorted him to the door. Dame dug a wad of napkins out of the dispenser and tried to soak up the dark stain above her knees. Felski sat down and wiped his hands on his jacket.

"This fucking city ..." he muttered.

Eventually, Dame took her seat. Her jeans were damp, and the skin beneath stung. She sipped at her tea and cleared her throat. "Where are the photos?"

Felski reached inside his jacket and pulled out the familiar envelope.

Dame took it out of his hand and checked to make sure the pictures and negatives were in it.

"He isn't the one, is he?" Felski said.

Dame put the envelope down. "What?"

"You might fool Hobart with these photos, but I'd bet every last donut in this place that those two aren't fucking."

Dame didn't say anything.

"People think being a detective is about searching for some kind of truth" — Felski shook his head — "but it's just a pay-cheque like anything else. We all just want to get home and watch someone do it better on TV."

Dame reached into her pocket and slapped the lipstick-shaped device down on the table. "Stay away from my family and my friends."

She picked up her two dollar and forty cent orange pekoe and walked out the door.

DAME HEADED WEST on Queen, the cold cling of her jeans making her more miserable with every step. For the first time in a long time, she had no idea what her next move was. Without the evidence, she couldn't go to the police, but how was she supposed to go to work every day and act like everything was normal, knowing what she knew?

Dame wished she could talk to Dodge. Not through the broken telephone of his aphasia, but the quiet shorthand they once shared. She remembered the singular light that came into his eyes when he cracked a case, the reflection of some distant fire only he could see. That was the Dodge she needed now. The one who caught Dr. Nathan Wallace embezzling thousands of dollars from Princess Margaret Hospital. The one who uncovered the Sherbrooke Shipping Conspiracy. The one who learned the truth about Jill Weatherhead.

But that Dodge wasn't available. He was buried under a landslide of bad luck. And she supposed that, if she couldn't talk to the Dodge of her childhood, then the one that watched reruns and ate Irish stew from a can would have to do.

She stopped by Shangrila, where she ordered the egg drop soup, crispy cauliflower, beef momos, and a double order of chili fries. Dodge loved chili fries. It was warm in the restaurant, and the air was a fog of garlic and coriander. As she waited for her order, something inside her seemed to thaw. Some sense of urgency finally dissipated. Maybe in the end, this was what she needed to do — the thing that so many people had been telling her to do all along — let go. Above her, prayer flags hung suspended. As she watched them, she couldn't tell if they were moving or not.

By the time her food arrived, Dame was feeling drowsy and content as though she'd already eaten a full meal. She found her way back out onto the sidewalk, and for a moment, she couldn't remember which way she had to go to get to her father's apartment.

It was cold outside, but she couldn't really feel it. Even her still-damp jeans didn't bother her anymore. She started to walk, but then stumbled and fell on the sidewalk. Pushing herself to her feet, Dame laughed a little. She wondered if people thought she was drunk. Was she drunk? She couldn't remember having anything to drink.

She tripped again, but this time, Felski was there to help her up. Maybe Felski would know where she was supposed to be going. She tried to ask him but the words that came out of her mouth weren't quite right. And then, there were no words at all.

"You're doing great, sunshine," Felski was saying. "It's not much farther."

She was relieved to hear it.

"Chili fries?" Her bag of food was in his hands, now. "And momos?" He popped one into his mouth. "You don't mind if I have a few of these, do you?"

She didn't mind at all. And when he brought her to the curb and gently ushered her into the back of a white 1989 Chevrolet Caprice, she didn't mind that, either.

"WHAT DO YOU *see?*"

Everything was so bright. So bright and so loud. Without her glasses, it was all just a screaming orange fog, but as her eyes adjusted, she could make out the countless banners of fire unfurling from every surface. She squinted and pushed her way further into the merciless blaze.

"What do you see?" her father's voice echoed in her head.

The kid stumbled forward, scanning the room, trying to make sense of the strange and shifting landscape. There was a sudden groaning above her, and she spun around in time to watch some enormous, shapeless thing tear through the ceiling and crash where she once stood.

She called her father's name again and again, until the smoke stole her voice and all she could manage was a strangled cry against the monstrous roar of the furnace. Her eyes blurred with tears, while cruel eddies of spark and cinder swirled around her, biting at her exposed flesh.

The heat was unbearable, and it was getting harder to think straight. There was no logic in this place, only fire. And even as she turned to look for it, she knew she'd lost the exit. A racking cough bent her body and scrubbed her lungs like a wire brush. She pushed ahead, blindly, but tripped over a fallen beam and landed sobbing on her hands and knees. When she tried to get up, she found she didn't have the strength. She felt a slow surge of panic moving through her limbs like lava.

She could breathe a little better down there, and maybe if she closed her eyes, it would be easier this way. Maybe it would be over sooner. She thought about her mom, and whether she'd see her again. She thought about her dad, and how she'd broken her promise. How she'd left him all alone.

But then, when she opened her eyes, he was there. Crouched low and staggering, carrying a curly-haired boy in filthy Spider-Man pyjamas. The boy's arms were wrapped around her father's neck, as though he'd fallen asleep and the old man was just bringing him up to bed.

At first, the detective stared at his daughter like he didn't recognize her, like she didn't make any sense at all, but when he looked at her again, he collapsed to the floor. He laid the unconscious boy down gently and crawled over to her.

She had never seen him look so afraid, and suddenly, she understood just how weak he was. How little of him was left. She watched him turn back toward the sleeping form on the ground just a few feet away. The tears in her eyes turned to steam, and when she opened her mouth, there were no words to say. Suddenly, there was a roaring in her ears, a terrible rending sound that climaxed in a blue explosion. The last thing she saw before she lost consciousness was the ceiling collapse, and a flaming curtain of debris fall directly behind her father.

There was nothing but darkness then, for what seemed like a very long time. When she woke up, she was in her father's arms, and she could feel the slow, shuffling rhythm as he dropped one foot in front of the other. He was carrying her somewhere, but she couldn't remember why. The cool damp of the alleyway was a balm for her lungs, and ahead she could make out the pulsing lights of emergency vehicles.

She tried to ask her father a question.

"Shh," he said. "Easy, partner."

His own voice was a hoarse wheeze, barely a whisper. His jacket was missing, his clothes ruined. His face and body were streaked with black, and most of his hair was gone. She could see ugly red lesions through the holes in his shirt. Behind her father, a thick wall of smoke was erasing the night. She put her arms around his neck and felt his body break into a spasm of coughing. They were safe. But still, something wasn't right.

"Where —" She forced the words out. "Where is he?"

"Shh," her father said again.

She looked up at him, but his eyes were fixed ahead.

"There was a little boy," she said. "Where's the little boy?"

The detective didn't say anything. With his daughter in his arms, he made his way toward the lights at the end of the alley.

CHAPTER FORTY-FOUR

WHEN DAME WOKE up it was dark and cold and she didn't know where she was. Her joints were stiff, and her hipbone ached where it lay against the unforgiving floor. A fresh headache gripped her brain with barbed fingers. As she propped herself up on one hand, she tried to bring the other to her aching temple, but found she couldn't. A steely clank told her that one of her wrists had been handcuffed to something metal.

Her stomach swirled. Something inside her wanted out, and she heaved blindly into the darkness. She heard the splash of her own vomit against the floor. She coughed and spat the awful taste out of her mouth.

"Hello?" The sound of her voice bounced around the cavernous black. "Is somebody there?"

No answer.

She fixed her glasses on her face. Before she could identify the cross-hatch of ruined roof above her or the dark cage of the elevator, Dame recognized the smell. The familiar stink of failure and decay. She knew she was inside the Sainte-Marie Hotel.

The evening came back to her in glimpses. Archives. City Coffee. Shangrila. *Felski.*

With her free hand, she patted her body down, terrified by the possibilities of what she couldn't remember. At the very least, she was fully clothed. But her phone was gone. And the once-soaked denim of her jeans was mostly dry. Another thought occurred to her: how long had she been out?

She traced the smooth plating of the cuffs. It wasn't a difficult lock. A hairpin — even a paper clip — would make short work of it. But when she searched her pockets and felt around on the filthy ground, she found nothing useful. She thought back to Dodge's lessons: *This stuff I'm showing you — it could help you. It might save your life one day.*

A fat lot of good it was doing her now.

She pulled hard against her restraints and felt the metal dig into her wrist. At the other end, the wrought iron of the old elevator was unyielding. Panic, which she'd been shoving down into her guts, was now climbing its way to the surface. A scream was boiling in her lungs. She was about to let it all out when she heard the sound of something wet hitting a wall and the trickle as it ran down to the floor. Then, a new smell filled her nostrils, sharp and unmistakable, cutting through the Sainte-Marie's sad reek.

The smell of gasoline.

"Felski?" she said. "Is that you?"

There was another splash and trickle. The stink of the gas got stronger.

"Felski?" she said again.

Splash. Trickle.

"*Felski!*"

Something plastic and heavy hit the ground. She heard the sound of boots moving through the grit. Eventually, Anton Felski's face appeared in the pale moonglow. He switched on his flashlight and the whole world was suddenly one blinding bulb. Dame shielded her eyes with her free arm.

"Thought you'd be out for at least another couple hours." He shook his head. "Too bad. Might've been easier that way."

"What the hell did you do to me?"

Felski played the light over her body. "Rohypnol. Put it in your drink when you were busy cleaning coffee off your jeans."

"You *drugged* me?"

"That guy outside the coffee shop kept asking for a dollar sixty-five. I said I'd give him twenty if he came inside and bumped into me. Course, I didn't give him shit." Felski's phlegmy laugh gargled through the darkness.

"But why?" Dame struggled to sit up. "You got what you wanted."

There was the skritch of Felski's feet in the dirt. "Dame, you of all people should get what's happening here. I mean, you saw what was on that doohickey, didn't you?"

"Fischer's being blackmailed. Someone sent her that security footage to make sure she'd approve development plans."

"Not too shabby." Felski disappeared back into the depths of the hotel. All Dame could see was the darting of his light.

"When Fischer knew she couldn't get approval, she freaked out and got her son involved. Gus burned down the buildings she couldn't destroy herself."

"And they say you can't fight City Hall."

"But how did someone like Fischer get mixed up with someone like you?"

"Well, Good Samaritan that I am, I made a point to introduce myself to Ms. Fischer after that high school went up in flames." Felski's voice echoed in the black. "Eventually, she hired me to follow you and retrieve the property you stole, but as your friend Lewis discovered" — from out of the shadows he came carrying a water cooler jug — "I offer a wide variety of services."

A dark vein of horror opened up in Dame's body. Felski took the jug in two hands and continued splashing gasoline over the floor and walls.

"But, you're not —" She tried to control her breathing. "— you're not just working for Fischer, are you?"

"Look at you, figuring things out all by yourself."

"When the cops realize Gus set the other fires, he'll get the blame for this one too. And for whatever happens to me."

"Afraid so."

"Fischer wouldn't want her son charged with murder. She may have hired you, but she's not the one picking up the tab tonight, is she?"

"Oh, hon," a familiar voice came from the back entrance. "You always were a little too smart for your own good."

CHAPTER FORTY-FIVE

"WATCH YOUR STEP, Ms. Beckers," Felski said. "It's a bit of a mess in here."

"Oh, wow. It sure is." Peggy switched on a flashlight and stabbed around in the dark with its beam. When she found Dame by the elevator cage, she crouched down in front of her. "Well, I hope Anton was at least more careful with you than he was with poor Lewis."

"Yeah" — Dame rattled her handcuff — "he's been a real gentleman."

"You know, for all the trouble it took me to get you here, Dame, you don't seem very surprised to see me."

"I didn't want to believe it," Dame said, struggling to sit up. "Even when it was right in front of me."

"Well then, tell me how you did it. Tell me how you solved the *big case*."

Dame shook her head.

"Oh, come on, hon. Let's not do this." She prodded Dame's shoulder with her flashlight. "I've seen this part of the movie too many times. First, you act all coy, and then I threaten you with my *hired goon* — no offence Anton."

"None taken, Ms. Beckers."

"I mean, if you were stalling for time, I might understand. But no one's coming, Dame. No one even knows you're here. So, let's just skip to the part where you explain what finally gave me away, and we can" — she cleared her throat — "move on."

Dame was quiet for a moment. Finally: "Chocolate-covered raisins."

"I'm sorry?" Peggy frowned. She looked at Felski and then back at Dame. "I didn't catch that."

"Chocolate-covered raisins," Dame repeated. "You always do something sweet to make up for something shitty."

"I do?"

"A few days ago, Sharon Fischer returned the original blueprints for Loyalist Collegiate, Good Shepherd, and the Sainte-Marie Hotel. But this afternoon, I found out she never borrowed those blueprints in the first place. You did. Even though you were blackmailing her, you were still nice enough to save her a trip to Archives."

"Well, that place is always a bit of a nightmare." Peggy put her fingers to her curls. "But Sharon's boy wanted those plans, and — I have to admit — he really seemed to know his stuff."

"What I still don't get is why. *Why* are you doing all this?"

Peggy reached over and took Dame's wrist in her hand. She soothed the red mark where the metal had bitten into her flesh. "You know why I'm doing this, Dame." She glanced around the dark hotel. "Just look at this place. Isn't it time we put an end to all this nonsense?"

"They let this happen," Dame said. "Marinetti — the developers — they could've restored it, but they let it rot."

"Aren't we just as much to blame? We make monuments out of pretty things, but in the end, they always fall apart."

"You spent your whole career trying to save these places."

"For a time, I did. But eventually, I came to realize that we're just a teeny tiny part of a complicated ecosystem. An ecosystem that needs our help if it's going to survive. Luckily, I was able to find some like-minded folks who shared my vision for this city's future."

"Developers."

"There's some private interest involved. There has to be. But there's a lot of people in this city who understand what's at stake."

"And what's that?"

Peggy stood up. "Do you know that by the time I retire, Toronto will have a million more mouths to feed? A *million*. Can you imagine cramming that many more people into this city? Not to mention the *kinds* of people they are. Catholics. Immigrants. People who, despite all medical advice to the contrary" — she levelled a look at Dame — "*insist* on pushing another screaming child out into the world. It was clear to me that if our little garden was to keep growing, we needed to pull a few weeds."

"How many weeds, Peggy?"

"Only what was necessary. Most of it was by the book, of course — special permits and corporate exemptions — but there were times when we had to think a little outside the box: St. Paul's United, Deacon House, The Empress Hotel —"

"You've erased hundreds of years of history."

Peggy sighed. "If there's one thing I've learned doing this job, it's that history takes care of itself. We remember what we want to remember, and forget what we want to forget."

"You didn't let Gus Morrow forget."

"Phil Marinetti wanted to bring that security footage to the police years ago. Who do you think stopped him? I told him, *wait*. Wait until you can do some *good* with it. It took a little convincing. These men" — Peggy shook her head — "they slap their names on a few buildings and call themselves city fathers. But what this city really needed was a *mother*. Someone to clean up the messes and throw away the broken toys. Someone to do all the ugly, thankless jobs."

"Thankless? Aren't they paying you?"

In an instant, Peggy brought her hand down across Dame's face. "How can you even *ask* me that?" Her eyes were wild. "I've given *everything* to this city."

There was a cold ache where Peggy's wedding ring had connected with Dame's cheekbone.

"But they are paying you, aren't they?"

Peggy took a deep breath and smiled. "You know as well as I do that the cost of living here can be" — she looked down at Dame — "quite high." She cleared her throat. "Anton, were you able to retrieve the USB drive?"

"Sure was." He walked over and put the device in her outstretched palm.

"We made copies of it," Dame lied. "All the files. And the video. If anything happens to me, I guarantee it'll go viral. Everyone's going to see it."

Peggy dropped the flash drive into her coat pocket. "Well, if that's true — and, to be perfectly honest Dame, I doubt it is — it'll just save me the trouble of doing it myself."

"Bullshit."

"I can't trust Sharon anymore. And her son has become a bit of a liability. Broadcasting your evidence to the world would certainly shine a light on his unfortunate *tendencies*."

Dame heard a familiar, wet sound. Her eyes had adjusted to the darkness, and she could see Felski, throwing more gas at the walls.

"In the end, I guess we used Sharon as a bit of — I'm sorry, what's it called, Anton?"

"Misdirection."

"*Misdirection.* Right." She shook her head. "You were going to ruin everything, Dame. So, when this opportunity presented itself, I couldn't really pass it up. You'll be gone and Sharon's son will go to jail for a long time."

"Two variables that cancel each other out." Dame smirked. "Sounds like a real tidy equation."

"Tidy?" Peggy looked incredulous. "Do you have any idea how much trouble I went through trying to *protect* you from all this? I warned you — over and over again — not to get involved. I moved Heaven and Earth to get you that promotion. To make you one of us. And when you refused, I had Anton drive all over the city to scare you off. But, you couldn't let it go. You *insisted* on snooping around and stirring things up."

Peggy took a deep breath. "You remind me so much of your mother, you know that? When Rosie found out about our little operation, she couldn't let it go either."

A high-voltage hum burned through Dame's brain. "What do you mean?"

"It's a good thing she never had a chance to tell your father." Peggy shook her head. "I know he had his suspicions, but even he couldn't make sense of such a random act of violence."

The room rushed toward her. "Peggy, what are you talking about?"

"I begged her to walk away, but she was bound and determined to turn it all into another headline. Another feather in her cap. It broke my heart to do what we did, but in the end, she left me no other option."

Dame felt numb. Her body sagged against the metal of the black elevator as though a great weight was pinning her down.

"Life is full of impossible choices, Dame. Sometimes, to save what you love, you have to let something else die. You should understand that better than most people."

"She was your friend." Her words came thick and slow.

"My friend." The strange, faraway look came into Peggy's eyes again. "My friend who stole the man I loved. Who had his baby." The look vanished and was replaced by something darker. Something familiar. "He should have been mine. *You* should have been mine. But you're not. You're just your mother's daughter, through and through. I think I've finally come to accept that."

Dame stared back at the woman in belief and disbelief.

Peggy looked away. "Anton? Are you finished yet?"

"Just about, Ms. Beckers."

"Well then" — she turned back to Dame — "I'm afraid it's time we said our goodbyes."

Tears finally spilled down Dame's face. "You don't have to do this, Peggy."

"My smart, brave girl." The silver-haired woman bent down in front of Dame. With a tissue, she gently blotted her eyes. "We both know that's not true."

Peggy stood up straight and pulled the hood of her coat over her head. As she made her way toward the door, she looked back only once.

CHAPTER FORTY-SIX

FELSKI DUMPED THE rest of the gas at Dame's feet. The fumes scorched her sinuses. He hurled the plastic jug into the darkness and it gonged off some unseen obstacle.

Dame sniffed. With her free hand, she adjusted her glasses. "Was it you, Felski?"

"Was what me?"

"Behind the wheel of that car — the one that killed my mother."

He paused for a moment. "*All things truly wicked start from innocence.*"

"You read that on a bridge, too?"

"It's Hemingway. Means I didn't do it."

"Who then?"

"What does it matter, Dame? There are a lot of guys like me out there."

"It matters to me."

Felski sighed. "I don't know for sure. But there's this older guy. Kind of strange looking. Has two different-coloured eyes. I know he used to do most of Ms. Beckers's wet work."

Dame shuddered. "So, you didn't kill my mother."

"No."

"But you're going to kill me."

Felski cleared his throat. "You know, I had a hard time finding work after Dodge fired me. He made sure of that. Told people I was 'unstable' and 'dangerous.' But Peggy Beckers gave me a job. She was good to me. And maybe I didn't always feel good about what she had me do, but —"

"Bullshit," Dame said. "You like hurting people."

"Look sunshine, I tried to warn you, but you just —"

"That's why they wouldn't let you be a cop, isn't it?"

"Might be time to shut that mouth of yours."

"You know, I happened to read a copy of your psych profile. What did it say again?"

"I know what you're trying to do, Dame, but it's not going to —"

"A 'lack of self-control'? A 'predilection for sadism'? Is that how they put it?"

"I told you to *shut up*!" Felski was pacing back and forth, rubbing his knuckles with his hand. He let out a long, slow breath. "You know if it was up to me, I'd knock you out cold. Just a little bump on the noggin. Real quick. You wouldn't feel a thing. But Ms. Beckers — she said she wants it to hurt you as much as it hurts her."

He reached into his coat and produced the green Bic. A cold fist squeezed around Dame's heart.

"Come on, Felski" — she tried to smile through the tears — "I'm Dodge Polara's daughter. Isn't that worth something?"

"Sorry, sunshine." Felski put a cigarette in his mouth. "I need that paycheque like everybody else."

She watched in horror as he thumbed the lighter once, twice, a third time.

"This fucking thing." He shook it and tried again. For an instant, there was a brilliant spider of sparks, and then nothing. "*Fuck.*"

He took a deep breath. "Okay. No problem. I think I've got some matches in the car." He looked down. "Don't go nowhere."

As she watched Felski walk through the exit, Dame's heart did a drum solo. She gave one last desperate heave against the metal of the cuff until she thought her wrist would dislocate. At last, the scream hiding in her chest burrowed out through her throat. Not a fierce blast of righteous anger, but the desolate cry of a trapped animal.

She thought longingly of Dodge's lockpick kit. She could almost feel the cracked brown leather in her hand and hear the rattle of precious tools inside. She pictured the delicate machined hooks and the tension wrenches her father jerry-rigged from rake tines, windshield wipers, and the arm of an old pair of —

Dame's breath caught in her lungs. With her trembling free hand, she took her mother's glasses off her face. She wedged the frames under her boot and twisted the arm away from its hinge. The lens broke with a heartless crack, but she came away with a long, thin blade. Dame bent the metal into the handcuff, and in the grey light of the neighbourhood, she got down to work.

CHAPTER FORTY-SEVEN

"SORRY ABOUT THE delay." Felski bustled in through the back door. "Apparently, it's impossible to find a light around here. Had to go to the store up the street. Two bucks for a pack of matches. Can you believe that?"

Dame was quiet. She kept her back to him.

"Cold shoulder, huh?" He struck one of the overpriced matches and held it against his cigarette. "Well, not for much longer, I'm afraid."

Still, Dame said nothing.

"Where's that potty mouth of yours now, huh? This is your last chance to use it."

"Let me ask you a question, Felski." Dame cleared her throat. "Why can't women parallel park?"

"What? What are you talking about?"

"I said, 'Why can't women parallel park?'"

Felski started to laugh. "You're going to tell me a joke?" His laugh turned wet and ugly. "Okay, I'll bite. Why can't women parallel park?"

There was a quiet click and Dame took a steadying breath. She turned around to face Felski. "Because men keep telling us that *this*" — with two free hands she made the insignificant measurement — "is what seven inches looks like."

Felski's mouth fell open. "How —?"

To Dame, everything that happened next seemed to happen in slow motion. Felski's cigarette unglued itself from his bottom lip and fell end to end onto the gasoline-soaked floor. When it made contact, there was an impossible moment of silence and then, a great whooshing sound. Almost instantly, the room blossomed with blue and yellow flames. Dame took a couple steps back. The once-dark hotel was now a riot of colour and light. A howling chorus filled the air.

"*There's no way out, Dame!*" Felski hollered over the noise.

He had a point. The private investigator stood between her and the back exit, and everything else had long been blocked off or boarded up. So Dame ran — not toward the door — but toward the southwest corner of the building.

Felski chased after her. "*Where do you think you're going?*"

The heat was intensifying, and the smoke thickened with every step. Fire billowed all around her. She hurtled closer and closer to the wall — twenty feet, fifteen, now ten. She waited until the last possible moment before she made her move: an abrupt left turn. She looked over her shoulder and saw Felski trying to corner, but knew it was too late. She heard the rotten crack of the floor giving way, and heard his scream end abruptly as he hit the concrete below.

Dame stumbled back to where he fell. She tried to catch her breath, but there was too much smoke. In the chiaroscuro light of the fire, the hole looked like a mouth full of bad teeth.

What's it called, Anton?

A low moan came up out of the blackness.

Misdirection.

The fire climbed the wall now, snapping at the timber, tonguing the already-damaged ceiling. All around her, flames advanced

like an ambush of bright tigers. She unzipped her jacket and removed the photographs of Aki and Howlett she'd tucked inside.
She tossed the pictures into the fire and watched the heat swallow
them whole.

Dame doubled over coughing. Ashes circled her head like a
swarm of late-summer flies. She pulled her shirt up over her nose
and started toward the exit. There wasn't much time.

And then from above, a flaming rafter came hurtling down
and sent Dame sprawling into a pile of rubble. She tried to push
herself up from the filth, but her arms buckled beneath her, and
she collapsed back onto the floor. Her breath was coming in short
gasps now, her lungs searching for air but finding only smoke.
Her eyes closed against the sting of it. She struggled to stand, but
the heat had an impossible gravity that dragged her to the ground.

Dame realized she was alone. Her father wasn't going to pull
off another one of his magic tricks this time. He wasn't going
to appear from the smoke and carry her out in his arms. Dodge
couldn't save her anymore. No one could. And part of her wanted
to stay where she was, in that strange vacancy, so close to the
beating heart of the fire. Maybe, it was just what she deserved.

But then, when she opened her eyes, there was someone else
there — the curly-haired little boy — standing across the room in
his pyjamas, watching her.

"Get up," she heard him say.

Dame tried to speak, but the words wouldn't come.

"You have to get up," the boy said again. "You don't belong
here anymore."

She blinked and the boy was gone. Summoning the last of her
strength, Dame put one foot on the ground, and then another.
She found her balance and stayed low. And for the final time, she
made her way out of the Sainte-Marie Hotel.

"UGH. IT'S TOO *hot in here.*"

The kid leaned her head back against the seat of the Buick and fanned herself.

"*Open the window,*" *the woman said.*

"*Couldn't we just buy a car with air conditioning?*"

"*No, but you could open the window,*" *the woman said again.*

The kid sighed. She cranked the handle and let the evening into the car. Her mother did the same. Ahead of them, a convertible honked and a streetcar clanged. The day was about to end, and as they headed west on Queen, the chrome and steel of the traffic flashed white with sunlight.

"*Are we ordering takeout tonight?*" *the kid said.*

"*It's Friday, isn't it?*"

She nodded. "*Is Peggy coming over?*"

"*As far as I know.*"

"*With dessert?*"

The woman smiled. "*Maybe.*"

"*Hey.*" *The kid sat up in her seat.* "*Why is there a truck sticking out of the side of that building?*"

"*That's the* CHUM-*City Building. They make* TV *shows there.*"

"*Like* Read All About It?"

The woman shook her head. "*I think they film that in Brampton.*"

A few minutes passed in silence. Eventually, the woman pointed out the window. "*You see that park beside us?*"

The kid nodded.

"*There used to be a huge college there. Trinity College. White brick and Ohio limestone. It would've looked like a castle from here.*"

"*What happened to it?*"

"*There was a fire. And then the city didn't want to take care of it anymore, so they tore it down. The foundations are still there, buried somewhere under the ground."*

"That's kind of sad." The kid stared out at the park as they drove past. She tried to imagine a castle in all that empty space. Traffic moved slowly, street light to street light, until they came into view of the Dufferin Street Bridge. The kid pointed up as they neared an old hotel.

"You told me about this one, right? It has some kind of weird metal elevator or something?"

"Yeah, that's right. Want to go have a look?"

"Do we have time?"

"Of course," the woman said, switching on the turn signal. "We've got all the time in the world."

CHAPTER FORTY-EIGHT

THE DOOR OPENED, and a man walked into the little room, followed closely by a steely-looking guard.

"Visiting hours are over at four o'clock," the guard said.

He closed the door and left the two of them alone.

"Hey," Dame said.

"Hey."

The man stood there for a moment, while she stayed seated at
the metal table. Neither of them said anything. For someone she'd
once undressed, Dame had never seen Gus look more naked. He'd
lost about fifteen pounds, and his standard-issue jumpsuit hung
off his frame, a size too large. His face was pallid, unshaven, and
there was a yellow smear on his cheek — the fading memory of
an ugly bruise. He seemed to be having difficulty looking at her,
and in the light of the fluorescent tube above them, his green eyes
were a dull grey.

"I hope this is all right," Dame said. "My father pulled some
strings so we wouldn't have to talk through Plexiglas."

Gus sat down across from her but kept his eyes on the table.
"To be honest, you're the last person I was expecting to visit me."

Dame cleared her throat. "How are you?"

He shrugged.

"I'm sorry about what happened to your mom. I know that job meant a lot to her."

"Yeah. Well, at least she didn't have to spend any time in here." He glanced around the little room.

"I heard Anton Felski took a plea deal," Dame said. "I guess he rolled over on a lot of high-profile people. He'll still have to do some pretty serious time, though."

Gus nodded. "What about … that woman?"

Dame adjusted her new glasses. They still didn't feel quite right on her face.

"Peggy Beckers is still missing," she said. "Apparently, no one's seen her since the Sainte-Marie burned down. I had to meet with the Crown Attorney last week. They're going to charge her with a bunch of things: extortion, arson, fraud, and —"

"— conspiracy to commit murder." Gus finally met her eyes. "Look, I want you to know I didn't have anything to do with —" he looked back down at his hands "— with what they did to you."

"I know."

The room was quiet again.

"They charged me with four counts of arson, and one count of involuntary manslaughter, for what happened before. After the trial, they'll probably send me to Penetanguishene. It's supposed to be" — he took a deep breath — "a little better there."

"You're pleading guilty?"

Gus nodded. "My lawyer thinks he can get me twelve years minus time served. It's probably the best I can hope for."

Another silence hung between them, punctuated by the distant sounds of slamming doors and men shouting at each other.

"Why did you do it?" Dame finally asked. "When you were a kid, I mean. Why did you set that first fire?"

Gus kept his eyes fixed on the surface of the table. "It was a few months after my dad died. My mom didn't really know how to —" He sighed. "She was spending more time with that old hotel than she was with me. I was angry. I didn't know where to put it all. So, when another one of her meetings ran late, I siphoned some gas from our car." He cleared his throat. "The place was supposed to be empty. But it wasn't."

Gus took a deep breath. "I was reviewing the old police report with my lawyer earlier this month. It said there was a man injured in the fire named David Polara. Was that —?"

"My father."

"He tried to save that little boy."

Dame nodded.

"I used to see that boy, you know? Like a ghost. On the street. In crowds. Sometimes, in the middle of fighting a fire, I'd see him in the flames. Like he didn't want me to forget. Like I ever could."

Dame could feel tears welling in her eyes, but she blinked them away.

Gus sat back in his metal chair. "Did you know, the first time I saved someone's life, I wasn't even on duty? I was having a beer with a couple friends, and this woman a few tables away stood up and knocked over a glass. She had her hands around her throat" — he put his own hands to his neck — "so I went over and asked if she was okay. But she couldn't talk or anything. I yelled at someone to call 911, and my training sort of kicked in. Started doing back blows, then the Heimlich. Popped a piece of chicken out of her like a champagne cork."

He paused for a moment and smiled at the memory. "She was okay. And for a little while, I felt okay, too. There were high-fives, and drinks, and the owner of the place picked up our tab. It was a good night.

"But then, I woke up the next morning and nothing had

changed. And I think I finally understood that what I did could never be undone. I could save a hundred lives, and that little boy would still be dead. I took something out of the world, and there's nothing I can do to put it back."

Dame's fingers touched her stomach. There was so much she wanted to say to him, but she didn't know how to do it. And she didn't know if it would make things any better.

"When I set those other fires, I got the blueprints out and combed those places top to bottom. Made sure that no one was —" He took a deep breath. "I figured, if someone had to burn down those buildings, it should be me. That way, no one would get hurt. Guess I messed that up, too." He looked around the room again. "You know, I always knew I'd wind up in a place like this. One way or another. It's like some part of me has been in here since I was sixteen."

They were both quiet.

"But hey," Gus said. "It's not all bad. I finally quit smoking."

Dame smiled, but her eyes betrayed her with a pair of tears. She pushed them off her cheeks.

"Why did you come here?" he asked.

She started to speak, then stopped.

"Did you want me to apologize?" he asked. "I mean, I'm sorry. I'm so sorry. But we both know there's nothing I could say that would ever —"

"No. It isn't that." Dame felt a flutter of movement in her belly.

"Then what?"

"I think —" There was another little nudge, something she hadn't felt before. "I think maybe I just want to know what kind of person you really are."

"I'm not so sure myself." He tried to smile. "Guess I've got twelve years to figure it out. Minus time served."

CHAPTER FORTY-NINE

LEWIS LOOKED UP at the clock. "You sleep in this morning?"

Dame collapsed into her desk chair. "No. I had another doctor's appointment. Did I miss the meeting?"

He shook his head. "Meera's still out running a few errands."

"God, she's so busy these days."

"Heavy is the head that wears the crown."

Lewis bit into his bagel and started chewing. Dame could still see the pink scars Anton Felski had left on the side of his face. "So, what's it like being married to the boss?"

He swallowed his food. "She's only the boss when we're at work."

"Yeah" — Dame smiled — "let's keep telling ourselves that."

The office door swung open and the new team leader of Heritage Planning came bustling through it. In her hands was a white cake box. "Am I late?"

"We were both late, so it doesn't count," Dame said.

"I was on time," Lewis grumbled to himself.

Meera put the box on Dame's desk. "Breakfast is served."

"What's this?"

"It's to celebrate your last day. I couldn't exactly bring you a bottle of mezcal, could I?"

Dame lifted the lid. "*We'll Miss You, Dave.*"

"Dave?" Meera took a closer look. "Shit. That's the last time I order a cake from Costco."

"We really are going to miss you," Lewis said.

"Come on, guys. I won't be gone all that long. It'll be like I never left."

Meera looked at Lewis.

"Dame," he said, "do you ever wonder if working for City Hall is your true calling?"

"I don't know. Is it really anyone's 'true calling'?"

"You exposed a multimillion-dollar arson conspiracy," Meera said, "when the police and the Fire Marshal couldn't."

"Yeah. And I almost got killed doing it."

"Still. Your picture was all over the news. We got slammed by reporters wanting to interview you. I'm just saying — you might want to give this whole private investigator business a little more thought while you're off."

"Maybe" — Dame's hand rested on her stomach — "but right now, there's more pressing business to attend to."

"Fair enough," Meera said. "Lewis, can you get some knives and forks from the break room? Dave's cake isn't going to eat itself."

Lewis stood up with a sigh. "Yes, boss."

As he lumbered out of the little office, Meera turned to Dame. "You text me updates every day, okay?"

"Sure. But it's not like —"

"I'm serious. If you need anything — *anything* — podcast recommendations, bottle of Advil, ice cream sandwich from Bang Bang — you let me know, okay?"

"Meera, I —"

"*Okay?*"

Dame smiled. "Yes, boss."

WHEN DAME GOT home from work that afternoon, she wasn't particularly surprised to find the door to her apartment hanging wide open. As she walked up the front steps, she wondered why she bothered locking the place at all.

"You know," Aki said, "you should probably have those locks changed."

"Yeah. I've been meaning to talk to the new landlord about that."

She was sitting at the kitchen table, turning the ceramic tiger over in her hands. Its smooth orange surface was interrupted by a network of white cracks where it had been glued back together.

"I heard about you and Ray," Dame said. "I'm sorry."

"I'm not. I spent twenty years being someone I didn't want to be. I couldn't do it anymore."

Dame nodded.

"Anyway, I wanted to thank you," Aki said, "for letting me work things out on my own terms."

"All things considered, it was the least I could do. How's Hank?"

"It's been tough," she said. "Tougher than I thought it was going to be. But he's got two bedrooms now and he's managed to double the size of his Lego collection, so that helps a bit."

"And Charlotte?"

"*School Colours Never Fade* just wrapped up shooting a few days ago, so we'll have a bit of time off together. It'll be nice to see who we are when the cameras aren't rolling."

"Think there's going to be a second season?"

"Guess we'll have to wait and see." Aki held up the ceramic tiger. "Is this your handiwork?"

Dame nodded. "It broke, but I couldn't throw it away."

"You did a nice job."

"I don't know. You can still see all the cracks."

"I think that's what I like about it." Aki put the glued-together tiger back on the kitchen table. "In any case, I should get going. I've probably overstayed my break and enter."

She got up and started heading toward the door. Dame followed her.

"You know," Aki said, "I'm really glad I managed to keep this place in the separation agreement."

"Me too." Dame smiled. "My old landlord had some serious boundary issues."

Aki laughed. "I love what you've done with the spare bedroom, by the way."

"Thanks." Dame's hand found the new roundness of her belly. "I'm kind of fond of it myself."

CHAPTER FIFTY

DAME WAS TIRED. In the year since the Sainte-Marie Hotel had burned down, it seemed she was always tired. Still, there was something about the hard light of the parking garage that made her feel especially exhausted. She leaned against her father's Buick and stifled a yawn. "So, you're sure this thing's running okay? It's not going to break down halfway to Paint Lake?"

"My cousin's a licensed mechanic," Fatima said. "He told me it's in excellent condition. For its age, at least."

"And how about this one?" Dame pointed at her father. "What kind of condition is he in?"

"He's running okay, too" — she put an arm around Dodge — "for his age."

Dame's father frowned. "*All p-packed?*"

"You two can't wait to get rid of me, can you?" Dame smiled. "But, yeah" — she looked inside the car window and nodded — "I think I've got everything."

"Oh, shoot." Fatima turned to Dodge. "We forgot the —" She pointed up at the ceiling and, presumably, the apartment six floors above.

Dodge nodded, and Fatima bustled off in the direction of the elevator.

"Don't you leave 'til I get back!" Her voice echoed off the concrete.

Dame looked at her father and raised an eyebrow. The old man smiled back.

"So, are those Michelins still good?"

Her father gestured at the car, as if to say, *See for yourself.*

"Well, you can't blame me for asking. Last time I checked, half your tires were flat." She looked back toward the elevator. "And things are still good with Fatima?"

Dodge nodded.

"I'm glad. Just — don't fuck it up this time. Not for a couple weeks, anyway. I won't be back until Marinetti's trial starts and I need someone to keep an eye on you."

He smiled, but the smile grew tight across his face.

"*P-P-Peg —?*"

Dame also had trouble saying her name these days. "She's still in the wind."

Dodge frowned.

"Look, with all the publicity this trial's going to get, she won't be able to poke her head out without someone chopping it off. They'll find her eventually, Dodge. She's not our problem anymore."

The old man didn't look convinced. And if Dame was being perfectly honest, she wasn't either.

"Oh hey," she said, changing the subject, "is it okay if I hold on to Loretta a little longer? I thought it would be nice to take some pictures at the lake — you know — fall colours and everything."

He nodded. "*Y-yours now.*"

"I couldn't, Dodge. You love that old camera."

"*For*" — the old man held up an insistent hand — "*next c-case.*"

Dame started to protest, but Fatima materialized looking sufficiently winded. She fanned herself with one hand and held something out with the other.

"Can't believe we almost forgot these."

From Fatima, she took a small yellow case and unfastened the snap. Inside were a pair of glasses, nearly identical to the ones she had lost in the fire.

"David found them in an old dresser. They were your mother's backup pair."

Dame tried them on.

"Your new glasses are nice," Fatima said, "but I think these ones suit you better."

"Thank you." She gave her father's girlfriend a hug.

Dodge opened one of the back doors and stuck his head inside the car. When he re-emerged, there was a smile on his face. He closed the door with a gentle push.

"Everything look okay back there?"

He nodded.

Dame put her arms around her father. "You take care of yourself, okay?" She stepped back and opened the driver's side door. "Looks like the weather up there's going to be amazing. Do you remember how cold it was this time last year?"

The old man glanced at the car and ran his fingers through his white hair.

"You worry too much, Dodge." She sat down behind the wheel. "I promise I'll take good care of her."

"Drive safely," Fatima said.

Dame smiled and pulled the door shut. She started the engine and let it run. All around her, the upholstery was perfumed with the smell of ancient cigarettes. She waved at Dodge and Fatima, and then eased the old car out of the underground lot. The sky was an unrelenting blue, and above the apartment buildings that lined her father's street, Dame could make out the latticed boom of a crane, sweeping across the sky like some unhurried, prehistoric monster.

She followed Jameson until it met up with the Gardner, and then headed west. For a long time, she fought the stop-start of late-morning traffic, but when she hit the 427, a minor miracle occurred. The road opened up, and she shifted into fifth. It was then that she heard a soft gurgling sound coming from the back of the Buick.

Dame glanced at the rear-view and saw the little girl stirring in her seat. "Hey, Rosie," she said. "You finally waking up?"

She heard a sneeze and checked the mirror again.

"We're just going for a little car ride."

Her daughter was staring out the window with her father's bright green eyes.

"What's going on back there, partner?" Dame adjusted her glasses and looked out at the highway ahead. "What do you see?"

ACKNOWLEDGEMENTS

Thanks to my partner Sarah Wyche for her immeasurable support.

Thanks to Walter and Ezra, my parents, Elyse Friedman, Sam Hiyate, and my early readers and advisors, including A.J. Devlin, Mark Fortier, Andrew Hood, Erik Luscombe, Lisa Miszczak, Lee Puddephatt, Mark Rhyno, Leanne Toshiko Simpson, Russell Smith, Nicole Stoffman, Diane Terrana, and Carolyn Van Sligtenhorst.

Thanks to Marc Côté and Cormorant Books for taking a chance on me.

The following people were also responsible for various acts of cool along the way: Justin Armstrong, Matt Bowes, Dionne Brand, Catherine Bush, Fraser Calderwood, Rose Cullis, J.E. Hewitt, Jeremy Luke Hill, Amy Jones, Kelvin Kong, Mathew McCarthy, Aefa Mulholland, Walter Palmer, Christina Ray, Leslie Vermeer, Karmen Wells, Michael Winter, and the Wyches. Much obliged.

An earlier draft of this novel was a thesis project for a Master of Fine Arts degree through the University of Guelph. Thank you to all the instructors and writers who helped wrangle it into shape.

I'm grateful to the Social Sciences and Humanities Research Council which helped fund the creation of this book.

Thanks also to the North Writers Group: Chris Bailey, Diana Biacora, Kris Bone, John Currie, Simone Dalton, Radha Menon, Ashish Seth, and Aaron Tang.

And last, but certainly not least, thanks to the 2019 graduating class of U of G's MFA program: Claire Freeman-Fawcett, Alexandra Mae Jones, Rebecca Kelly, Hajer Mirwali, Stephen Near, Marilo Nunez, Oubah Osman, Kaitlin Ruether, Bardia Sinaee, Leanne Toshiko Simpson (yes, again), Zack Standing, and Ambika Thompson. Best. Cohort. Ever.

The title "Who By Fire" is a reference to Leonard Cohen's song by the same name featured on his 1974 album *New Skin for the Old Ceremony*. Cohen's song echoes the Jewish liturgical poem *Unetaneh Tokef*. I borrow this sacred language with the utmost respect for Jewish people, culture, and faith.

We acknowledge the sacred land on which Cormorant Books operates. It has been a site of human activity for 15,000 years. This land is the territory of the Huron-Wendat and Petun First Nations, the Seneca, and most recently, the Mississaugas of the Credit River. The territory was the subject of the Dish With One Spoon Wampum Belt Covenant, an agreement between the Iroquois Confederacy and Confederacy of the Ojibway and allied nations to peaceably share and steward the resources around the Great Lakes. Today, the meeting place of Toronto is still home to many Indigenous people from across Turtle Island. We are grateful to have the opportunity to work in the community, on this territory.

We are also mindful of broken covenants and the need to strive to make right with all our relations.